TWO SHIPS SAT ON THE FIELD—

leggers and pirates equipped with the standard box of tricks. Tractors to lock them on to a ship or free-floating cargo, guns that could angle to protect a ship on the ground. And a nasty sense of civic duty.

They was going to hold us on the heavy-side and hammer us to death.

They hoped.

I gave *Ghost Dance* all the go-devils in the inventory, to where I was sure something was going to cut loose and blow. She started pulling away, and the view-screens went fade-to-black as the darktraders on the field gunned their engines to hold her.

I opened a wide channel. Both ships would hear it.

"This is *Ghost Dance*. We've got fifteen plates of goforth and nothing to lose. You boys want to be serious nonfiction you just hang on; I guarantee to wrap you around the first lamppost in angeltown."

No answer. Just the howl of an open circuit. *Dance* was starting to shake.

"I mean it. When you forged your First Tickets, anybody tell you what happens you Jump too deep in a gravity well?"

Silence.

"Want to find out?"

The finest in DAW Science Fiction from
Eluki bes Shahar:

HELLFLOWER (Book One)

DARKTRADERS (Book Two)

ELUKI BES SHAHAR

DARKTRADERS

HELLFLOWER #2

DAW BOOKS, INC.
DONALD A. WOLLHEIM, FOUNDER
375 Hudson Street, New York, NY 10014

ELIZABETH R. WOLLHEIM
SHEILA E. GILBERT
PUBLISHERS

First Printing, March 1992

1 2 3 4 5 6 7 8 9

DAW TRADEMARK REGISTERED
U.S. PAT. OFF. AND FOREIGN COUNTRIES
—MARCA REGISTRADA.
HECHO EN U.S.A.

PRINTED IN THE U.S.A.

To Dora Schisler,
Butterfly's role model
and to
Jean Stevenson,
for Library Science
above and beyond the
call of duty.

Contents

In a Hellflower Garden of Bright Images

I was minding my own business doing what was more or less any Gentry-legger's stock in trade—delivering a kick to a client. Only the kick was my buddy the live political hotrock Tiggy Stardust, hellflower prince, and the client not only didn't know he'd ordered the delivery, he might blow both of us wayaway when he got it.

"I do not like this, *Kore*."

"Is this supposed to surprise me, bai?"

I hadn't told Tiggy that. Tiggy was sure his da would protect both of us—but then, how much did you know about life when you was fourteen?

"It is demeaning."

"If you'd left the damn knife in the ship, you wouldn't have this problem."

"It is not a 'knife.' It is my *arthame*."

It was my idea he could get to be fifteen with a little help.

My name is Butterflies-are-free Peace Sincere and I'm a moron.

* * *

We'd hitched a ride here on a pirate ship hight *Woebegone* on account of a promise her captain Eloi Flashheart had made to Yours Truly in the not-too-distant past. But Eloi's charity stopped at the spaceport gates, and now Tiggy and me was on our own. In beautiful theory it wouldn't be for long. Kennor Starbringer was here to open the new Civil Year from the Ramasarid Palace of Justice in Low Mikasa. Kennor Starbringer was Tiggy's da, the man who wanted Tiggy back.

I hoped.

"Soon we will be with my father once more. His vengeance on the Mikasaport Authorities will be terrible. How dare they use a servant of the Gentle People thus? Is not my word sufficient bond?"

"I guess some people just got attitude problems, bai."

It's like this. A long time ago—when I still had a partner, a ship, and a future—I went and did the dumbest thing in a life career of doing dumb things and rescued a hellflower from some roaring boys in a Free Port. Only the hellflower turned out to be the Honorable *Puer* Walksby-Night Kennor's-son Starbringer Amrath Valijon of Chernbereth-Molkath, Third Person of House Starborn— that's Tiggy Stardust for short—son of Kennor Starbringer the well-known and very truly sought after Second Person of House Starborn and Prexy of the Azarine Coalition and the roaring boys had been set on to kill him.

And the only thing I knew about the killers for sure was that they had to be somebody what'd been with Tiggy on the alMayne consular ship *Pledge of Honor* when she was orbiting a little place called Wanderweb. And that left room for a lot of rude surprises.

"It is not right."

"Bai, you going to tell me right's got something to do with the way the universe is run?"

And if I didn't take Tiggy back to them anyway—House Starborn in general, Daddy Starbringer in particular— Tiggy was going to die of a bad case of hellflower honor.

"Perhaps not among the *chaudatu*, *Kore*. But my honor cries out for vengeance!"

"Je, well, tell it to keep its voice down. If the proctors tap us, you going to be honorable in the morgue."

You see, our boy Tiggy—which is to say Valijon Starbringer of alMayne—is a hellflower, and hellflowers ain't like real people. What you got to know about hellflowers, first bang out of the box, is that they're crazy. What I found out about them, back when I had free time and a partner I could trust, was that hellflowers—which is flashcant for our galactic brothers the alMayne—is just this side of an Interdicted Culture. They'd be deliriously happy to be dictys, too, except for the little fact that their home world isn't anywheres near the Tahelangone Sector and their home delight in life is to hunt and kill Old Fed Libraries, of which nobody but Tiggy and me has seen zip for the last millenium. So they spend the part of their time that isn't spent hiring out as mercenaries making everyone else in the Empire real, real nervous on account of two things.

"Soon we will be with my father, *Kore.*"

They're the best at what they do, which is killing.

"And his vengeance will be terrible. Je. I heard you the last time."

And you can never figure out when they're going to do it, on account of hellflower honor.

"I would even have challenged them honorably for the right to pass, but the tongueless ones would not duel."

"Je. Magnanimous."

But in about a hour-fifty, tops, this was not going to be my problem. Kennor Starbringer was at the Ramasarid Palace of Justice, and me and Tiggy was going there.

"I do not like this, *Kore.*"

* * *

Low Mikasa Spaceport was the biggest thing I'd ever seen in my life, and it wasn't even the biggest thing in earshot. All you had to do was look up and there was High Mikasa hanging overhead, looking ripe and ready to fall with all kinds Imperial topgallants, Company big-riggers, and other stuff in all stages of built hanging around it. The Mikasarin Corporation holds the patents used for most of the shipbuilding done in the Empire and High Mikasa builds them. You use Mikasarin technology or you don't fly.

I looked around. Tiggy was right behind me. He had not been a happy hellflower since we came through De-barkation Control. Hellflowers does not go anywheres without their knife. Period.

I hadn't even bothered to try getting my blasters through—Low Mikasa being capital of the Mikasarin Di-rectorate, it's rife with all the bennies of civilization like

a weapons policy that boils down to "don't even try."
But Tiggy-bai'd been sure they'd let his *arthame* through,
and they had. Sort of. *"Cultural empowerer and object
of spiritual focus"* they called x-centimeters of ferrous
inert-blade. And then they glued it into its sheath.

I hadn't stopped hearing about it since.

"Soon we will be with my father, *Kore*," Tiggy said
for only the thirtieth or so time since breakfast. Usually
he wasn't a chatterer, and all of a sudden I realized what
was different now.

Soon he'd be with his father.

And he wasn't any more certain of what Kennor'd do
than I was.

* * *

The Ramasarid Palace of Justice is this big ornate cer-
emonial thing in the Low Mikasa Civic Center that looks
like a Imperial starshaker crashed into a fancy dessert.
The walkway we was on dropped us the other side of the
plaza where we could of got a good look at it except for
all the people in the way. The last time I'd seen so many
bodies in one place there'd been a riot going on.

Tiggy and me fit right in, so nobody gave us any more
look than Tiggy's hellflowerishness accounted for. We
worked our way up to the front. It was just a good thing
wasn't neither of us carrying anything worth stealing;
priggers must be having a field day here.

"*Kore*," Tiggy said in my ear, "the *chaudatu* lied.
He said it was not lawful for the people to carry weapons
here, and he lied."

"T'hell he did, 'flower. S'matter, somebody try to
clout your knife?"

"No, but that man is armed, and thus the port *chaudatu* lied."

I tried to look around and see where Tiggy was looking, but we was both jammed in tighter than furs on a
Riis run. I couldn't see anything.

"Where?"

"Back there, and—"

About then they let the palace doors open and everybody started shoving.

* * * * *

Valijon's Diary:

I am a servant of the Gentle People, whom the *chaudatu* call alMayne and hellflower.

I am the Honorable *Puer* Walks-by-Night Kennor's-son Starbringer Amrath Valijon of Chernbereth-Molkath, born within the walls of the Gentle People, Third of my House, whose tradition is service, even among the *chaudatu* without souls, and the *Kore* San'Cyr thinks that I am mad.

It is only meet that the *chaudatu* think the Gentle People mad, for thus they do not envy us and that is a kindness to them, but the *Kore* is not *chaudatu*. She has hunted the Machine as the *chaudatu* dare not. She has taken my honor into her own mouth and offered to die for me. She has shed her blood in my defense and made herself naked to my enemies.

Are these the acts of a *chaudatu*? No one among the Gentle People will say so.

And yet she says that I am mad. Perhaps—only perhaps—this is humor, a custom of the *chaudatu* that the Gentle People understand as little as the *chaudatu* understand honor.

But if she who was and is no longer *chaudatu* may understand honor, perhaps I who am her *servites* must understand humor.

I will consider this.

The *Kore* also thinks—she does not say this—that I am stupid, and I am no more stupid than mad. Fools do not live to become people upon my homeworld, and I have been a Person for six gathers of the Homeland seasons.

She thinks I do not know how it was that I was abandoned at the place she found me. She thinks, like the *chaudatu,* that the Gentle People know nothing of treachery—yet did we not learn it from her kind, and learn to despise it? Were we not betrayed again and again by *chaudatu* in the service of the Machine until to know *chaudatu* is not to trust?

The Gentle People understand betrayal. The less-than-human betray. The price of humanity is eternal vigilance. Many are born to seem human who are not.

And many who were once human cease to be.

I pray that I am still human, but I fear. My father foretold me that to go among the soulless hellspawn was a hazard to my *arthame*—and though all my father's words are truth, still I did not understand. Now I do. I have been among the *chaudatu* and seen abomination. The *chaudatu* leaders betray their people and open their hearts to the Machine. The *Kore-alarthme* has said this, and she does not lie.

The machine in all its hellshapes first was made by the *chaudatu* to serve the *chaudatu*. It has always betrayed them, as the unknown traitor in my father's house has betrayed me. The Gentle People have counted a hundred generations since the Machine was defeated, and we do not forget. If my *arthame* has been occulted, I will be purified and made whole, and my name added to the songs the Starborn sing at the burning *ghats*. But before that time, I will bring my father word of treachery.

I was meant to die, and the only possible betrayers are our own.

*   *   *   *   *

We took the first bolt that came along. Everybody else was heading into the Audience Chamber where the free floorshow was going to be and didn't miss us. We was still in a part of the Palace where it was legit to be, but soon or late the *legitimates* would trip over us and wonder what we was doing here instead of there. I hoped we found Kennor-bai first.

From what I knew and what Tiggy'd told me, he'd be traveling with a hellflower garden slightly larger than the crew of the *Woebegone*, all nice-minded as hell and armed to the earlobes. And Kennor was here, so they'd all be here, too.

So where was one now, when it would do some good?

Finally we saw a 'flower dressed up real legit in House Starborn blue leather and Tiggy sang out in helltongue. The Junior Brother of Mercy was dressed with the complete disregard for local customs and weather character-

istic of hellflowers abroad. The local Peacekeepers must
be having peristaltic strophes over him, too; he was
wearing a pair of heavyweight blasters in a crossover rig
with a rifle slung over his back. And his hellflower knife,
of course. *Not* glued down.

Him and Tiggy choodled back and forth for whiles.
The word *"chaudatu"* figured very fine and free in the
conversation, and by now I'd picked up enough helltongue to be able to figure out that Junior Brother's name
was Blackhammer and he wasn't buying Tiggy's story
about being Valijon Starbringer the missing son-and-only.
The *"chaudatu"* in the case was Yours Truly: *chaudatu*
means, sort of, "nonperson who not only doesn't have a
Knife, they are never going to be honorable enough to
even stand next to somebody who's got a Knife and ought
to just off themselves now." If a hellflower likes you, he
calls you *alarthme,* which also means Got-No-Knife. Go
figure.

"Look here," I interrupted, "maybe you don't know
by eyeball Missing Heir Baijon, but his da does. Why
don't you just take us to Kennor-bai and let him arrest
us?"

Blackhammer didn't want to admit he savvied Interphon, but Tiggy added something nasty about walls and
shadows in helltongue so Blackhammer fingered his Knife
and finally agreed.

We went wayaways to a place with "personal and private place for very important sophont" stamped all over
it in Intersign glyphs. Blackhammer slid open the door.
There was about a dozen hellflowers around the place,
and I'd rather of walked into a cycling hyperdrive. Seen
as a group, hellflowers was stunning—tall, light-haired,
dark-skinned, trademark hellflower-blue eyes. Inbreed-
ing that'd make any dicty-colony turn green with envy,
and gorgeous.

Not to mention insecure. There was enough hardware
here to fill a pretty good Imperial armory and more cold
iron than in the entire Starfleet—this in spite of its being
illegal for civilians to carry heat anywhere in the Directorate. If I'd cared especial about getting out of here alive
it would of worried me.

Blackhammer and Tiggy and me went through another door into a room with a desk, but wasn't no Kennor Starbringer there neither, much as I'd hoped.

The woman behind the desk was hellflower, older than Tiggy, and wearing enough flashcandy to make her a top-seeded member of the garden club. Her hair was chopped short and she wore a eyepatch and her face was stippled with white scars she hadn't bothered to fix. Burns, looked like. She took one good look at the two of us and sent Blackhammer out quick, and I realized Tiggy and me was dead meat. She turned on Tiggy.

They fell into each other's arms.

The yap got pretty thick but the general idea wasn't too hard to follow: Golly, we thought you was dead, where you been? Well you see it's like this, I met this *chaudatu*. . . .

Eventually they stopped playing old home week and she turned to me. Up close and personal like this I could see her scars was real recent, and it nagged at me like a old enemy. There was something about burns at the edge of my mind . . . .

"House Starborn owes you its thanks for preserving the life of the Honored One Valijon and returning him to us. Ask what you will in *weregild* and it will be granted to you. Come, Honored Valijon, your father will rejoice to see that you have been restored to him."

Or in the lingua franca of deep space, thanks awfully and get lost.

Tiggy backed up against me. "*Kore* Winterfire, I am sworn to obedience to the *Kore* San'Cyr until my father himself accepts me back." He sounded average-to-pretty-well distressed about it, but stubborn.

"Surely the woman excuses you from this pledge." Winterfire looked poisoned gimlets at me, but it wasn't my look-out if she couldn't keep her hands on the son-and-heir in first place.

"*Ea dzain'domere!*" Tiggy pointed out in helltongue. He'd promised.

"A promise is a promise, Honored Valijon, but it is ill-done to promise in words of power to those not of the Gentle People. If the Honored Kennor must give the *chaudatu* an audience it cannot be now. He is already robing for Court and cannot see it until after the ceremony. The *chaudatu* may wait if it wishes.''

Winterfire gave me a monocular glare indicating I better have business elsewhere. Too bad I never learned to take hints like that.

"Oh, we wait all right," I said. "Got nothing better to do."

"Then perhaps you will wish to view the opening ceremony." Winterfire was all smiles now and it should of worried me. "I will tell the Honored One that you are here, and have *Puer* Blackhammer find places for you. After it is over he will conduct you to your father, Honored Valijon."

I could see Tiggy wasn't too thrilled with that idea, but I liked the thought of watching the show a lot better than I liked sitting around backstage with a bunch of hellflowers all post-meridies.

"Yeah, yeah, reet—c'mon, 'flower, lets go watch your da make nice with the Imperials, j'keyn?"

"Ea," said Tiggy, sounding tired.

Brother Blackhammer slid Tiggy and me into the Audience Chamber of the Palace of Justice through the side door marked *"Important People Only."* Blackhammer locked it up tight behind us and we took seats in the very important sophont section up front.

I couldn't shake the feeling I'd seen Winterfire somewheres before, but the only hellflowers bar Tiggy I'd seen lately had been on a planet called Kiffit and trying to kill me.

It was just too damn bad I didn't remember then what I knew about the hellflower smile.

2

When Hell Was in Session

The Audience Chamber was pretty thoroughly jammed with a cosmopolitan mixture of races and sexes and there was something just the least bit bent about it all. I put it down to me not being used to the way things looked in the Directorates. I'd done lots of strange places and been lots of strange things in my misspent etcetera, but the frontier of even a decadent culture looked different from darkest civilization. I wished Paladin was here to tell me that. I wished Paladin was here to tell me anything.

But my good buddy and partner Paladin wasn't going to be around anymore. That was the price of a lot of things—like the death of an Old Federation Library named Archive.

And I could worry about it on my own time—after I was shut of Tiggy Stardust.

"Was good thing you know that Winterfire jilt," I said to him. "Now you be hellflower back in good standing Real Soon Now."

Tiggy didn't look like he thought so. Tiggy looked like he thought he'd left his honor somewheres and wasn't sure where.

"*Kore* Winterfire is the chief of my bodyguard, and before that, when I was not yet a person, it was *Kore* Winterfire who raised me to adulthood."

Terrific.

"Yeah, well, don't worry about it. Everybody makes mistakes." I just hoped we wasn't everybody. We couldn't afford to be.

Because once upon a time the Nobly-Born Governor General His Imperial Highness the TwiceBorn Prince Mallorum Archangel, that busy child with the interest in

Library Science, decided he wanted to put the Azarine Coalition in his pocket and walk off in the direction of becoming Emperor his own self.

For any number of rude reasons, the only way to do that was to rewrite the Gordinar Canticles that govern the Coalition and abrogate the hell out of Azarine Coalition Neutrality.

He couldn't do that while Kennor was president of that same Coalition, Kennor Starbringer being a Constructionist who took Coalition Neutrality to bed with him at night, but Kennor's next-in-line for alMayne's seat on the Coalition was the bright hope of LessHouse Dragonflame, Uncle Morido, and Morido Dragonflame was real pliable. It was obvious that time had come for Kennor Starbringer to retire.

But Archangel was smart—or maybe somebody was smart for him. Offing Kennor direct would just stir up bad trouble back on alMayne. So nobody was going to do that—they was just going to arrange for Kennor to become a Official alMayne Nonperson and Imperial criminal.

That was why all the disproportionate interest in Our Boy Tiggy stopping breathing that had occupied my lately life. Once he did, Kennor'd either have to avenge his death (illegal in the Empire) or not avenge it (illegal on alMayne). Either way his actions was actionable. Neat. Archangel was picking out his best fly-vines for attending Kennor's funeral when one little thing interfered.

Kennor didn't avenge his kinchin-bai. Kennor didn't un-avenge him. Because Tiggy wasn't dead or murdered or any other little thing, and as long as Tiggy wasn't guaranteed dead, he wasn't Kennor's honor-problem, and that could of stonewalled His Mallorumship for years. Tiggy'd just disappeared, courtesy of Yours Truly.

And now he was back. And fresh from being seen by Archangel right in the middle of Archangel's Library project. One whiff of "Library" and even Dragonflame would bolt, because if there was one thing hellfowers hated worse than death and hell and *chaudatu* it was what they called the Machine and the rest of the universe called Libraries.

I just hoped Kennor's hellflower traitor felt the same way, because that put paid to Archangel's dreams of putting the Coalition in his pocket. The bottom line was: Archangel'd made the latest of many grabs for the Coalition—and missed. Now him and Kennor and everybody was back to Square One.

And that meant it was time for Archangel to try again.

*   *   *

About the time I was getting bored sitting here taking symbolic part in the glorious pageant of Imperial rule there was a real loud blatt of trumpets and a Imperial lackey in Space Angel black came out on the balcony where Kennor'd be standing Real Soon Now and read off a long prolegomenon.

Waitaminnit.

Sure as I knew trade-routes, His Nobly-Bornness the TwiceBorn Lord Prince and Governor-General Mallorum Archangel (second in line for the Phoenix Throne, collect 'em all) 's writ only ran in the Outlands, which the Directorates wasn't. He was the courtier of last resort for the Sector Governors, but they only had nominal power in Directorate Space. Directors and Shareholders ran the action here. Mikasarin Corporation should be overseeing the opening of the Mikasa Civil Year, or a TwiceBorn from Throne. Not one of the Governor-General's hired guns.

Besides which, Archangel was last seen declaring martial law in Roaq Sector and pretending he didn't own part-shares in the Old Federation Library of terminal illegality that I'd relieved him of. He would have to of moved hell-and-High-Jump to get loose of that and beat the *Woebegone* here.

But even if there was trouble right here in downtown glittertown, free citizens of Imperial Mikasa was as likely to make it at a Imperial bean-feast as they was to ask for high taxes, and the place was crawling with *legitimates* besides.

So why did I wish so damn much I had my blasters—or even a vibro?

''*Kore,* I do not like this.'' I bet they didn't have riots on alMayne, because that was what this was going to be in about twenty seconds and Tiggy didn't look half worried enough.

Which was oke as I was worrying plenty-enough for both of us.

The Governor-General's Space Angel finished his screed and left the stage. The crowd started making mobnoises real quiet-like. I forgot about any spare problems I might of had.

''Tiggy-bai, think we maybe wait outside and see your da later whiles, if all same to you.''

He started to get up. Just then there was a booming noise behind us. The Court bailiffs had slammed home the big ornate bars across the doors closing off the Audience Chamber.

We was locked in.

''Trouble,'' I said to Tiggy, and started moving him toward where we could get a wall at our backs.

The inner curtains on the balcony swept back and Kennor Starbringer stepped out. He looked like Tiggy, but he looked even more like he'd had to put up with lots of things in life he didn't like. He was overdressed like every hellflower ever born and had his Court of the TwiceBorn robes on over that, open down the front to show off the hellflower glitterflash. All of a sudden I knew I'd been played for a greenie and by who and it was all my own fault, too.

The free citizens of Imperial Mikasa let out a yowl like a scalded theriomorph and came forward over their seats shouting death to extra-planetary mercenaries and Azarine Coalition headmen.

Somebody let off a blaster.

''*Kore*—what is this? What is happening?'' Tiggy had his back to the wall and looked wild-eyed.

''Shut up and run!''

Only there wasn't any place to run to. The citizenry was a mob now but the mob wasn't interested in us. Yet. Soon enough they'd stop trying to get at one hellflower and settle for any hellflower. I looked up at Kennor.

There was six 'flowers up there on that balcony all armed to the teeth and all looking to him to order open fire.

Somebody was counting on Kennor shooting back. And he wouldn't, because dusting citizens of Low Mikasa'd get him gigged under the Pax Imperador as sure as avenging his murdered son would. And Kennor Starbringer was going to hold on to the presidency of the Azarine Coalition at all cost.

"Move!"

I shoved Tiggy hard and pointed. If the ornamental screen fronting the balcony'd hold our weight, we could get up off the killing floor.

"I'll cover you!" Tiggy said.

"Dammit—"

"Kore! I am armed!"

I looked. He'd tore the glued-on sheath of his *arthame* off in shreds and the inert-blade glittered sharplike and next to no good at all against crazies with real heat.

But it was still more than I had. I started up the carved pillar that led to the balcony and hoped Kennor wouldn't kill me when I got there.

The world narrowed to where I put my hands and feet, without point nor end. Boot on garland. Stop and pull off gloves for better grip. See mob surge back and forth below like a liquid in null-grav, making up its mind. Balcony shakes; brawling underneath and somebody taking my lead and starting up the pillar on the other side.

Somebody'd got tired of waiting for Baijon Starbringer to become an Official Dead Person. Somebody'd decided to come up with another reason for his da to retire. Somebody'd bought a riot.

I reached the edge of the balcony and hooked one arm through the railing. Smelled burnt rock where a blast-charge'd spattered against the wall and started dust filtering down. Innocent citizens and bought roaring boys was muddled all together on the Audience Chamber floor, and all in about the time it would of took for Kennor to get through the first sentence of his speech.

"C'mon, you godlost glitterborn!" I braced myself and reached down. Tiggy sprang up and grabbed my wrist. Damn near pulled me in two before he caught hold of the same ornamental stringcourse I was wrapped around and scrabbled over me and up onto the balcony.

The mob hit the space where he'd been and started feeding on itself. All that took about as long as the second sentence of Kennor's speech would of.

Kennor's 'flowers closed up around him when Tiggy vaulted over the rail. I could see from where I was that Tiggy was shouting something but all sound was wiped out by mob-roar. The balcony shook again and gave that definitive lurch of structural weakness. Tiggy grabbed my elbow and dragged me up, yelling at the others in helltongue.

The first wave of the climbers reached the edge of the balcony and started scrambling through the rail. The floor lurched and the tiles underfoot started to buckle. Kennor ordered his people back into the alcove toward where the back stairs was. He pointed along the buckling seam of flooring. A couple of the bright hellflower lads got an idea and fired. The balcony tore lose.

There was a crash, silence, and then some dispirited screaming. Kennor said something I still couldn't hear and looked amused.

Hellflowers smile when they're about to kill something. That's what I should of remembered.

By now a couple of the bodyguard had cut open the access door to the back stairs, which seemed to of been accidentally sealed from the outside.

"To the Embassy!" Kennor shouted in a voice that carried. He hadn't turned one hair at Tiggy's return from the dead. The hellflower bodyguard formed up again with Kennor, Tiggy, and me in the middle. I was elbow-high to the lot of them and I couldn't see a damn thing, but that didn't matter much because then we started down the back stairs and it was pitch-dark.

About now we heard sirens outside and all power to the building was cut. Standard riot-control protocol: no lights, blast doors over windows rolled shut, computer access shut down.

The last one through the balcony access door wedged it shut again and the mob-noises and the sirens cut off like you'd sliced it. The only noise I heard at first was my boots on the treads, and I got the idea of stopping about the same time everyone else did. There was noise ahead of us.

More mob, I thought first, but no. This area was closed to citizenrabble, and any of the kiddies barred into the Audience Chamber would of come from behind.

Professionals, then. The last backstop. The hellflowers I was in the middle of flowed around me like air and made slightly less noise.

In the pitch-black indoor dark of the back stairs of the Ramasarid Palace of Justice, Kennor Starbringer's hellflower bodyguard hit an unknown number of armed and dangerous professional, experienced, and fully briefed sellswords with orders to kill.

The sellswords didn't stand a chance.

I heard Kennor order no survivors, and I knew it was because if there was no survivors, Kennor could make up any fantasy he pleased and go on farcing the Court of the TwiceBorn about him being on the right side of hellflower honor.

And no survivors was eventually going to mean me.

Funny; until I met Tiggy I always thought nighttimers had the monopoly on bending the Pax Imperador. But what I'd seen lately made us the junior league. Archangel dancing with High Book, some hellflower glitterborn buying half Mikasa's *legitimates* to ice the president of the Azarine Coalition, president of the same doing mass wetwork to hold onto his job.

If there'd been anything but sudden death on the other side of the Audience Chamber door I would of gone that way and not stopped running until I reached Port and *Woebegone*. But there wasn't. So I stayed where I was, and five minutes later none of the mercs was left alive.

When the shouting was over someone lit a torch and Kennor's hellflower hardboys started searching what was left of the bodies. I'd seen worse, but not lately. I stayed where I was.

Blackhammer was one of the deaders. Kennor looked at him, then looked at Tiggy and me. I could see the wheels turning behind those hellflower-blue eyes and wished I knew what he was thinking. The hellflowers finished their work and we went on.

Got to the bottom of the access stair and out into a Palace of Justice restricted area. The hallway was deserted and everything was quiet as guilt.

In a sane universe Kennor would of gone back to the rest of his hellflowers, or made a public fuss to the *legitimates*, or at least complained out loud. But Kennor was hellflower, and hellflowers is crazy. Kennor just smole a small smile at the big empty and him, six hellflowers, Tiggy, and me faded into a corridor meant for tronics at the back of the Palace of Justice.

The illegal transponder I got put in my jaw for reasons too complicated to go into here buzzed a little as it took transmission on a near-miss frequency, but even if I couldn't hear anything it gave me the good word. Imperial Space Marines or something else real heavyweight was down and around and chatting itself up. A Remote Transponder Sensor is what only them is supposed to use.

But if Space Marines or something like them was here in a Sector-Capital-and-Directorate-Homeworld, they couldn't of arrived after Tiggy and me'd left *Woebegone*—no time—and Eloi would of told us if they'd got there before.

Unless they'd been shipped in secretly, because somebody knew a riot was going to be on offer. Somebody name of Mallorum Archangel, who was sponsoring Kennor's little jaunt to Mikasa and oh by the way his assassination, too. Because he'd got tired of waiting for Baijon Starbringer to turn up livealive or dead.

Or because now that Tiggy'd seen his Library, Archangel couldn't afford to have him and Kennor meet again in this life.

Terrific.

Kennor seemed to know where he was going, and that was outside into an alleyway at the back of the Palace. The alley had a pretty good view of the police cordon that'd been thrown around the block. Air scrubbers was hovering in place over the fire, and if I'd been brain-dead everything would of looked normal.

I'd heard of treason. They was fighting it all the time in the stories in Thrilling Wonder Talkingbooks. I never thought I'd actually see some, and I wasn't sure if I had now. Only Kennor was the for-sure real live law, and it was my kind of people what hid from the *legitimates*, not his.

I'd used to think.

The bodyguard was stripping off their weapons and piling them in a corner of the alley. Kennor started shucking his TwiceBorn robes and most of his hellflower glitterflash and then pulled his hair out of the roached topknot alMayne high-heat wore.

Leaving now would be the smartest thing I ever did. It wouldn't even matter that I got gigged for illegal emigration, unlawful appropriation of contract warmgoods, possession of illegal technology, and six other fatal warrants the minute I hit the street—there was a *chance* I wouldn't, which was better than I had here. I knew it.

But I didn't move quite fast enough. I stood there like a jerk holding the blaster I'd picked up back on the stairs until Kennor looked at me and reached for it.

"The carrying of personal armament on Directorate worlds except by authorized personnel is forbidden under the provisions of Chapter II of the Revised Inappropriate Technology Act of the Nine-hundredth and seventy-fifth Year of Imperial Grace. As a duly-commissioned representative of the Phoenix Throne, I must ask you to surrender your weapon."

I looked at him. He smirked—or whatever hellflowers do with their mouth that couldn't be that because they is just too damn noble. I handed him the blaster and he tossed it into a discard pile that looked like somebody'd boosted a Imperial armory. Even if hellflowers had the diplomatic permit to carry all that fire-iron, I bet they didn't have a permit to leave it around lying loose.

Kennor turned back to his bodyguard. By now they was stripped down to just knives and one of them was passing around a tube of goo so they could fake the Mikasan peace-seal on those. Kennor's people was real pros at farcing *legitimates*, and I would of been real interested in that if I ever planned on being interested in anything again.

When they was all done making themselves up to look like citizen hellflowers and nobody related to the riot of the week at the Palace of Justice, Kennor gave them their orders in handsign. I could follow that easier than I could helltongue: *Scatter. Regroup at prearranged point. Say nothing.*

Then six hellflowers, looking like anyone's nursery of innocent unarmed unofficial children, faded off smartly and vanished into the crowd that was starting to collect around the riot-police, and Kennor, Tiggy, and me was the only ones in the alley.

"Look here, your Honorship—" I began.

"Now," said Kennor, laying hold of my wrist in your basic inarguable fashion, "we three will go together and quickly—before the Imperial *chaudatu* find us here and we all suffer unfortunate accidents while in protective custody."

I didn't bother to remind him I had a guaranteed accident coming no matter what. Kennor took off with me attached, and Tiggy followed.

* * *

My partner Paladin always used to say I never thought enough, and that wasn't fair. I'd always thought as much as I had to, only I'd never before needed to think as much as I did now. I had plenty of time for it, though, slinking acrost Low Mikasa with Kennor and Tiggy and the three of us trying not to be seen—or if we was, to look like ship-crew wayaways from Port.

Fact: One hundred days ago, Gentry-legger me rescued what I thought was a solid citizen what had wandered into the wrong street of my friendly neighborhood Free Port.

Fact: The citizen was actually Tiggy Stardust, *aka* Valijon Starbringer of House Starborn, in the throes of his first murder attempt. Somebody'd let him shag off from his consular ship without ID in the pious hope that either the law or the natives of Wanderweb Free Port would sign the lease on his real estate in short order. Probably the same person who arranged front-row seats at the riot, come to think of it, and I knew which *Puer* Blackhammer I was betting on.

Fact: In my neverending quest to get Tiggy-bai back to the arms of his tender loving da, we took a real round-about detour, and tripped over the fact that Mallorum Archangel, Imperial Prince, Governor-General, and second in line for the Throne if the Emperor ever took the Long Orbit, was hand in claw with an Outlands nightbroker in a scheme to 1) use infinitely-illegal Old Federation Technology to take over the universe and 2) ice Tiggy Stardust as part of a squeeze-play to gain direct control of the Azarine Coalition to use it as his own private army.

Fact: There still wasn't any other place in the universe for me to take him, so I'd brought Tiggy back to Kennor Starbringer's unhealthy vicinity anyway and run into hellflower trouble—and the answer to a question that'd been bothering me for whiles.

Who'd sent Tiggy out to play in traffic on Wanderweb and made several attempts on him since?

Easy. Who was better placed to do it than a member of his personal bodyguard?

* * *

"Now shall I be happy to accept the TwiceBorn's sorrow for what has happened at the Palace of Justice today," Kennor said. I looked around.

We was in the very best bolt-hole of the alMayne Embassy, following a nervewracking several hours sneaking acrost town on foot. The suite was done in what was probably alMayne high style. Hellflower chic was heavy behind ornate fancywork in edged metal and one whole wall used for nothing but displaying handweapons. My idea of chic was fine vintage neurotoxins, and I had hopes of being very chic Real Soon Now.

"Yeah, your Honor, I can explain some of that," I said, and stopped. It was a little late in my career to be making up to the *legitimates,* even if they was bent hellflower *legitimates.*

Tiggy burst out in a breathless sing-song that I followed not very and flung himself facedown at his da's feet.

"And who knows who in the end may be discovered to be responsible for woefully disturbing the civil peace?" Kennor went on all mournful and just like Tiggy wasn't there.

"Now look—" I said, which wasn't politic maybe but I didn't get the chance to compound my errors.

"Ea comites, hjais koriel!"

Because just then Winterfire came out of the inner room and headed straight for Kennor.

And everything clicked into place.

Kennor was standing there flat-footed, not even going for his knife. I'd known it was a member of his personal guard as set up Tiggy and the riot. But I'd picked the wrong one.

Nobody was looking at me. I crossed the room with a bound and ripped open one of the wall displays.

Everything seemed to take a thousand years. The first thing my hand closed on was a little Estel-Shadowmaker rechargeable—one shot and it takes forever to recycle but I wasn't going to get two chances anyway. I pulled it up and turned and fired all in one move, and I could still see Kennor standing there like he wasn't armed.

Fired. Missed. Oh, not quite; she staggered a little and her tunic caught fire and I smelled burning hair and burning flesh and suddenly I was back in a bazaar in a place called Kiffit where I'd killed two hellflowers who'd been trying to kill me because I'd saved Tiggy's life.

And one of them was her. That was what'd lost her the eye and covered her face with those pretty burn marks she must of had some hellflower reason for not removing.

Winterfire didn't even try to put out the fire. I saw her bring her hand up slow and Kennor, damn him, didn't move. Kennor Starbringer would be dead and the Azarine Coalition would belong to Mallorum Archangel and Archangel would use it to make a war like the one that pulled the Old Federation down. A war like Archive's.

So I got in the way. My timing was good. I moved and Tiggy moved and I heard him scream and thought for one crazy second he'd caught a plasma-packet and then I realized she hadn't fired yet. Then I saw the muzzleflash from Winterfire's gun and then I didn't see anything at all.

* * * * *

Valijon's Diary:

I think Father must have known from the moment he saw Blackhammer's body who the traitor within our walls was. He told me later that She Who Will Not Be Named had asked especially that Blackhammer be sent from the Homeland to aid her—the child of her body, loyal to his line and his LessHouse first of all things

So I learned later. Then I saw only the gun.

It was a *chaudatu* ploy, to forge honor into a knife against the Gentle People. She Who Will Not be Named called *comites* with my father—he could not strike her down until she gave him cause; the first blow must, in honor, be hers. And if he must bide so, then it was twice-over my place to void a quarrel in which I had no place. Her life was not mine until she struck, and the Law was clear: I might not assume that she would.

So I, too, was helpless, though it was I whom She Who Will Not Be Named had first betrayed. She had promised me safety, and was false—and sacrosanct, until the moment she chose to strike at the *Kore-alarthme,* whose honor was mine to keep.

Then her life came into my hands. And then I did what honor demanded, to tell those of House and clan and line that She Who Will Not Be Named had forfeited what it is to be human.

* * * * *

I was someplace that I knew wasn't real, not like organics know about real. For a minute I didn't know who I was, then it came back like putting together the pieces of a cargo.

Butterflies-are-free Peace Sincere. Ex-Luddite Saint, ex-slave, escapee from the Interdicted World Granola, darktrader, Librarian, human. The place I was in was out of my own private dreambox—a imagination of what a computer core would look like if a memory-bubble had eyes. I'd been here before. A hallucination, caused by a piece of Old Fed Tech that nobody should ever have woke up again.

Archive. Fully-volitional logic. Library. Killer

* * *

About a thousand years ago—back when your Phoenix Empire and mine was still a Federation about four times its present size—some bright kiddy came up with the notion of putting pure intellect in a box and calling it a Library. And since the *Federales* thought they had more important things to do with their time, they turned over the running of their Federation to the Libraries and made it so Libraries could build more Libraries.

Mistake. Because—so the story goes—the Libraries had more important things to do with their time, too, and thought that organic life clashed with their decor. There was a war. And ten centuries later the Empire is still hunting the nonexistent surviving Libraries from that war.

Mostly nonexistent.

I'd never been anything special, but I'd done one special thing. In the midst of a misspent career of moving *chazarai* from here to there for people who might not be its original owners, I'd gone and rescued and rebuilt an illegal Old Fed Library. I hadn't known what I was doing. I'd never heard of Libraries then. It was a damn good thing I lucked into maybe the only pacifist Library there ever was. Paladin was my friend, my partner, the edge I needed to stay alive in the never-never.

Until I went and rescued Tiggy Stardust.

And Paladin left me.

"Go, and live a human life among your own kind." I heard his voice—I could touch him here, I could see him, but all he wanted was for me to walk away and then everything vanished like smoke and stardust and I was alone.

And he'd made a mistake. It was important, more than

his feelings or mine, and I had to tell him about it, but I had to wake up first, and—

"*Kore! Kore-alarthme!* Don't die—*Father*—"

And my dreamworld shattered into dancing points of light.

I opened my eyes. Tiggy was hanging over me like High Mikasa Shipyards, spattered in blood. I couldn't think why, but I was glad he wasn't hurt. Blasters cook, not puncture.

"You *will* live," he said, like someone was giving him argument.

I tried to move. I felt too light and too heavy. Unbalanced, like somebody half in armor. Something was missing.

"Get out of the way."

I recognized Kennor. The ends of his fancy silver hair was wicked in blood. Why is it there's so much blood when hellflowers is around?

"You are injured," said Daddy Starbringer like he was reading out the late-breaking news. "What is it you wish to say before you die?"

So that was why I felt so good.

"Winterfire set you up. Archangel had a Library. And I brought your son back, you son-of-a-"

Then the floor tipped sideways and I fell off.

*   *   *

I was back in the dream computer core again, having a long conversation with Paladin about what happened when me and him and Tiggy went up against Archangel's Library.

"You know I had to set that blast, bai. Couldn't trust what might of happened with Archive Library if I didn't."

"And what did you think that would be, Butterfly?"

"You know, Pally-che-bai." But he didn't. Paladin didn't know things he ought to know, and then I realized it wasn't Paladin at all.

I opened my eyes. It looked like a cluster galaxy seen from realspace.

Things flipped into focus.

"Go on," said Kennor Starbringer.

"Go to hell," I said. We was face-to-face; I must be standing and on a box at that, but I tried to twitch a finger and I couldn't feel a thing. Nothing.

I tried not to let it bother me any more than scaring me half to death.

"You will delight to know that we rejoice in *Malmakosim* Archangel's tender *chaudatu* concern, and in his assurances that reprisals for the regrettable and unexpected civil disturbance will be as swift as they are severe. He shares with me also my dismay at the death of She Who Will Not Be Named."

I'd thought I'd been talking to Paladin and instead I'd been giving Kennor all the answers he thought to ask. It bothered me from someplace far away enough so I knew I was drugged, and I guessed I hadn't said anything too incriminating or we wouldn't be having this conversation now.

And if Winterfire was Archangel's chief catspaw in House Starborn, she couldn't be the only one. I wondered, in a far-off way, what Archangel'd paid her.

"I guess you be both just as torqued at that as each other is," I said, since Kennor was looking at me.

"My doctors assure me that you'll recover."

"Where's Tiggy?"

The question seemed to surprise him. He frowned.

"Your son. I brought him back, remember?"

"Yes."

We looked at each other whiles until it occurred to me that it was my turn to say something.

"You wanted him back, right?"

Kennor showed his teeth in that alMayne expression that is not a smile.

"No. I wanted him alive."

I wanted to answer that but couldn't. I saw the path back into the computer and took it, down deep inside where even Kennor couldn't find me to question. And Paladin was there.

* * *

Time passed. I got used to it. I saw Kennor a couple more times and Tiggy not at all. On one of Kennor's visits I got some of the pieces filled in. My buddy Winterfire, *aka* She Who Will Not Be Breathing No More, had died a traitor to the hellflower cause and had her head shipped home to hang on Kennor's gates. Quaint local custom.

I wondered what Kennor had in mind for me. I didn't know what I'd blathered to Kennor whilst he was rummaging in my brain, and if Kennor's people was any good their fetch-kitchen'd told them what I was. Interdicted barbarian—shoot when found. They must be saving me up to put on a show.

I didn't really care.

Finally Kennor's pet bonecracks let me out of the giant economy size finestkind biopak I'd been welded into for longer than I wanted to think about and put me in a luxury accommodation prison instead. And I finally found out just how far Winterfire'd got toward trying to kill me.

Cybereisis prostheses. You don't catch a plasma-packet off a hot blaster and keep your original inventory. Winterfire'd took off half my left arm and Kennor's hellflower cyberdocs had done for the rest. Glass and plastic and brainjinks laying up along my spine and a left arm that nobody but me could tell from the original.

I cared about that. It gave me the creeps. But I was healthy enough to kill now, if they was going to. I wished they'd left me asleep.

But wishes aren't cargo, and darktrade was not exactly a career where you made old bones in the first place, and there wasn't no place for me anywhere except in the never-never—a second-rate darktrader to a third-rate nightworld broker. Fast ship and faster blasters, untrustworthy luck and a knack for other people's trouble. I'd lost all of them now except the last.

* * *

I was looking out a set of armored one-way holosim windows at nighttime Low Mikasa Prime. Prime was a great big prettycity full of people born here, with a right to be here. None of them'd know what a candle was, or a horse-drawn plow.

Or a blaster, maybe.

Wet beaded on the pick-ups referring the image I saw. Kennor'd told me there'd be rain tonight, like it was a big treat. Even told me when it'd start.

I looked down at my hands and wiggled my fingers. Big treat. Only now one set of them was real and one wasn't.

The door made that sound they do here when they open and Tiggy—which is to say, Prince Valijon Starbringer of House Starborn all fine and nice and real friendly—and Kennor-his-da came in.

I could see them reflected in the holosim but I turned around to where they was anyway. Tiggy looked fine. He looked happy. He was back in finestkind hellflower dress-up like I'd first seen him, weaponry (legal inside the Consulate) and bright-polished *arthame*.

I ground my teeth and imagined I could feel the damn expensive useless hardware of my RTS down in the bone. But Kennor'd made a point of telling me they'd took it out. Damn him.

"*Kore!*" said Tiggy. He looked young and excited and no part of me. He never had been, really.

"I bid you welcome to my walls, woman not of the Gentle People. Peace to you in my son's name while you abide here, and joy to you for seeking the walls of Starborn. Your shadow will be cherished while you remain, and if you must in honor depart to the Land Beside, know that you will not die unknown and unmourned," Kennor perorated for the official record.

It took me a minute to unknot that and another one to decide that the sentiments expressed was not maybe as comforting to us *chaudatu* as it might be to hellflowers. The cognoscenti would note that it contained not one word about getting out of here alive.

"It is a great pity that there is no *chaudatu* proof that Archangel consorted with the Machine," Kennor went on like I'd done the pretty right back. "On alMayne, the word of an Honored One would be enough. Here, words

mean very little.'' He sat down in a chair. Tiggy stood.
I leaned.

''Next time I'll save you the pieces,'' I said. ''Look,
bai, brought you kinchin-bai, got shut of all comme-tays
farcing and I'm golden. If you was going to ice me Ti—
Baijon wouldn't be here, so I guess you're letting me go.
So tell me the whistle you going to drop and we call it a
night, oke?'' And I'd be dead by the time I found which
way the spaceport was, but never mind that.

''Not quite,'' said Kennor. ''Amrath Valijon of
Chernbereth-Molkath, what do you have to say in your
defense?''

''My fault was grievous,'' said Tiggy like he'd been
rehearsed. ''I owe my life four times to the *alarthme*
woman, called *Kore-alarthme* San'Cyr, and I have not
redeemed it.''

Kennor smirked at me.

''Shut up!'' I said real loud. ''Don't you shove me
none of your hellflower honor, bai, or—''

''And what is the price of a son of the Gentle People?''
Kennor said encouragingly to the son of the Gentle People just like I wasn't there.

Maybe I could get out of here unnoticed whilst they
was bandying the book of the Law back and forth.

''*Weregild* to the worth of his family; service to the
length of his years; or another price set,'' said Tiggy
happily.

No hope; he was between me and the door.

''And *Kore,* I am no longer constrained to stay shut of
the damfool honor nonsense since my pledge of obedience to you has been redeemed,'' Tiggy-Baijon said to
me.

''So,'' said Kennor, turning back to me. ''What will
you claim, *Kore* Sant'Cyr? My son tells me you have
saved his life four times, and this is so. Each time must
be bought back, for his honor.''

''Tiggy's honor ain't nothing to do with me. I don't
give a damn about honor. And there's something you want
from me, Honored One Kennor Starbringer, or you
wouldn't be staging this Quaint Folkways wondershow
about our galactic cousins the alMayne.''

"Kore-alarthme!" yelped Tiggy, but Kennor waved him down. And smiled for real. Hellflowers was awful pretty when they smiled right.

"Very well, *alarthme* Sant'Cyr. I will speak to you as if you were one of the Gentle People. In truth you are owed what has been said. In honor, it will be paid. To *chaudatu* we offer coin; they have no souls and are satisfied. But to you I offer the choices of our own, and should you claim blood or souls my House will honor the debt. But there is more, as you have said. My child is precious to me—"

"About as much as the Azarine Coalition," I said. Tiggy flinched.

"Yes," said Kennor, slow. "As much as that. As much as your care for the Coalition when you stepped into the path of the weapon of She Who will Not Be Named."

That was a accident. I promise.

"Archangel wants war," I said. And I'd already lived through Archive's version of a war. Memories real as my own crowded in—of slaughter on a scale that'd make Mallorum Archangel pack up his toys and go home for sheer envy. The war between the Libraries and the Old Federation—the war that outlawed the Libraries and let the Phoenix Empire be. It was in my head like it'd happened yesterday.

The Empire was a lot smaller than the Federation Paladin and Archive remembered. If Archangel got his war, this time there wouldn't be anything left.

"The Lord Prince Mallorum Archangel wants war, and an army to wage it," Kennor agreed. "The neutrality of the Coalition endures as long as my life, and even if I tell the Homeland of his traffic with the Machine, the alMayne are only a part of the Coalition."

"Baijon's life ain't going to be worth much when the dust clears, is it?"

I looked over Kennor's shoulder at Tiggy. Political hot-rock, and I'd been too stupid to realize that the best thing to happen to him was to never go home. Because now there was just going to be another godlost hellflower traitor to ice him and nothing I did was going to matter.

"My son's life is valuable to me, *Kore* Sant'Cyr. If he stays here, he will die," Kennor said.

It took me a minute to figure out what he meant, what he wanted, why I hadn't conveniently died and why it was I was getting fed this amazing line about being almost a real person, alMayne-style.

"You want me to take kinchin-bai back to the Outfar and pretend he ain't coked trouble with trouble chaser. No."

As much as I meant to do anything, I was going to look for Paladin, which would be a little bit dicey with a technophobe hellflower breathing down my spine. And none of my plans involved being arrested and tortured by the Governor-General.

"Then he dies," Kennor said.

"Could of died lots of places. You tell me why I care—and farce me no honor cop, glitterborn, you *sold* yours for the Azarine Coalition."

That was a very bad thing to say. Kennor stopped moving like he'd been shoved into stasis. Tiggy went white under his hellflower bronze.

Kennor took out his knife and looked at it.

"Then take this, and do better for the Gentle People than I have done."

He held it out.

I backed up so fast my head hit the holosim and made it ring. Everything I knew about hellflowers said they didn't act like this. Kennor Starbringer was *crazy*.

No, he was right. He was right and I was right and everything was a godlost mess.

"I don't give a damn—" *about your "Gentle People,"* I was going to say, but my mama always told me not to tell lies to armed strangers.

"What do you *want*, dammit?" I said instead.

"A war that doesn't come this year. My son, alive for longer than I can keep him so. He is yours. His life is yours. Will you not cherish it?"

Through all this Tiggy was silent as mumchance.

"How?"

"Will you accept him into your service for honor's

sake, and take him with you?'' Kennor asked me. And then I got it.

Only in talkingbooks does a passing alMayne noble-man—which is what Kennor was—fork over his son-and-only to a passing space gypsy—which is what I was, or close as makes no nevermind. But Kennor was pushing real hard for it.

Why?

The answer came all at once. It seemed to come from somewheres outside, and it was as cold as space.

Kennor Starbringer must/must not avenge his son's death. Vengeance would ruin him politically. Mercy would crucify him with the hellflower vote. Either way he'd lose the Coalition.

But if *I* killed Tiggy—

—and died in the murder—

Kennor would and would not have his vengeance. He could even declare hellflower seven-ring vendetta over my bones and satisfy the conservatives back home: I didn't have any family to complain to the Emperor.

So someone was going to murder Tiggy—and if not me, then Kennor's hand-picked someone else. Because once he'd showed up in public again, Tiggy *had* to die, and in a way that didn't implicate Kennor. That was Kennor's only way out.

Tiggy was his weak point. He must of kicked and screamed before letting the Emperor make him haul Tiggy out of whatever box with locks the kid'd grown up in. But once Tiggy'd cleared planetary atmosphere and was outside alMayne civil law, he was dead meat.

No matter, even, if Kennor loved him.

And that was real too bad for Tiggy and Tiggy's da, but it was even worse for Yours Truly, because I had a stone hunch that if I didn't agree to have Tiggy for my new partner I had a life expectancy that could be measured in inches.

''You done asked babby-bai if he wants to be dark-trader what Teasers and *legitimates* home delight is for to shoot? 'Cause that's what I know; that's what I am. You send him along of me that's what I make him—not anti-war rescue project for good of Azarine Coalition.

Not glitterborn sob-story pet. Partner. You want job, Tiggy-bai? In a hundred days we probably make good start on committing every crime in the Calendar in glyph-abetical order. Don't need to know much. Just some pi-loting and be good with blaster. I can teach you everything else. Might even learn some sense to go with your honor.''

Was longest speech I'd made in slightly more than so long, and Kennor et fils could of been wall-paintings for all the visible interest they showed. Then Tiggy smiled.

''To circumvent the false laws of the *chaudatu* is an honorable profession. We will be very successful smug-glers.''

He crossed over to where I was. He looked like he'd just been offered a three-day pass to the Ghost Capital of the Old Federation for high adventure, and dammit, by now he should of known better.

I turned and looked at Kennor.

He had to believe it. He had to let us go.

Kennor put a hand on Tiggy's shoulder.

''Run far and fast, *alarthme,* and Archangel will hunt you—but carefully, for Archangel has enemies as highly placed as he.''

Damn Kennor. He was hoping, naked like he'd said it flat out. Hoping that he could make a difference, could matter, could outwait Archangel—and hoping, maybe, that somehow Tiggy and me'd get away.

From Archangel.

From *him*.

3

Hell Is a Very Small Place

It was three hundred twenty hours since I'd been at Mikasaport last, and six hours since I'd agreed to a cross with so many doublings I couldn't even remember who was betraying what anymore, and my main concern was how to walk in my new high-ticket footwear without falling flat on my face. The clothes I was in would of made a serious down payment on a new ship, but I wasn't going to have to worry about that.

Tiggy Stardust—who said his name was *Baijon*, thank you very much—and me was going to alMayne.

It was raining. The streets was deserted, all but for Kennor's great big land-yacht with Kennor driving. The yacht would also make a serious dent in the price of a new ship.

Which we would get. Kennor'd promised me a ship and papers, along with anything else I wanted to ask for to set us up in the Trade, in the nearest place Kennor hauled cubic and didn't have the Pax Imperador looking over all of our shoulders.

alMayne. And at the moment I couldn't promote a better idea.

I didn't have a ship and I didn't have a partner who could forge me clean registry on a stolen one, or launder my First Ticket, or anything useful like that. And I didn't have hope of buying a ship outright, even in my new crown jewels. A ship costs credit. *Lots* of credit.

I remembered back when I'd been willing to do a lot of killing just for the chance to wrap my stolen pilot skills around a forged First Ticket. Not even for a ship, mind—just for the documents that'd let me fly one. That'd been a long time ago. Before Paladin.

And now it was like that again. A ship was freedom. A ship was survival. So I had to get a ship any way I could—and that meant going to alMayne with Baijon he said I got to call him on the off-chance that Kennor was going to do at least some of the things he said.

I had papers identifying me as a *alarthme* of House Starbringer, one Butterfly Sancerre by name. They got my name wrong but enough of the facts right that it was a cleaner ID than any I'd ever owned. The rest of my earthly possessions consisted of a pass to travel from Mikasa to alMayne, and then freely through Washonnet Sector. alMayne's a Directorate even if it doesn't hold any client worlds or control any more than its own system space—you mind your manners in Washonnet when hellflowers say to.

The *Pledge Of Honor* was highbinding Mikasa, but that wasn't how we was going off to hellflower-land. *Pledge* was still going to Throne with Kennor. By rights Baijon should of gone with him, but talking his way out of that was Kennor's business.

Kennor's personal particular battle-yacht wasn't here either, having gone home whiles ago with Winterfire's head and the news that she wasn't quite as human as he'd originally thought.

This left only one way for us to get home to alMayne. We was taking the galactic bus.

To be strictly accurate, it was a Company highliner. The highliner was named *Circle of Stars*, and Kennor'd held it here for ninety hours waiting for me to be well enough to make up my mind. So now we was in a helluva hurry to leave.

I watched Kennor watching me. He was disappointed the rain didn't bother me, *chaudatu* as I was. Baijon was now promised to serve me for the next fifty-six galactic standard years, that being his age (14 gsy) times the number of times he said I'd saved his life (four). Never mind the fact that if I lived that long I'd be ninety-one and dead for the past thirty years. Honor was honor.

And I hoped Baijon was stupid enough not to realize just how stupid this was as a concept, galactopolitically speaking. Heirs was heirs; they had more things to do with their lives than spend it prenticed to a pirate, or whatever Kennor thought I was. Because if Da Kennor needed Babby Baijon at all for the family business (reasonable), he'd just put him out of reach for ever and aye (stupid).

Only the only way Baijon was going to be of use to his da now was dead. And even if Kennor gave up the Coalition yesterday, it was too late to save his beamish boy. Baijon had his deathmark: he'd seen Archangel's Library.

Archangel knew by now that Baijon'd talked to Kennor. But Kennor hadn't cried Library, so Archangel didn't know how much Kennor knew. Not knowing was going to give him happy days and busy nights and maybe take his mind off us.

At least, that was the plan.

We drove past all the restricted parts of the port and got to the docking ring whiles I was thinking that unfair must be the default setting for reality because there's so much of it.

The gig for the *Circle of Stars* was bigger than my whole last ship had been. She was a rickety piece, all flashcandy for the groundlings, and you could see her half a klik away. Lit inside and out, stuffed with inertial compensators, and not a goforth in sight. Her pilot was wearing a comic-opera version of a Company man's uniform—silver boots and gauntlets and a helmet with blast-goggles and a transmitter-crest that he wasn't ever going to need. He got out of the gig when we got there, and bowed, and opened the door, and everywhere he stepped the crete went dry because of the personal shield he was wearing.

Kennor hugged Baijon and Baijon hugged him back hard like he knew that wasn't none of us ever going to see each other again. Not if we was lucky.

Then Kennor hugged me, and that I didn't expect. His *arthame* and one of his blasters dug into me in a lot of soft places.

"Run far, Butterflies-are-Free. Run fast."

Then he stepped back and I stepped back and tripped over the doorsill to the highliner's gig, and Baijon caught me and I sat down fast and started looking for the straps and by the time I found out there wasn't any we was way above Mikasa and I couldn't see Kennor Starbringer no more.

*　*　*

The shuttle moved like a lead pig. High Mikasa was synchronous over the capital and the port; we slid sideways along the gravity until High Mikasa vanished and *Circle of Stars* appeared.

I'd never seen another ship in orbit except in the hollyvids. For one, I never spent a lot of time dawdling in orbit, and for t'other and for sure I've never gone coasting up to another piece of high-iron just to say hello. In my line of work that could get you killed.

Circle was big. I'd expected that. She was also lit up so she glowed like a planet in sunlight and she was all glazed the same color, smooth and even and like somebody was taking care about it. No rust, no rot, no six colors of atmosphere seal peeling at different rates. And even if she was never going to hit atmosphere, she was smooth and sculpted and polished like somebody was going to look her over outside up close and personal.

We didn't circle her half long enough for my liking. The pilot wrapped the gig around her until he lined up with her bay, wafted the ship into *Circle's* tractor-field, and sat back while she pulled us in.

Paladin always told me the level of technological sophistication varies inversely with the distance from the center of civilization. Eventually he told me this was a fancy way of saying the farther out you go the poorer everything gets. Even if he'd made a big point of saying it was true the other way round too, I might of believed it but I wouldn't of *known* it.

The Outfar was the edge of the Empire. Mikasa was the center of the Imperial Midworlds.

Circle was magic. We'd flown right in from cislunar space and it'd been through shields, not doors, and the bay was light and warm and pressurized. If there was anything like machinery on offer, it wasn't nothing I recognized.

Baijon was traveling as Third Person Peculiar of House Starborn his own self. There was two other flunkies and a bunch of A-grav units there to meet the shuttle. What they knew about us was that Baijon was alMayne high-heat and I was his entourage. This was not the truth by hellflower standards—by them I was the high-heat and Baijon was my chief werewolf—but Baijon had no objections to "breaking the false laws of the *chaudatu.*"

Yeah.

Baijon spent whiles being rude to the rubes for expecting him to live up to their standards—it's wonderful what you can get away with if you've got the political clout not to get arrested—whilst I ground my teeth and tried not to chew my nails and wondered how many days to Washonnet, home, and murder.

If Kennor meant to pin Baijon's sudden death on me it'd have to be on alMayne, where he could trust everyone to act like honor-mad morons and he didn't have to worry too hard about the Pax Imperador. Out here it was too damn likely some other citizen'd take the rap for me—at least if I had any say in things—and then Kennor'd be up to his *arthame* in honor-problems again.

Assuming Archangel didn't get him first.

If I was managing to think like Kennor—or viceyversy—I was safe for now.

At least, I thought so at the time.

Circle was like a downside city for sheer mass cubic but we didn't have to walk far—which was just as well considering Kennor's taste in footwear for *alarthmes*. Soon as we got out of the dock area a floater waffled up and the four of us—me, Baijon and two professional cowards—went for a little ride.

It was depressing. All this stuff just lying here and no place to sell it even if I could pry it loose.

We got to the rack and ruin Kennor thought appropriate to send his son and stalking horse home in, and the shippies hovered until I assured them that His Honorability was just waiting till they was out of sight before expiring with ecstasy. You could of parked my last ship in the main room and it wasn't the only one. There was half-a-dozen more besides: rooms for sleeping, and eat-

ing, and wet-bathing, and a few other perversions I hadn't
had time to acquire. We had either a exterior cabin with
eight meter high hullports (unlikely) or else the main
cabin bulkhead referred the exterior hull pick-ups when
everything else was shut off, like now. Anyway, according to the walls we'd already made the Jump to angeltown
and I hadn't felt a thing.

This was out of my league. I knew about rich and I
knew about showing off how you had enough power to
do what you damn pleased and devil take the TwiceBorn,
but what I didn't know was if I was ever going to understand what kind of sick depraved mind could afford to
jump this much cubic to angeltown without a damn thing
useful occupying it. And Baijon didn't know a damn thing
of any mortal use.

Who could I bully and who could I bribe and when
was I being insulted? Who knew the truth and who was
buying in on Kennor Starbringer's chosen fiction?

Paladin could of told me. But instead of looking for
him, I was going to alMayne where a bunch of rude
strangers was waiting to punch my one-way ticket.

"Baijon-che-bai, we take lookaround, do gosee, je?"
At least it'd take my mind off my problems.

* * *

I'd meant he should show me the bridge and the black
gang—the parts that make a ship a ship—but what Baijon
showed me was a series of fancy hooches where they
didn't know coked R'rhl from *biru-deska,* and places to
buy clothes that looked unwearable and jewels you'd just
get tossed for if you wore them on the street. I couldn't
find any place that sold boots.

The gravity was a work of art. There was two "downs";
the one I was standing on and the one overhead, and
there was two tiers of shops oriented to match. I wondered if I could jump high enough to get captured and
reoriented by the other field, and decided not to try. I
caught Baijon looking up and thought he must be thinking the same thing. There wasn't much in the way of
signs, and damn near every one I saw—except for things

like Ship's Services—was in Imperial Script, but you could tell what was what because all the shops was displaying holosims out front.

I stopped, staring into one of them filled with items I might even have freighted at an earlier stage of their careers—valuta made wearable.

"*Kore*, do you want them?"

I looked at Baijon. He looked like his spike-heeled sandals was too tight.

"What would I do with them?"

He thought about it.

"You could smuggle them," he said hopefully.

"*Sssst!*" I looked around, but wasn't nobody close enough to me to hear. "I don't—do that," I said, when I could keep my voice down.

"But—" Baijon looked puzzled—and indignant.

"I don't *tell* nobody I do that," I corrected.

"But I already know what you do, *Kore*," Baijon said helpfully. "You circumvent the false laws of the *chaudatu* and participate in the freemasonry of deep space, the brotherhood of open economic frontiers—"

One of us had been auditing too many talkingbooks.

"And anyway you want me to just walk in there and *buy* them?" I said to shut him up.

"Why not?" said my hellflower.

"With what?" I said. So he told me.

It turned out we was riding Baijon's credit rating, and as a shareholder of the Starborn Corporation (or a scion of a hellflower royal house, take your pick) he could sign for anything *Circle* had loose and take it away. Anything.

This gave me a case of Divine Inspiration.

We was *not* going to alMayne, very sorry Kennor Starbringer.

We was going to the ship's casino.

* * *

The TwiceBorn all lead soft boring lives, so I'm told, an so's they don't get too bored they have entertainment. I was going to promote me some, too. Where there's casinos there's valuta, and where there's valuta there's hard credit, and where there's hard credit a good chunk of it could naturally fall my way. I knew *Circle* ought to be stopping between here and alMayne, and wherever it stopped Baijon and me was getting off. With enough hard credit we could ride his ID to the place we could both disappear.

Like most of my bright ideas, if reality'd cooperated it would of worked.

*   *   *

The casino probably wasn't as big as it looked. I'd seen *Circle* from the outside and then spent a couple hours being dragged around inside. I knew how big the compartment *could* be, and this wasn't it.

What it was, was big enough even so to probably hold most of *Circle's* live freight, and here they all was: drinking, eating, and betting credit in colors I'd never knew existed. I'd seen black, white, and green—once I'd seen silver. The lowest thing being shopped around these tables was gold.

And all I had to do was walk up to a mechanical and ask for some. That didn't mean I had to waste it on the chancery: there's fools, damn fools, and people what try to make money in a "honest" casino.

On the other hand. . . . The games was so honest it'd make a cat laugh, because they didn't have to be rigged to make a profit for the house. The place looked like your goforths would if you was to run them without shielding, so any game requiring quick recognition and quick reaction was naturally going to favor the dealer. There was sound baffles and photon walls and every other thing to trick your senses. Everything that wasn't holosim was mirrors. But I'd been a pilot, and if you follow your body's perceptions in space you're dead. I could look where the *Circle's* gameplayers didn't want me to look.

I could beat the house. I knew the odds the house offered, and the number of playing pieces in each of the games, their frequency of play, their value, and the odds against a winning combination.

How?

All of a sudden my skin was on too tight and the air was the wrong mix. The native funk and glitterflash was more alien than any thing I'd ever seen: these were *breeders*—organics—and they had to be destroyed so that my kind could survive. Odds and possibles crowded my head like might-be-maybes in a navicomp before Jump.

"*Kore?*" said Baijon. He put a hand on my shoulder and I was left with a jarring hole where the conviction I was god had been.

Some *thing* was wrong. Something important was wrong.

But the feeling vanished even while I tried to pump it up. For once I was going to use my brains, draw credit up to the limit, and then go arrange to be first off at the next stop. I was tired of this shooting gallery and twice-tired of breathing air that had somebody else's finger-prints on the mix. Kennor Starbringer could whistle for his political cats-cradle and his homicidal set-piece. Mama Sincere didn't raise any daughters *that* stupid.

I was so busy congratulating myself on my brains that I almost missed the guys that showed up to kill us.

* * *

I've always said I could smell trouble coming. Paladin says that all human events are patterns that the human mind can follow, just like solving for the next number in a mathematical sequence. And just like you can know when you've numbercrunched the wrong answer, you know when a pattern's got too many databits—or not enough.

Me, I know when to duck and when to gape at life's great mysteries. The pattern in the casino was wrong. I ducked.

"We got trouble, Pally!" I sang out without thinking. Baijon figured I was talking to him and came back as smooth as if we'd been partners forever. I heard his rings click on the hilt as he grabbed holt of his *arthame*.

"Through the foodservice—that way." He pointed, keeping his hand low so no one could see the move but me. He made a shape in handsign: *who?*

The Cardati assassin shimmered visible right in front
of me. His cham-suit was a flashy purple in the casino's
lighting. It looked liquid, picking up and pulling power
from all the broadcast and induction ergs bouncing
around the *Circle of Stars*. He had a vibro in his hand.

I kicked him in the face.

But I wasn't wearing my bar-fight boots. My sandal
shattered like cheap formfit (which was a disservice to it
as it was bloodydamn expensive formfit) and the trendy
spike heel left itself in the Cardati's throat. He gargled
and his cham-suit powered back up, only now it had
blood on it so it was half-visible, half not. I grabbed the
vibro he'd dropped and looked for Baijon.

He was halfway across the casino and a good distance
up the side of one of the gaming towers. It held a game
where the betting was on different weights falling through
variable gravity fields, and another Cardati was crouched
on top.

The Cardati had something I wanted more than home
and mother in his arms—a blast rifle.

And I was about to get it—bolt-first.

Killdozer #2 swept the casino with plasma valentines
and then settled into the serious business of retiring Yours
Truly to the dead letter office forever. Not Baijon, you
understand. Me.

The compartment changed its looks violently as all
kinds of holothings overloaded. Lights flashed on and
off. I decided to get up that betting tower before Merry
Goodnight there decided to let a little starlight into Baijon, which would mean letting a lot of starlight into me
in the sweet bye-m-bye.

Overhead one of the big chandeliers was drifting. I
climbed up on the nearest table and jumped, losing my
other sandal in the process. The glitterflash sunsilk I was
wearing split in as many places as it possibly could but
I didn't care. I was up.

The fixture groaned and sank and tried to go out when
I climbed it, and when I cut the cord mooring it to the
ceiling it dropped with a jerk.

But it didn't go all the way down. I shinnied around to
the central brain and vibroed open the controls. Payday

and hallelujah: it *did* have directional controls. I jimmied the lift to max and started motivating it toward the gaming tower. It'd make a great battering ram, and if I got close enough to the Cardati before he saw it he wouldn't dare fire and risk triggering a A-grav explosion.

On the other hand, he might be another of those toys-in-the-attic cases who put honor and duty above spending an honest earned paycheck.

People was starting to react. Back on Mikasa the *legitimates* hadn't shown up because the fix was in and the office was to set Kennor Starbringer up to take a very long fall. Here wasn't no suspicion of that: there was Ship's Security in bright red flashwrap all over everywhere. But mainly they was interested in getting the paying customers out safe. The patterns was all wrong for them to be moving against the assassins for a good two minutes yet.

I saw the one on the tower. And I saw the other two, the back-ups, the ones biding with their cham-suits fully activated. I saw them because of the way the databits—the *people*—was moving around them, oriented on them without even noticing. I saw them.

Was this part of some cute plan of Kennor's? Was *I* the one supposed to do for Baijon Stardust on account of some plain and fancy brainbending?

Were the Cardati there at all?

Get the rifle. Get the Cardati. And don't ask why or how. Not now.

It seemed like I could see six moves in advance, same illusion stardancers get sometimes plotting Jump, but that's just pure fourspace maths and this was human beings. But I believed it enough to jump off the chandelier a long time—seconds—before the Cardati on the tower found it and blew it up.

I might of been omnipotent, but I was still barefoot. I hit the side of the gaming tower and slid down the sides grabbing with both feet. I slid maybe half a meter and my stomach went flip-flop as I slid through the variable grav fields. Baijon was somewhere above me telling a bored professional killer to prepare to die without honor. I started to climb.

The casino was empty now and looked more like a honest ship's hold than anything I'd seen so far. The peculiar thing was, it contained not one red silk *legitimate* waving heat and demanding all of us to surrender. It didn't take time or genius to figure why.

I hackled all over when I felt the pressure drop and hung on to the side of the gaming tower. Atmosphere leak, all my instincts said. But the casino was big. It had to be along the central axis of the ship; they couldn't just void it to angels.

But they *could* pump all the air out. And they was.

It'd take whiles, but they had whiles. And after all, whoever was the baddies' targets was safe outside, right?

Wrong. They was in here trying to do their own wetwork, like a couple of right morons. And anybody want to cover the bet that the Cardati came equipped with their own oxy-supplies?

I hit a patch of bad gravity that broke my hold on the tower and started me down again. As I swung round for a better handhold I saw Baijon circling the Cardati. Hellflowers is faster than anything human, but Cardati cheat. The assassin was augmented, coked on battledrugs, whatever you like. And maybe wearing armor.

But he'd slung his rifle back over his shoulder to deal with Baijon, and I was sure he'd forgot all about me.

I've been wrong before.

The top of the gravity ladder was about the size of a cantina table and not as much room to dance. I reached the top and had a leg up when the Cardati spun around and grabbed me by it and sent me all fees paid at Baijon Stardust. The Cardati must of jumped then—*I* would of—but all I can say for sure is Baijon didn't slice me and it was a long way down to the floor.

But that wasn't what bothered me. What bothered me came after the landing.

You can't throw a vibro point-first into anything. A vibroblade is a cutting edge that's so thin and moves so fast that it really cuts the connections between things and not the things themselves—a hairsplitting difference when it's your throat. But you can't throw it point-first because there's no air-resistance to the blade and no balance.

Nevermind. I hit, and rolled, and came up clutching the last assassin's vibro. I switched it on and threw it.

Not at where the Cardati was. I couldn't see him.

At where he *would* be.

There was enough noise at the right time to tell me something got hit. I headed for it on toes and fingers, staying below the level of the gaming tables and trying not to notice the air getting thinner.

Four Cardati in the casino. One dead for sure, one maybe dead. I tried to remember everything I knew about them, but all I could think of was they was members of the Coalition, just like the alMayne.

It wasn't going to be much longer. There was a thin wind like bad air scrubbers blowing across us toward whatever vent was recalibrated for "suck." Already I had all the symptoms of exposure to a bad hull-leak, and telling myself they was all ignorant groundlickers and doing this on purpose didn't make it any better.

The vibro'd gone in and started to tumble until the inert matter of the hilt stopped it. It'd cut enough of the cham-suit to power it off. Cardati #2 was a Official Dead Person, all right. He was laying on the rifle.

How had he got it inboard? I reached for the barrel.

"The honor was mine!" yelped Baijon, snatching the Aris-Delameter right from under my lunchhooks. "The battle was mine, and—"

"There's two more," I said, and he shut up like his throat'd been cut. I took the blastrifle away from him and raised up slow.

Bet it one way, they wanted Baijon dead and me alive to frame for it.

Bet the other, and they might want anything at all.

"*Kore*, they are tampering with the air," Baijon said soft behind me.

"Yeah. We got about five minutes before we gray out. Then there's only two things to worry about."

Out of the corner of my eye I saw Baijon make the handsign for "*query.*"

"Whether they decide to pump air back in. And whether this was set up by the crew."

Empty room, and cold. Dark and getting darker as all

the trashed playpretties gave up the ghost. Here, somewheres, two invisible assassins in chameleon suits that I
couldn't of seen, that I was betting life and limb that I
had seen. And I was going to do my damnedest to ice
them before they weaseled out on me through Imperial
Mercy, because hired killers was a language I knew, and
when somebody sends them you don't let them walk. Not
if you want to get older.

I checked the rifle. Full charge. And all kinds of bells
and whistles for heat-seaking and target-acquisition and
all that cop, with calibrations I couldn't read any too well
for the way my eyes was blurring. And somewhere in six
cubic hectares of casino, high-tech sudden death.

The air current broke to my left. I swept the rifle that
way, switch forward for continuous fire. Everything went
up like the Imperial Birthday and then damped out for
lack of air to burn. I couldn't see what—or if—I'd hit.

But pattern demanded the second one be coming from
behind and to my right. I swung around that way. The
rifle made big gold blossoms of expended plasma-
packets. One of them hit something, outlined a hominid
form just as all the troubleshooting lights on the rig went
on and it overheated and jammed in my hands.

He was still out there. Their drag-man. The one who'd
mop up if things got messy. His suit was dead, but he
was alive and well and real soon now we wouldn't be.

Run, I 'signed to Baijon, and stood up. The Cardati
was in plain sight about a dozen meters away. He was
carrying a rifle.

My heart was pounding, but I could tell myself it was
anoxia, not fear. I might even of been right. Down below
the level of the tables, Baijon slithered out of sight.

The last Cardati took his time. He'd seen me throw
away my last two weapons, and even if he knew Baijon
was still alive and biting, he also knew that Baijon's whole
armament consisted of one X-centimeter inert-blade sacred knife. I watched him raise his rifle.

Then Baijon leapt up onto one of the tables a few
meters away with the war-ululation of House Starborn
(for all I knew) on his larynx. He didn't even try to close
the distance. He whipped his hand back and threw—right

for the soft underside of the jaw where even a man in an armored collar is vulnerable.

Never depend on high-tech when low-tech will kill you just as dead.

* * * * *

Valijon's Diary:

It is fortunate that, in the company of the *Kore* San'Cyr, I have been to many far-distant outposts of the Phoenix Empire and observed a wide variety of *chaudatu* customs. Doing so, I learned that one must hold one's self prepared for anything, and so I was not surprised to find that the *chaudatu* captain of the Company Highliner *Circle of Stars* held the *Kore* and me responsible for the attempt made by bought dogs upon our lives.

I made it known to them that they were tongueless fools not worthy of death at the hands of a servant of the Gentle People, and that by their careless act they had nearly taken from my *comites* her right to slay those who had insulted her.

They said that the false laws of the *chaudatu* permit them this, and that I know to be true, but I know also that many times the *Kore* has slain those who have occulted her honor. She speaks of the bureaucracy as inept and corrupt, therefore rather she would do her own slaughter than leave it in the hands of those who might fail.

They said, then, that it was only care for my honor and the *Kore's* that caused them to place us in this chamber which, though honorable, has doors that do not open. The *Kore* says it "looks like jig to her," but I do not know what "jig" is. I only know that soon we will return to the Homeplace, where I may say farewell to my promised wife.

I wish I had never left it. But the Emperor stretched forth his hand at Archangel's bidding, and at the Emperor's beck even a son of the Gentle People must hasten to do his dishonorable bidding.

Once it was not so. The walls of the Gentle People were strong and unbroached, and the Pax Imperador was kept in the safest place for it—behind the walls of Zerubavel Outport. We would have kept it elsewhere if we could, but to do so would be to immure us on the Home—

there are no starports in the Empire save those the Empire holds.

But in my ten-grandfather's time the Peace was kept. And now it is not kept—and all for the ambition of an ignorant beast-man.

We are not a wealthy people. Ours is not a rich planet. When I became a Person I learned the true history of the Gentle People all the way back to the time of the star trek. The Home Planet was chosen because it had nothing anyone would wish to take from us. We are a people of peace. Our only enemy is the Machine. There is no honor to seeking a lesser foe.

Without doubt the Emperor knows this, and Archangel with him. For a thousand years we have been left alone, tithing the Empire in our minds and bodies. We asked to be left alone, and there was no profit to be had in doing otherwise.

Now the Empire forces its will upon us—and it is a symbol of the shadow in our walls that Amrath lets them. The Delegate-my-father may not intervene; Delegate to the Court of the TwiceBorn is an Imperial title and holds no force on the earth of the Homeplace. In the Homeplace FirstLeader Starborn rules; or as the *chaudatu* name him, Director Amrath Starborn of the Starborn Corporation, ruler of Washonnet Directorate.

But he rules lightly. And each time the Imperial Phoenix spreads its wings he retreats before it. And each generation more of the power to speak for the Gentle People slips from the fist of our leader into the hands of the Delegate.

My father tried to stop that. He is Amrath's cousin—many chose to be insulted that our GreatHouse should take such insult from the *chaudatu*. Others, I know now, wished to be so insulted themselves. But the Delegate-my-father, Kennor Starbringer, President of the Azarine Coalition, Second Person of House Starborn—Lord Protector of the children of Amrath Starborn's bonding—could not give back the power Amrath had let fall into the fist that Amrath had closed.

So now the Phoenix presses in on us, for now, at last, we have something it wants. It wants our body and blood to help it go to war—to set the Machine to rule men once more.

My father has set his will upon this battle, but my part

in it is not yet. Now the *Kore* will fare far, as agent of justice against the Librarian Mallorum Archangel, who would bring the Great Death back into the world.

* * * * *

Baijon and me spent the rest of the tik to alMayne in *Circle*'s brig. I woke up to find out we'd been tried in absentia and convicted of being inconvenient. If Baijon hadn't been who he was, it would of gone further than that. As it was, we got put in a very plush box with locks that wouldn't be opened until we hit Washonnet space.

True-tell, I didn't try very hard. Wasn't no point to it. *Circle*'d already decided to skip any stops she might of made before Washonnet in favor of getting us offloaded un quel toot de sweet.

And I had bigger kicks to ship. Like who was I really, and for how long?

This wasn't just idle curiosity.

I didn't need the RTS any more.

I could hear Paladin now. Without it.

Oh, not like it being him anywhere near; not like *talking*. Just I could hear what I guessed he'd sound like thinking to himself: all kinds words I didn't know put together in ways I wouldn't of thought them.

If you can run an organic brain in parallel with a computer—if you can run a pulse from one to the other—if a Library can be resident in a computer—

Could a Library live in a human brain? Or part of one?

Was what I'd done in the casino because Paladin wasn't gone at all?

Or was it *Archive* that wasn't gone?

And what did that make *me?*

Once upon a time they transplanted a human brain to run a starship. The smartship went mad. They can borg a person down to thirty percent of the original tissue—is it human?

Where does born stop and made start, and which is a Library?

I spent a lot of time asking that question of a Library that wasn't there. And sometimes he asked me back.

"Butterfly," Paladin didn't say, sometimes at night, "what is human?"

"Human is what the Empire says it is. You know that," I'd answer.

Breeding populations are Imperial-rated on the Chernovsky scale, and if you slide off the end you're a wiggly, with no chance of being a citizen, ever. Some special cases—like mine—are "fully within the acceptable range" like it says here and still can't be citizens—are red-flagged, in fact, for execution or instant deportation to planet of origin without a spaceship. I've spent a lot of time fooling Chernovsky scanners in order to stay alive. I know what human is. Seeing what isn't there and shooting things where they're going to be isn't human.

"What's wrong with me, bai? What am I going to do?"

But Paladin never answered that, because he wasn't there—just a ghost-dance in my head indicating a few fatal errors on the hard-drive that was going to mean quietus for my bare bodkin Real Soon Now.

Paladin should of been here. That's what friends are for.

But he wasn't. He'd left.

I been left a good many times one way and another, run out on and sold out and plain and fancy deserted. And each time I made plans to make the significant other sincerely sorry for such a suicidal error in judgment.

But even when Errol Lightfoot sold me into the Market Garden slave pits, I hadn't ever been hurt this bad—like a sweet ship with her goforths candied and her jumptank nothing but broken glass. And I wanted to get Pally back and tell him so—only how do you catch something with no mass and no volume that's invisible, moves at the speed of light, and doesn't want to be found?

You don't. You sit in highliner jig. And you wait for them to put you off somewheres where every third person is out to kill you.

Which left me plenty of time to think and plenty to think of. Like, if it would of been stupid beyond permission for Kennor to let Baijon get iced before he made it to home and honor, just who'd sent me four Cardati assassins as a bon voyage present?

4

All for Hell and the World Well Lost

Zerubavel Outport is the Imperial toenailhold on al-Mayne. The alMayne don't like it, but Closed World status has headaches of its own, so they roll over for it. Inside the cantonment, by treaty, *both* Imperial and alMayne law are equally valid, which makes for some interesting times around the justiciary. Outside the cantonment, it's alMayne law only and every sophont for himself.

I was not losing sleep over this. I had no plans for leaving the port in any direction except straight up, whether Daddy Starbringer was keeping his word or no.

What I knew was that Baijon livealive was Baijon all set to be topped by Archangel again and dandled at Kennor until he geeked. Baijon had to be ungettable and that meant dead to any sensible way of thinking and that meant somebody taking the fall for it.

I could be wrong. And if I was I'd apologize, very truly sorry Kennor Starbringer thanks so much. But from a safe distance, and after I had proof. Until then, I had it in mind to stay alive.

And that meant outguessing Kennor Starbringer.

I'd missed the first time. I hadn't got us out of where he expected us to be. The only holecard I had left was I knew he was out to kill us and he maybe didn't. The only way I could see to play that was make sure Baijon didn't go anywheres I didn't and hope I could find us something to ride angels in before Kennor knew we'd got here.

That holecard folded up and died about six seconds after we stepped out of *Circle*'s lighter and saw the reception committee.

"They do you great honor, *Kore!*" said Baijon all excited. "My father will have told them we were bound here—and, see, FirstLeader Starborn comes to accept you as if you were one of the Gentle People!"

And even if Kennor hadn't, they could of got Baijon's name at least from the passenger lists in the ships-in-port directory that *Circle* would of sent on ahead of her.

I looked where Baijon was looking. Brother Amrath was waiting for to accept somebody, all right—him and about six dozen of his best buddies. They was spread out all round the docking ring—took up half the field and glittered like a jeweler's shop window—carrying flags and banners and everything in the way of heat up to and including a light plasma-catapult.

There was no way they could miss us.

I took a lungful of alMayne. The air was dry, sharp, high in oxygen. The sky above was hellflower's-eye-blue except for the bit where the sunscreens occulted the primary and left a darker-blue blotch that hurt your eyes to look at it. It must torque hellflowers to be stuck on a place that needs high-tech just to make it livable.

Gravity was a heavier pull than inboard the *Circle*, but nothing you couldn't get used to in an hour or so. I stepped out after Baijon, keeping a weather eye on the sun. Shadows is important on alMayne—step on the wrong one and I wouldn't have to worry about second-guessing Kennor.

The serious doubts I had about these hellflowers' intentions didn't trouble my buddy Baijon—that's Prince Valijon Starbringer to you—at all. He went bounding acrost the crete toward them, leaving me exactly nothing to do but follow. Baijon, in case nobody's noticed, is the cousin of Amrath Starborn, First Person of House Starborn, FirstLeader of alMayne, chairman of the Board of the Starborn Corporation, Managing Director of the Washonnet Directorate . . .

King.

I hoped Paladin, wherever he was, was having as much fun as I was about to.

* * *

The galactic paradise alMayne, if you missed out on hearing about it in school which I did, is too close to too hot a star (the catalogs say a Type 6 white dwarf) to be much use to anybody. If you dig far enough and careful enough through the not-really-proscribed stuff, you will find that the alMayne settled Washonnet 357-II from Somewhere Else. You can't find out where no matter how hard you dig: that tidbit is lost in the before-the-war time. Once they got here, they renamed the place and planetoformed the whirling fusion out of it.

Despite which (and this is the important part for those of us what have livelodes riding on a loose interpretation of the Trade, Customs, and Commerce Handbook), hellflowers don't *like* tech particularly, and most of what the Empire does best is on their list of Proscribed Imports. alMayne is one of the few places in this sophont's galaxy where you can walk a load of plasma grenades right past the Teasers and not get more'n a pained look, but take a hologenerator one meter off the port cantonment and you'll be hung from Zerubavel's walls on hooks. I've seen pictures of people who tried.

I stopped behind Baijon and looked at Amrath Starborn, hellflower high-heat, over his elbow. Amrath looked at Baijon and then at me. It's funny to think about a hellflower being soft, but next to Kennor he was. He didn't have any problems that ran beyond the atmosphere of alMayne, and I think I was maybe the third alien barbarian he'd ever seen in his life. But he talked Interphon at me and he did it himself without any kind of a translator.

"We welcome you, woman-not-born-of-the-Gentle-People."

"My heart lifts to see the walls of the great wall," I said in helltongue that was probably worse than his Interphon. But I gave it my best shot and the most antique response I knew. alMayne don't have protocol exactly, but they've got right conduct, and god help the rest of the universe if it can't guess what it is.

Trouble was, I did know exactly what to do now. I should offer him my *arthame*, to show him I knew he was so wonderful that it was a positive joy to put him in charge of my honor for a nanosecond or so.

Only I didn't have one. So I handed him the only thing I *did* have, which happened to be my travel permits and fake ID. I stood up straight as I knew how—bow to a hellflower and he'll likely kill you just out of pure reflex.

Oh, I was just a traveling wondershow of alMayne folk wisdom, all right.

And there wasn't no place I could of got it from.

I had the sick feeling you do in nightmares when you remember you forgot something but can't remember what, and I almost missed the exciting part where Amrath handed my tickets back.

"You will have a chance to earn better," he said, putting his hand over mine. *"And be no more knifeless,"* he added in helltongue, which should of worried me more than it did at the time.

Probably I should of taken more interest in this exciting, once in a lifetime, never-before-seen-by-*chaudatu*-eyes sight, but I was a lot more interested in the musical question of if I was remembering things I'd never learned, what had I forgot that I used to know?

Amrath went on to chaffer with Baijon. The troops closed up around us and we started off acrost the crete to where there was a bunch of open airbuses and sky-horse two-seaters all blazoned with the Baijon Stardust family crest.

There was nothing in sight that looked even a little bit like a starship with my name on it.

What it did look like was a family picnic shaping to shag Baijon and me off to darkest in-country, with no-body knowing where we was except just how ever many of Kennor's spies was hanging around getting restless.

But what it didn't look like was real healthy to interrupt a king when he was making up his mind what would be fun for Yours Truly. I could either make a fool out of Amrath Starborn in public or get into one of the airbuses.

I got into the airbus.

Somebody took the controls and Amrath's private fleet took off, looking like a miniature Imperial battle-array and about as well armed.

Something was not going the way it was supposed to go. I'd had that feeling before and I'd always been right, but then I'd always had some idea of how things ought to be going instead of how they was, and I didn't this time. I just hoped it was wrong for Kennor and not wrong for me.

*   *   *

Zerubavel Outport and Trade City was set in the middle of a jungle which was partly there to keep the *chaudatu* in line and partly there to ranch. alMayne don't do much in import-export, being technophobe, but they've still got to have enough on the galactic credit standard to pay their taxes. The part that doesn't come from mercs comes from med-tech. Botanicals.

The plantation surrounding Zerubavel covered several zillion hectares of green and leafy, and when it finally stopped it stopped like it was cut with a vibro. The other side of the cut was silica desert. The next best thing to ground glass hung in the air, blowing against the windbreaks and sliding down them with a hissing sound like poured sugar. Flying through the force-screens made my teeth hurt.

Maybe I could leave Baijon here.

I wanted to be back in a way of life I understood, without alien etiquette kicking a hole in my plans every two minutes. Baijon looked really happy. He belonged here.

I was farcing myself. He'd be dead in a kilo-hour.

On the other hand, Yours Truly was—in the words of the credit-dreadfuls—"instinct with the hellish taint of the preternatural Library," which Baijon if he found out'd like even less than becoming an Official Dead Person and would lead to even more unpleasantness for my favorite dicty-barb.

I hadn't known my brain was scrambled when I promised to take Baijon with me to keep both of us from getting killed.

I wondered how much else I hadn't known.

"Kore-alarthme?"

I spun round on Baijon fast enough so that he went for his *arthame* and I slapped leather. He looked embarrassed.

I looked around. The airbus was full of his nephews and cousins and aunts. None of them'd noticed.

Kids, they was. Soft downsider glitterborn, even with being hellflowers.

I looked back at Baijon.

"I came to enquire if you were well, *Kore.*"

"Je— Yeah. Am reet. But Baijon, we got to talk sometime."

He looked around at his collection of relatives and back at me. If I didn't trust them I was going to have a lot of explaining to do.

"They are blood of my blood."

Yeah, and so was Winterfire. "Look, bai, old home week is real, but wasn't we promised a ship and all? What is this?"

Baijon frowned, looking like a hellflower doing his level best to think like a *Kore-alarthme*.

"We are going to my home, *Kore.* To Castle Wailing. The LadyHolder of Wailing is the giver of all good gifts; surely my father meant her to disburse this ship; you will see. And there I will go before the Court of Honor and bear witness that *Malmakos* is among us once more, and bring tidings to the Gentle People that *Malmakosim* Mallorum Archangel is forever *al-ne-alarthme—*"

Terrific. I wondered just how Prince Mallorum Archangel, Imperial Governor-General, was going to like having his name dished all over the Empire. *Malmakosim* means "Librarian," *al-ne-alarthme* means Nonperson Forever, and alMayne is one-fifth of the Azarine Coalition and usually has the swing vote.

"The whole idea, Baijon-che, is that we is supposed to be escaping, not blazoning selfs with Intersign glyphs for 'shoot here.' "

"I must do what you say," Baijon said like it hurt his teeth.

Sure he must. But the cute little kink in all this hellflower *comites* was that if I carried on in what the home team's pride and joy thought was too dishonorable a *chaudatu* fashion, there was only one thing he could do.

Ice me to save what honor I had left.

And then kill himself for turning on his *comites*.

Fortunately for my reputation and nonexistent honor, right about then the airbus sideslipped and free-fell about a thousand feet. I was about to go over the side and take my chances when the para-gravity cut in and dropped us right in the middle of a courtyard surrounded by walls and stuffed with hellflowers.

Welcome to Castle Wailing.

* * *

Everything in sight was solid stone and two meters thick, including the hellflower hired help which showed up to help the hellflower high-heat say hello to itself. There was more this-is-not-protocol-because-we're-hellflowers, of which a darktrader has to put up with more of in the course of doing bidness than you might think. The high point was six hellflowers carrying a canopy under which two more hellflowers walked.

"The Lord Warden Daufin Swordborn of Wailing, and the LadyHolder Gruoch Starbringer of Starborn, come to welcome the FirstLeader back within walls," Baijon told me.

The Lord Warden looked distinguished but stupid, and the LadyHolder didn't. She had a face that could of been some kind of thousand-year-old tomb portrait: risto and serene and set for life. She was wearing a diadem with stones the color of her eyes and a fur tunic dyed to match. When the sun hit the fur it sparkled off the crystals in the guard-hairs; an offworld import and not dyed after all.

"*This* is what House Starbringer has pledged itself to in *comites*?"

And probably the first and last offworld thing that would haul any ice around Baijon's aunt. She'd even said it in Interphon to be sure I wouldn't miss how glad she was to see me.

"I greet you in honor, *Kore* Gruoch," Baijon said. "And I greet you in the name of my *comites, Alarthme*

Butterfly San'Cyr, a friend to the Gentle People and a
foe to the *Malmakos,* who gave me her walls when I was
naked. My father himself has said this.''

Gruoch did not exactly throw up on our shoes, but she
looked tempted.

"*Puer* Valijon brings frightful news to shadow our
walls, LadyHolder—but we have no cause to speak of it
here," chirped the Lost Daufin. More Interphon for my
benefit.

Gruoch chirped something long and involved in helltongue at Amrath and everybody around me relaxed. Him
and her and the Lord Warden went off together, leaving
me to wonder how much she'd meant to insult me and if
Baijon'd noticed.

A pack of kiddies with "Old Family Retainer, Hellflower Style" stamped on their warranties advanced on
Baijon. They stopped dead when they saw me, and Baijon crisped out the situation in a few well-chosen helltongue polysyllables. After that they looked like they
didn't know whether to commit suicide or tap-dance.

What I will always admire to my dying day is the way
people like Kennor and Paladin always overlook the important nuts-and-bolts of a situation whiles they're setting up their wannabe cloud-castles. There might be no
such thing as scum among the hellflowers, since you was
either a Gentle People or not worth discussing, but there
was for sure some 'flowers what hauled more cubic than
others.

A glitterborn—say, the Third Person of House Starborn—
might come to swear *comites* to someone he wouldn't
normally pass the salt to. I bet it was a hot topic for the
hellflower talkingbooks, providing they had any. And
when something like that happened, everything got honored about in a way very satisfying to the hellflower psy-
che so that the prince (except hellflowers don't have
princes) wasn't unduly disrespected, the pigherd (which
they don't got either) didn't get too set up in the world,
and everything was fine and nice and real friendly.

Only they couldn't do that this time, because I didn't
fit into their damn archaic dreamworld and the only class

I'd ever had was Acculturation Class in the Market Garden slave-pens.

What does a hellflower do when he runs into something in the honor-line he's never seen before and just shooting it would be too much trouble?

Right. He talks about it.

We stood right there in the middle of the courtyard where the airbus'd come down. First the chief Old Family Retainer told a story full of antique words about The Hellflower Who Swore *Comites* To A Tree, about the wisdom of fraternizing with your own species. Valijon answered back to that with detailed claims of my right to *alarthme* status.

So somebody else told a long story about how *their* great-granther took as *comites* a perfectly nice hellflower from the LessHouse next door who turned out to be another sort of etiquette problem I couldn't follow.

So much for the home-life of the most savage human race the Universe has ever produced. The serious money to be made out of this was in keeping the word from getting out. And none of this got me one meter closer to a way off this rock.

Eventually Baijon finished telling them I was as terrible as an army with banners and more powerful than a loco motive. The judges' decision seemed to be that I could be Baijon's twin sister with no taste (provisional), and if they'd guessed wrong their vengeance would be terrible. On me, you understand.

At least it meant we got in out of the weather. The lot of us finally went inside, heading for Baijon's boyhood rooms. The guards on the door homaged him and tried not to see me. Baijon walked through the door. Something dropped on him with a shriek. I cleared leather without a thought and threw myself down. Light flashed off my handcannon as I flung it up and aimed.

The guards hadn't moved. *They hadn't moved.*

I eased off the trigger just in time. They hadn't moved, and Baijon was on top of whatever jumped him, and the old family retainers was standing around like indulgent grannies.

I got up and put away my heat and walked over.

The floor was decorated in Early Galactic Weird but I
had no trouble spotting the pistol flung down on it. I
picked it up. Small and light; the barrel was jeweled and
some alMayne family crest was carved into the butt-
plates.

Baijon looked up.

"I damn near iced both of you, you know."

The hellflower underneath him saw me and let out a
mortified squeak. Baijon sat back and looked guilty, and
exasperated, and all the things you do when you're caught
between your kin and your life.

"But— This is my cousin, *Kore. Shaulla* Ketreis."

Child Ketreis eeled out from under Baijon and scrambled to her feet. She topped me by a good handspan.
Ketreis was still too unfinished to bear any resemblance
to the opposite sex, but it was plain that Baijon intended
to wait.

"My betrothed," he added.

"But— But is *this* your *comites*, Valijon? It *can't* be;
the WarMother has sworn that no more alien barbarians
would come to pollute the sacred Homeplace!" She gog-
gled at me like she'd never seen a *chaudatu* before and
didn't want to see one now.

"Ketreis!" thundered Baijon just like any mortified
bridgegroom.

"But she *is*," Ketreis protested. "She's *ugly*—and after the alien spy came the WarMother promised that the
first would be last and that they would come never again
to the sacred jurisdiction of the Homeplace and that when
I was grown and had my *arthame*—"

"The *Kore* Butterflies-are-Free is my *comites*," Baijon
said, giving each of the words a lot of space to roam
around in. This time it seemed to penetrate. Ketreis
stared at me in horror.

"I have offended," she suggested in careful Interphon,
staring down at me, and what else'd been said crowded
out everything else the WarMother—that's LadyHolder
Gruoch when she was t'home—had found to tell anybody.

Betrothed.

As in *"we're going to get married Real Soon Now, at*

least we was before I promised to spend the next fifty-six years in the never-never.''

"You could of got your damn hellflower self killed,'' I started up, but Ketreis flung herself on Baijon again, laughing at him and saying about how she'd won and now he was just a less-than-never-you-mind. I had obviously got all the attention from Ketreis I was getting this incarnation and Baijon looked like he had better things to do, too.

Kids' games.

I went away.

The next room was a bedroom. There was a solid stone bed covered with furs, a couple carved chests, a desk with a self-contained computer uplink. There was rifles and spears on the walls, looking ready to use. The window was big and wide open; you could see buildings and open land and the forest growing up to the edge of the Wailing plateau and then the savannah beyond. Baijon'd probably looked out that window every day of his life until he'd left to go with his da to Throne.

He came in a few minutes later looking like he'd just got another mail-order lesson from the College of Hard Knocks.

"I have offended,'' said Baijon. "She is my cousin, *Kore*—it was only a game. She is a child yet—her words are windflowers. There was no harm done.''

"Like hell. You maybe is the fastest B-pop on the heavyside and jumping each other is your indoor sport, but you do it around me and somebody's going to get hurt, even if I don't hit who I'm aiming at. Could of flashed that doxy of yours, you know.''

"*Shaulla* Ketreis,'' Baijon corrected me. "We are . . . we were to have married as soon as she became a Person.''

Were.

"Does she know?''

Baijon looked torqued. "What is there to *know*, Kore? I do not reject her or her brother. Perhaps I will come back.''

"You start farcing yourself, Baijon-che-bai, your life's going to be real short.''

High-caste hellflowers don't leave home, said the Child's Golden Encyclopedia of Galactic Wisdom I was wearing in my head—and when they do, it's in a whole hellflower garden and not schlepping around the Outfar with one lone dicty-barb. Baijon wouldn't be back to alMayne again. He wouldn't be the same enough for them to let him back into their insulated little hell'risto paradise.

I wondered if he was grown-up enough to know it.

"Perhaps I will come back. Perhaps we will come here again when Archangel is dead. With a large ship, *Kore*, and Ketreis . . ." He stopped and looked away.

"Yeah, sure."

"And tonight I shall tell all of our adventures, *Kore*—and warn the People against Archangel. Your name will be glorified among the Starborn as the wisest and most cunning of *alarthme*, who sees the Machine no matter its disguise. The LadyHolder will see that you are worthy, that your name is fit to hold in the mouths of the Gentle People—"

"Are you out of your mind? I am not interested in free publicity covering all the ways to commit High Book and low treason. All I want is for her WarMothership to give me what Kennor said. A ship, right? And then I am nonfiction, oke? You can suit yourself."

Baijon looked stubborn.

"The *Kore* has said what she has said, and her *comites* will look for wisdom in her words. Now I beg a boon. *Shaulla* Ketreis has asked my company. Is it your wish to release me from your service for this scant time?"

"Look, bai, it's not like I don't think your kin is a real wonderful bunch of hellflowers—"

"It will only be for a short time, *Kore*. I know my duty. I shall follow it faithfully. I shall return to serve you, as I am bound, at the feast the Gentle People give in your honor tonight, do you not scorn to attend it."

"Get out of here." Which might not be a real longevity-based idea, but if I had to put up with any more hurt dignity I'd shoot him myself.

So Baijon went off to canoodle with his girlfriend, and I stayed home and tossed his crib.

There was hardbooks, hand-written in hellscribble that I couldn't read. There was a dataweb uplink, looking damnall out of place in all that retro, and everything you cared to want in the way of junk jewelry, and some stamped pieces of metal I guessed was probably hellflower money. There was all kinds pieces of sharp and dangerous metal, and buried under all the furs on the bed there was a little private cache that Baijon didn't want anybody else to find.

Talkingbooks.

Them I could read real well—there was *Thrilling Wonder,* and *Amazing,* and *Weird Space Romances* . . .

Proscribed imports to alMayne.

I thought about the kid that'd got them smuggled in, never mind how—who dreamed about Outside and broke his teeth to get there, and even if it turned out to be horrible was still dreaming—of a ship big enough to carry him and his ladylove out to where the stars are born.

I put the talkingbooks back where I'd got them. And then I did what I should of done in the first place instead of weeping over the misspent enthusiasms of youth.

I didn't really believe in Kennor's ship anymore and if I did I didn't believe Gruoch was going to give it to us. I bet any credit we'd originally never been meant to leave the Port, much less come home to where all Winterfire's cousins was waiting to finish up what she started. I bet things was going wrong in all directions, if I could only see it. Assuming Kennor'd ever meant anything for me but a shallow grave, of course.

And we'd come home nice and public. Stay here long enough, and Archangel's assassins could find us and get to us if they had to walk here.

If I ran and left Baijon, he'd be dead.

If I took him with me and he found out what was happening to me, I'd be dead.

But neither Gruoch nor Kennor held all the high-cards. Not when this Gentrymort shuffled the sticks.

Baijon's uplink had nineteen kinds of restriction on it for fear he'd find out something exoteric and the screen only displayed in hellscribble. But it had a voder, and it could access the ships-in-port directory at Zerubavel.

What I found when I got in to look made this a whole new game.

There was still another way out.

I'd even give Baijon a chance to come with me.

One chance.

I owed the kid who'd had those talkingbooks that much.

5

From Hell to Breakfast

Nobody bothered me when I decided to take a stroll around Wailing to see where they kept the skyhorses when nobody was looking at them. I found the vehicle pool stuck off at the edge of a sheer drop off the plateau. Nobody was anywhere in sight, and I bet no one would be. alMayne is run on the honor system. There is no heat. Every babby learns Right Conduct at his mother's Knife and when he grows up he just naturally goes on with it even if nobody's looking. It was just too bad for the local flower garden that mama'd butchered pigs with her knife instead of using it to instill in me the finer points of hellflower stupidity. I could get off this rock, no problem. I was already making up my nevermind where to go and what to do oncet I cleared alMayne's sky.

It wasn't that the thought of having had my own personal brain catch-trapped by an anonymous Library of dubious morals wasn't keeping me up nights. It was that it didn't seem like there was anything I could do about it. Who could I tell, and what would they do but shoot me? Maybe if I could find Paladin he could fix it—or at least tell me what was wrong.

If I went out of here with Baijon, did I dare even start looking for Paladin? Ever?

If I didn't he was gone forever. I didn't think I could stand that.

And even if I could put up with being left one more time, letting go might not be such a good idea. If I forgot everything I knew and remembered everything somebody else knew, who would I be?

And what would I do?

At least it didn't seem like it was getting worse. Maybe

it was just a temporary artifact of playing computer in Archangel's basement. Maybe it'd go away.

"Hello," said a voice behind me. "I'm Berathia. Are you Prince Valijon's *comites*?"

I got to stop worrying about it, though, and be scared out of six years' growth instead.

"Hello?" said the voice again. I turned around real slow.

She was dark-skinned like a hellflower but not as tall, and no hellflower born ever had those curves. I half expected to see navigational hazard beacons posted. Her hair was dark and worn long enough to be hiding damn near anything in it, and so was her eyes, which didn't look like hiding anything at all.

She was dressed like she'd just stepped out of Grand Central, and I could see the personal shield she was wearing so as not to freeze shimmer every once and a while. There wasn't a weapon in sight.

"I'm Berathia. Who are you?"

"Oh, me? I'm just your basic tongueless doorstop."

There was a pause whiles Berathia checked her hearing.

"Nevermind. It's a long story."

"You don't need to worry about being seen with me, you know," Berathia said. "It won't affect your honor. They've decided I'm not an adult. It's simpler for them. I would have met you at the Port except for that—they don't allow their children out of walls."

For an honorary child she looked real full grown to me.

"So what are you really?"

Berathia laughed, showing off a choice collection of little white teeth.

"I'm an anthropologist, of course." She beamed, like being a people-studyier was supposed to impress me. "Of course, it was very difficult to get permission to come here at all, and I imagine Father had to remind some people he knew where the bodies were buried, but here I am! And—"

You didn't have to listen to Gentle Docent Berathia Notevan, or even pretend to. She followed me back to

Wailing (there being no point in sticking out here with an audience) and with no work on my part I found out she was a scholar of the Imperial College of Man, a licensed Chernovsky technician, and was here studying about what hellflowers get up to whiles they're lonealone at home, to do which she'd had to put in all manner of fixes, and with which the LadyHolder was not particularly pleased, although King Amrath thought she was cute.

I didn't even really have to be here, I bet; she was determined to tell somebody about unscrewing the inscrutable.

"—of course the anthropology is a cover of sorts; my real interest in alMayne is the Old Federation Technology, and they have so much of it here. Libraries are very important to the alMayne; an active part of their ongoing culture. They're saying all over Wailing that Prince Valijon has destroyed an actual Library Archive— Are you all right?" Berathia asked with interest. "I'm sure it was my fault; I'm so clumsy—Father always says I'd be a perfect backup weapon for the Imperial Space Marines. Just send me in and destroy *anybody's* manufacturing capability for up to a dozen kilo-hours . . ."

I looked up at her. Berathia blotted out a good chunk of the sky; like a sunscreen but better looking. I didn't quite remember falling over anything.

"Library?" I said. "Chapter Five illegals?"

Chapter Five is Chapter Five of the Revised Inappropriate Technology Act of the nine-hundred seventy-fifth Year of Imperial Grace. It deals with Old Fed Tech in general and Libraries in particular. Around my neck of space it's known as High Book. Class One is the possession or concealment in fact simple or collusion to possess or conceal—or even just knowledge of the location of any part of if the Office of the Question is feeling nasty—a Library. A Old Fed Library. Old Fed Tech.

And they had so much of it here?

"Chapter Five?" said Berathia blankly. "Oh, the ITA. Don't worry about that, it's perfectly legal. And of course Prince Valijon's done no such thing, but I get most of my information through palace gossip and you know how distorted *that* is. If not for the logotek this trip would almost be a waste, but of course there are always the talkingbook rights.''

I'd got up, but I was still staring. Don't worry about the ITA, this *legitimate* glitterbaby says, like the thing I spent half my life running from was something nobody paid no nevermind to anymore.

''alMayne has one of the best research logoteks on Libraries in the Empire,'' Berathia said. ''Oh, I admit it isn't common knowledge—that silly prejudice—but it's all perfectly safe and I have a permit and everything. Say, didn't you travel with Prince Valijon? Can you tell me—''

''You came here to go and find out about *Libraries*?''

''Well, of course!'' said Berathia.

Sure, je, reet, j'keyn, don't everybody?

* * *

Irrelevant linguistic note: in helltongue the root word for child and outsider—which happens to be *t'chaul*—is the same. When I got back to Baijon's suite, my own pet candidate for both was waiting there for me.

''*Kore,*'' he said, ''I abase myself.''

''Yeah, sure. Who do you know what's named Berathia Notevan, and what's this all same along you 'flowers got a bunch of Libraries in your basement?''

''*Kore?*''

''You know, a anthropologist? Short, dark, and naked?''

Baijon ran a hand through his hair and looked baffled. They'd done him up hellflower-style, and hellflower or no, any experienced bar-fighter could rip him up in six seconds flat, from pretty looped braids and dangly earrings to stompable rings on six out of ten of his best fingers.

Prince of the blood. And young enough to be sure he could beat death, certain easy, now that he was back on his home turf with his kin all around him. Only even his kin was out to get him, and I didn't know why.

''The . . . A *chaudatu* woman?'' he finally said. ''She is a spy.''

It turned out, on sober consideration, that she was a spy along of cause she was going to find out things about the Gentle People (like what they ate for breakfast) and go tell it to somebody. Baijon felt this represented a serious lowering of hellflower social standards.

"In my ten-father's time it would not have been, *Kore.*"

"Je, che-bai, but was she true-telling or no?"

"The Gentle People were born to fight the Machine," Baijon said happily, "and walk in terror and fury of it all our days. We alone of all the people remember it as it was."

"But what about—"

"And so that we are not confounded, each generation Memory walks among us, and Memory abides in the logotek of the War College and schools us in the evasions of the Machine."

One of which Machines, incidentally, Baijon his own self had spent more than twenty days within a few meters of and hadn't twigged to.

But the War College I knew. It'd been pointed out to me on the Grand Tour: sort of a finishing school for hellflowers, and famous enough that even I'd heard of it. Sometimes it even sent experts out to show the Imperial Space Marines what to do on the heavyside, but nothing to do with space war. AlMayne aren't pilots.

Not for a thousand years.

I felt something roll over slow in the back of my mind, just waiting to make trouble. There was two things I wanted real bad.

One was to get out of here *now*.

T'other was to gosee what it was hellflowers knew about Libraries that I didn't.

"Baijon," I said. "Is a thing I want to tell you about getting out of here—"

But I didn't get the chance.

* * *

The banquet hall was at the center of Wailing; we went down a lot of steps. No suspicion of a A-grav drop here;

most of the systems in Wailing was passive systems, designed to run without power. I even saw torches and candles.

Just like home.

It had not been a good idea to come here, even if it wasn't mine.

The armorer for Starborn had interrupted me getting down to cases with my little buddy Baijon. It seemed Starborn wanted even social embarrassments to look their best.

Baijon said they was doing me honor. In that case, honor meant a lot of stupid clothes.

But that wasn't all it meant. And the rest of what they tricked me out in fit in with my life career plans so well it made me nervous.

There was a Aris-Delameter crossover rig that'd make Destiny's Five Cornered Dog weep. It had two fully-charged blasters rated to punch a hole in a brick starship strapped down nice and functional, and there was a third hideout blaster that the Starborn Armorer practically begged me to take slipped down the top of one boot with a set of throwing daggers in the other. I had a brand new replacement for my old inert throwing-spike down the back of my neck and half the jewelry I was wearing exploded if you pushed the right bit.

I looked like something out of the credit-dreadfuls. But I was in hellflower heaven all right, and everybody else was got up even gaudier.

I pulled Baijon aside as we was about to go in. The room was already full of hellflowers, and I had a hunch I was going to be put somewhere public.

"Look. I ain't got time to be reasonable. I'm getting out of here tonight. You coming with me or not?"

"*Tonight?* But *Kore,* you cannot mean—"

"Don't you be telling me what I mean, bai, got too much of that already. You coming or no?"

He was young enough to think it was fun. "I am with you," said Baijon Stardust. "I will tell the Lady-Holder—"

"You be telling her nothing, bai!" I grabbed his arm.

"We do this on the cheat, je? How long is this thing going to go on?"

Baijon looked over his shoulder at the banquet hall.

"Until dawn, *Kore,* but—"

"Oke. I wait one hour. First good time after that, I go out. You give it another half hour, you do a fade without nobody noticing. Meet me at the skyhorses, je?"

"Ea, Comites."

*   *   *

It was not one of my best plans, but it had the virtue of being quick and cheap. Baijon and me went in and got told off our places. For high formal dinners on alMayne you sat on backless benches at a wooden table. Just like I'd thought, I was going to be in plain sight. Well, there was ways around that.

This was actually the alMayne Court, cep'n there weren't no Imperial Legate here. I sat six down from Amrath at the High Table with Baijon standing behind me and could see the whole room. Wall to wall it was full of damn near genetically identical hellflowers.

Except one.

Berathia Notevan was sitting right beside Amrath, being stoically ignored by everyone there but him. The seat on the other side of Amrath had LadyHolder Gruoch's chop on it, and it was empty. Common or hellflower garden sense said it shouldn't be.

There was trouble in hellflowerland.

Local politics, I thought, and nothing to do with me, but anything that bobbles the Azarine Coalition ain't local.

*   *   *

You see, once upon a time there was these mercenaries, five races worth. They had a thing called the Gordinar Canticles, which same forbid them to take the field against Imperial troops, but other than that they was your common or garden play-for-pay kiddies, and anybody in the whole wide Empire with good solid credit could hire them.

This is what's called Azarine Coalition Neutrality. Coalition Neutrality is the basis for our way of life here in the Glorious Phoenix Empire, and Mallorum Archangel wanted to put an end to it. Not that he wanted the *coalitiani* to give up their way of life—he just wanted to be the only one who could hire them, period.

A private little army for a private little war, and the fact that Archangel was still after the legal transfer of polity in the Coalition did not mean quite as much to me as the fact that Archangel was after *me*—and LadyHolder Gruoch Starbringer, who probably wouldn't recognize Archangel if he turned up in her sock drawer, looked like sharing a number of his aims with regard to Yours Truly.

So I ignored the storm warnings in beautiful downtown Wailing in favor of plans for bidding a swift farewell to the land of a thousand sidearms.

Mistake.

6

The Haunted Bookshop

The horizon'd rose and cut off the primary some time before, and the sunscreen blotted out most of the stars. It was pitch-dark as I made my way past Wailing's sentries.

The party had degenerated into serious drinking and the telling of shaggy-*chaudatu* stories. Hellflower neurotoxin will cause damage to your liver that only hellflower fetch-kitchen can repair. Nobody'd noticed much when I left the party after the first round.

The House Starborn logo on my clothes made sure I wasn't challenged by anybody. On their home turf hellflowers is not the galaxy's most suspicious sophonts. At least not of other hellflowers, and it took some time for the news to trickle down that *chaudatu* weren't like real people.

It was bitter cold, and for the first time I was glad I was wearing a purple crushed-velvet surtout trimmed with green vair-fur for my stroll to the vehicle pool. Baijon would be a half-hour or so behind me, and then we could slide, reasonably free of charge, back to the Outport and Trade City.

And I was walking away from the biggest—maybe the only, outside Tech Police HQ—supply of hard information on how to find my buddy Paladin and what was eating my brains out.

Saving my and Baijon's skin was a strong counter-argument all the way to where the airbuses was parked. But after I jimmied one and bypassed the ID transponder, the flight computer, and the ignition—all idiot systems—there was still a good chunk of time before I could expect Baijon.

And the logotek was just sitting there. I could see it from where I stood: a darker patch of sky. Wouldn't be nobody there. Everybody'd be at the banquet, and hellflowers don't lock their doors. If there was anything I couldn't read I could take it with and have Baijon read it to me later.

I'd *need* to know this stuff.

Baijon'd wait for me. And wasn't nobody expecting us to do this in the first place so they wouldn't be looking.

I had the margin.

I thought.

*   *   *

A logotek is where you keep all the words nobody's figured out how to make into books yet. The War College logotek specialized in Old Fed Tech, and to hellflowers that means just one thing.

Libraries.

There was watchlights in wall-niches every few feet oncet I got inside—just fire and fat and string in a glass cup.

I hated them. They were cold and dead. They did not take energy from the Net. They did not give energy to the Net. They were cut off.

I took a deep breath and reminded myself I'd been born in a sod hut with a dirt floor, where you used animals to drag a piece of tree through the ground so you could stick seeds and roots into it to grow dinner for later.

A place that Libraries wouldn't like, because without computer dataports and tronic interfaces there was nothing for them to see or touch.

A place like alMayne was, even though it was an Open World with Imperial trade, because hellflowers was expecting Libraries to come to tea any minute and they didn't want them to feel too welcome.

Paladin'd always complained about the low-tech in the Outfar, but I'd just thought he was putting on airs. But all his information about the world had come from artificial senses, and those took hands to build and energy to run. Without them he was blind, deaf, dumb, halt, and imbecile.

Any Library was.

But I wasn't a Library, I reminded myself. I wondered how hard it was going to get to remember that, and if I'd even care when I forgot.

But I knew that trick too, and thinking about it doesn't change anything. The only cure is bidness.

* * *

I took one of the watchlights with me when I went downstairs. I passed a lot of signs that said the hellflower equivalent of "go away" and then a lot more explaining how insanity and mange would result from going one step more.

Then I was in.

It wasn't a big room, but it was still wider than it was tall. The walls had glow-strips in them, with a little plaque by one saying they was certified Old Federation construction. There was display cases around the walls.

What could I take that would do me any good?

I went up to the first case. It held pieces of Libraries, dead, and with everything they'd ever known gone.

If I forgot everything I knew I'd be dead, sure and simple. There might be something breathing, but it wouldn't be me, Butterflies-are-free Peace Sincere.

Wouldn't that be the same if the whole Empire forgot everything? They'd already forgot so much. What if they forgot more—or decided to just chuck it all? What would be left?

Death on such a scale it made me go weak in the knees to think about it—and nothing I could do to get in the way.

Nothing.

My hands shook like Archangel was right behind me, waiting to scoop the lot. I passed dioramas about places that was just points outside the Empire's borders on a better-than-average star-map these days. Places that was cinders and gas and had been a thousand years and more.

Places I remembered. Orilice. Miramolin. The Drift.

Harakim-Selice. Places where Libraries had taken over people somehow, and got them to let them in, and—

No. I had made a life career of not thinking about things, and I was going to put it to good use.

I passed a bunch of displays of weapons proof against Libraries, of catch-traps to load into your computer system to burke them, of sure-fire ways to spot a Librarian. If I didn't find something useful in the next five seconds, I was giving up. I already knew more useless stuff than I wanted.

That was when I found The Book. It was new manufacture—a flatcopy thing with pieces and pages like there wasn't much use for any more—and when I opened it it was written in something I'd never seen before. Not Intersign, not Interglyph, not Imperial Standard, helltongue, or even Old Federation Script.

The only thing was, I could read it.

Not like I was reading a page of Intersign. More like a talkingbook; I looked at the page and I could hear it in my head.

The first page said "A True History of the War." I skipped through, glancing at the pages, but it made me dizzy. Something about the Main Library Complex at Sikander.

I put it under my arm and left.

*   *   *

You could see a few stars through the sunscreen; I knew by the way they'd shifted I'd been down under the there longer than I'd thought. It was a good fifteen minutes past the time Baijon was supposed to meet me, but he knew to go to the airbuses and *wait*. He'd be there, or have left Sign that he'd been.

I got about six meters from the logotek when I realized trouble was up. I made it back to the inside of the logotek and to the first halfway oke place to hide The Book.

I didn't want to do it. I wanted to know what it knew. Knowledge must never be lost.

But by that glass slipstick, all what I knew should be kept around whiles longer, too. I hid The Book in a looked-like pile of other books and slid back out of the logotek.

This time I saw for true what I'd only intuited before. There was torchlights moving, which meant people was looking. And with a well-developed sense of peril-noia, I knew the only one they could be looking for was me.

Dry cold air rasped my throat as I jogged back to the airbus. There was nobody in sight and nobody around, and there hadn't been either. Baijon'd never got here.

Where was he?

I'd told him to be here. Baijon would willingly miss out on doing his *devoir* about the time he signed up to be a Space Angel.

I could run now. I might even have time enough to leg back for The Book first.

It was sort of comforting to know flat-out I wasn't going to do it.

* * *

But that didn't mean I was going to just walk back and lie down for the chop. I did my personal best to avoid everybody as was out looking for somebody, and finally came to a chunk of wall I recognized.

Baijon's room was dark but there was someone in it breathing. I stuck both feet through loops of vine and raised my head up over the sill slowly. I saw the faint flicker of a personal shield.

"You maybe want be keeping quiet, jilly-bai," I said.

"For heaven's sake, get in here before someone sees you," said Berathia Notevan.

* * *

"I hoped you'd come back here—you weren't seen, were you?"

The room was dark and empty. Someone else'd been through and found Baijon's talkingbooks and left them out in plain sight.

"Where's Baijon?"

"He's going to be all right," Berathia said, and if it

hadn't been for her shield I'd of grabbed and throttled her.

"You tell me how he's going to be all right."

"Look, that isn't important right now. The alMayne have a unique racial psychology. I'm afraid that Lord Starbringer accidentally made things rather difficult for you by allowing Prince Valijon to enter a state of *comites* with you. The LadyHolder is deeply offended, and—"

I got out a blaster and looked at it.

"You be telling me where Baijon is, 'Thia, or I fire this."

She twitched. A personal shield is just like what you wrap around the short-term controlled fusion reaction of a blaster-bolt, except it's bigger and it stays around longer. It's no particular use against a blaster, neither, because the first bolt overloads it and the second one cooks what's wearing it. Sometimes the overload is big enough to do a straight conversion to kinetic potential. Boom.

"Prince Valijon made the mistake of calling the Imperial Governor-General a Librarian," Berathia snapped. "They've locked him up until he can be cured. Now they're looking for you to find out what drove him mad."

Hellflower logic: The *comites* is responsible for every action by his *servites*. *Every* action. Fine.

Only I'd made two minor miscalculations tonight.

I'd thought Baijon wouldn't make a after-dinner speech titled What I Did While On The Lam With The *Kore-Alarthme*.

And I'd thought any pack of hellflowers would just naturally believe him when he got up on his hind legs and hollered Librarian.

But he had. And they hadn't.

On the other hand, Gruoch (who'd showed up just in time for all this) wasn't willing to call him a liar. She decided he'd been tainted by the Machine (the same one she'd just refused to believe in, mind.)

"He isn't crazy," I said.

Berathia actually stamped her foot. "That doesn't *matter*, I told you! To the alMayne, one of you must be— and they have only one way of finding out which. They'll purify both of you, and then ask both of you again—but *you're* not going to be alive to answer.''

I would not put it past a hellflower to ask me anyway and be meeved when I didn't answer him.

"You've got to come away with me *now*," Berathia said again. "I have transport hidden at the edge of the plateau. They aren't used to interfering with children. You can—''

Someone was coming. I knew it because I knew it was *time* for someone to come and try rousting Baijon's crib on the chance something interesting might be to home.

"Look. It's a cute idea but it ain't going to work. For the record, I guarantee Archangel's doing High Book. Now get out of here or they'll have you, too.''

Berathia started to argue when a little light on her belt blipped.

"I'll be back,'' she said, and went over the window-sill.

Anthropology must be interesting work.

* * * * *

Valijon's Diary:

The Loremasters teach us that the universe is a whole, and that being in all one thing, it can be studied from any beginning. To measure a circle, begin anywhere.

So it is true that what the beast-men do on their far-away thrones is visible within the House of Walls—though only philosophically so. One does not expect to see what the *chaudatu* do affecting the Gentle People. Space is too vast, or so I once thought.

Perhaps my eyes are opened even as my soul is shadowed—or perhaps the clatter of their tongueless souls becomes great enough to reach us within the walls of our first and last defense.

That the Phoenix Empire is corruption itself the Gentle People have always known. It could not be otherwise, governed by beasts. The Loremasters teach us that the simplest solution—to ourselves govern the Empire and make it a sure citadel against the *Malmakos* and its wiles—is folly. They say it is the Gentle People who would be destroyed, and so long ago the First-to-Seize chose that the alMayne would not seek the throne for its blood. For us and for all time he chose not to compromise with beasts.

In kingship there is always compromise. Between People it is safe and honorable. Between a Person and a beast it is suicide.

Many generations have praised the name of Lodir Starholder First-to-Seize and the hard path he chose for us. Thus we kept ourselves ready, so I was taught.

But now I do not see it so. The Libraries rise up again and we are not ready. Somehow our separatism has lost instead of saved us. We only pretend to honor while being as corrupt as the Phoenix Court.

The *Kore* said that I must go away with her this night, and so I promised, even though tomorrow the *Shaulla* Ketreis becomes a Person and might, in honor, choose to accompany us. But possibly it is better to go now, so that we may return, triumphant, when Archangel is slain as the *Kore* and my father plan between them.

So I thought, and so I promised as I was bid—they are *chaudatu* words, but the *Kore* knows no better. But equally I could not depart from among the People without alerting them to their peril: the Machine is awake and among us, and Mallorum Archangel takes up the cursed mantle of Librarian. My father knew this. My father bade me speak, and warn the Gentle People of the betrayal by this Emperor who forces our fealty.

And I gained nothing.

Before I was born it was known that, did luck not favor me, I must risk my shadow against the curious customs of the *chaudatu*. My father saw to it that I was instructed in history: the getting and holding and losing of dominion.

Now my father's aid has been turned against me. The LadyHolder spoke in all honor of the madness that festers in the abodes of the Tongueless Ones, of how things may seem to be but are not. She spoke of unwisdom in binding a servant of the Gentle People to one of whom no one may know the virture of her words, and how the *chaudatu* are as cunning as the *Malmakos*.

And when she was done, no one would listen to me. More, she swore that they *would* listen, once I was purified and fit to be among them once more.

I told her that she spoke as Alaric Dragonflame had

spoken, when he promised me the safety of his Knife and Walls and set instead the Wolves-Without-Honor to seek my life. And so I am bound, and they seek the *Kore* also, to prove her.

But she will have fled. I may, in honor, hope for this. Gruoch will not hear of the Machine—she will render the *Kore* tongueless forever lest she speak of it.

How could we fall so low, knowing our danger? Just as the human body weakens and dies, so do kingdoms and thrones. It was true also among the *chaudatu:* mad they may be, and tongueless, but they age and die and their political systems also. Long peace breeds decadence and rot.

But we *knew* this! Never did one GreatHouse hold power long: each was free to demand what service it would, if only the Pact against the Machine were kept.

Now it is not kept. No one of the Gentle People is free to disregard the claim I made, to swaddle it in *chaudatu* words until its truth is murdered. If I am wrong, let me die rather than bear the living shame—but test my words, not my body!

Gruoch will not. And thus all is over.

I have studied history. I know the marks of decadence and decay. They are ours, and we are dying: the People have been too long kept from the whetstone of battle, and have decayed.

Could my father have not known this? Or did he see only what he wished to see, and hoped for goodness in what he could not change?

Or did he send me to awaken the Gentle People once more?

On Mikasa he told me of the binding he weaves for Archangel; strand by strand and year by year, preparing his trap with the very *chaudatu* Archangel seeks to rule. My father prepares the battlefield against the day of battle when the Gentle People will be called to stand in judgment.

But when they are called, will they come?

I do not think so. I think they no longer wish to hear. The threat of our ancient enemy was brought forth, and no battle was offered, only lies. GreatHouse Starborn will fall for this cowardice, and not alone. I do not think this time that the Empire will let us be. Our ways are too alien.

Our intolerance of the Machine which they court dooms us in spirit or flesh.

If the *Malmakos* is to rule Man once more, the Gentle People must be broken to smooth its path. In a time that our walls should have been seamless, we have opened our gates to its hounds.

We have become the instrument of Imperial Peace. We have become the promise of war.

* * * * *

In a sweet gesture of unanimity with a Empire they can't see for dust, alMayne honored guest quarters for people they'd rather shoot is cold, drafty, locked, and surrounded by hostile irritated people—who was also crazy, because when they'd unilaterally decided I'd rather be here than in Baijon's old rooms they'd left me everything I was standing up in.

But even with three blasters, four throwing knives, a vibro and six kinds of grenade I wasn't ready to stage one of my patented usually successful escapes. Not without more information than I had or looked like getting.

Gruoch didn't like me; I knew that already. But (if I could believe Berathia) she hadn't believed Baijon when he'd pushed every hellflower's favorite button, and that was a little harder to figure.

I realized then I was actually trusting Kennor, who'd said, back on dear old Mikasa, that on alMayne the word of an Honored One would be believed. Well it hadn't been, and that left me two and a half choices.

He was wrong.

He was lying.

Or all three of us'd been set up.

Just what *had* Archangel offered Winterfire to go bent, anyway?

* * *

alMayne either doesn't have a moon or it stayed home that night. No stars through the shield from this direction, but a couple rainbow reflies—Wailing must be right on the approach route to the Outport.

I found out that the open window was a sheer drop and the door a) was guarded by people not interested in polite conversation and b) didn't open from the inside. About the only thing I could do was kill myself, and I didn't think that'd help Baijon's chances of being tried and found human. I even tried pushing for that weirdness living inside my head, but it was on vacation, too.

So here I was in the beautiful open-air dungeons of Castle Wailing, having done all the right things for the wrong reasons and still preparing to become an Official Dead Person sometime in the near future.

I decided I'd been wrong about Kennor. Kennor wasn't out to kill us (probably). Kennor didn't need to set up advanced plots to kill Baijon and me. All he had to do was send us back to alMayne.

Sometimes I'm too subtle for my own good.

And while I was being subtle, I bet I knew what Archangel'd offered Winterfire.

Hellflowers is xenophobes, and I know from xenophobes: my Luddite ancestors didn't like everybody else so much they climbed down a gravity well and threw away the key. But holograms can be regenerated from a single piece and so can cultures. Even Interdicted, the Population of Granola generated a few xenophiles each generation—enough to keep the Patriarchate in kindling.

But hellflowers wasn't Interdicted. And so there was an even better system in use here, to make sure the hellflower you sent out among the hellgods was the same one you got back. Baijon'd walked right into it. They was going to prove him until he fit right in with the rest of the hellflower rootstock or died trying. And I got to go along for the ride.

And how many hellflowers was tired of this little arrangement and wanted to close the doors on the Federated Imperial Galactic Union of Tongueless Doorstops, *Chaudatu,* and Social Cripples?

The Governor-General could get them Interdicted status. He could waive the escrow account and the filing fees. He could even seal them up and let them stay right where they was.

If he was real nice, he'd let them keep the batteries for their sunscreens, and I bet the conservative faction on jolly old Washonnet 357-II'd never thought about *that*.

I wished, all sudden-like, to know what relation Winterfire and Blackhammer was to LadyHolder Gruoch, and if they'd ever all sat around the Court of Honor drinking tea and talking about what little umpleasantnesses stood between them and Closed World status. Ketreis'd even mentioned it and I'd been too stupid to notice. "The WarMother is going to get rid of all the *chaudatu* for eke and aye," she'd said. How else could Gruoch do it but by getting alMayne Interdicted—and in a way that didn't put the question to an open vote.

Ice Baijon. Kennor stops being President of the Coalition. Morido Dragonflame—who might or might not be on the Interdict Party's side—steps up into the Presidency and allows the revision of the Canticles that makes the Coalition into Archangel's private army, with or without hellflowers. Archangel conquers the universe.

I wished that was all. Archangel could have the universe for all of me; I wasn't using it. But what he was going to do with it was fill it with brain-eating evil Libraries—and the Empire's guardians of truth, justice, and the organic way was stupid enough to let him do it as long as he promised them a planet of their very own.

Kennor couldn't know this. His son was betrothed to Gruoch's daughter, for Night's sake. And because he hadn't known, Baijon's and my run for freedom was going to be real short.

It was not much in the way of consolation to know I'd beat the odds by about twenty Galactic Standard Years of survival, or that Baijon getting the chop this way would leave Kennor whole and frisky in the astropolitical arena to fight Coalition neutrality to the last redoubt.

I'd promised I'd keep Baijon alive.

And if we both died, who was going to stop Archangel's war?

* * *

The horizon slid round and the primary changed relative position and nobody brought me breakfast. Around the time I managed to get myself thoroughly depressed and nobody brought me dinner the door opened, and a Very Large Person walked in and took what passed for my mind right off politics.

The alMayne (says Paladin) came here from somewheres else just after the Library War. They bought the Washonnet system (which did not have anymuch of a thing in it worth having at the time) and planetoformed its likeliest-looking planet, which they call *Home* and everyone else calls *alMayne*.

Whoever'd started the place did it with a gene-pool smaller than a Interdicted Colony's—hellflowers all look like each other's sister and is *hard* to tell apart.

Paladin says that along one time you could find just about every variation in genotype there was all together on the same planet. But even he couldn't remember just when that was and it sounds damsilly to me. Genetic drift'll get them every time.

NB: a lot of dicty-colonies fail because they don't have enough people to burke a run of bad luck. But they've paid hard credit for nobody to go in and help them, so when they all die the Empire sells the world again. Economical.

So all hellflowers is long and whippity and don't even bother to register hair and eye color on their ID, right?

Wrong.

The 'flower that came in to my box with locks was two meters and a bit and he could of made three or maybe six of Baijon. His eyes was gray—almost white—and the pupils looked like negative stars in a continuum I didn't want to visit.

He was carrying The Book I'd filched from the logotek.

"I am the WarDoctor Firesong of no House. Memory has heard that the *Malmakos* has returned." His voice went with the rest of him. I wondered which of my fingers he was going to break first, and I couldn't even tell for sure if he was mad.

"Je; pleased to see you, too. Where's Ba—*Val-i-jon*

Starbringer,'' I said, pronouncing it real careful so there couldn't be any adorable confusion over who I meant.

"Valijon is preparing himself. Tomorrow his person-hood is to be tested. I have come to speak to you of yours.''

I didn't want to stare at The Book he had in his hands but I couldn't help it.

"Purifying himself. And what exactly does that mean when it's t'home?'' I wanted to blast him but I needed information, and The Wall That Walked was the closest thing to a DataNet Terminal in sight.

"You are worthy in my brother Kennor's eyes, but you are an outlander, and soft. Valijon Starbringer has said words, but the Gentle People do not yet know if his shadow is his own. Valijon must be pure to fight the Machine. If it has touched him, I must know.''

Reality took a half-spin and I thought about a hundred things—allergies to the local food, poison in the drink. It was like trying to use somebody else's mind to think with, or tripping over a catch-trap somebody'd loaded into your navicomp. I'd been drugged, one time and another. It felt like this.

Pure to fight the Machine. I was thinking, but they wasn't my thoughts. The Machine—

Human personality is a lot more derangeable than the folks back home might think. On Granola, the only way to change a body that much was to kill him. I got out into the Empire and found out the question wasn't *whether* but *how much?*

Persona-peel. Memory-edit. Dreamlegging. And a whole hellhouse fetch-kitchen that can make you forget who you are, or who you were, or just what you did last week.

Or remember something you never did.

Organics, Paladin says, are the sum total of their ex-periences. Maybe they're more too, but if you take away a experience, you change a person.

And if you add one?

I remembered a world where organic life was the enemy. Spiteful, unreasonable, and ignorant, they had nearly managed to destroy what was destined to succeed them. If I had been human, I would have had a sacred trust. But I wasn't. So I had a job.

And I wouldn't stop trying to do it until I was destroyed.

Archive wouldn't stop trying to do it until Archive was destroyed.

Maybe not even then.

If I remembered what Archive remembered, was I still me? Because I did remember what Archive did, and I really wanted to know. . . .

I clamped down and stopped remembering all those things I didn't have the right to know. The cell stopped looking like part of a place I'd go a long way to nuke.

"No Machine touched Baijon. It didn't. I was there. I know. It didn't touch him, you— Look. There is not no *noke'ma-ashki* Machine nowhere for to touch anybody. I killed it, je? I blew it up—Baijon wasn't even nigh it more'n a minute fifty!"

"And before it died?"

I stared at him, and all I could think was: *he knows*.

But he didn't know, not anything at all. I'd be dead if he did. And he didn't even suspect me. He thought it might be Baijon with Archive looking out from behind his hellflower-blue eyes.

Just like it said in The Book.

Because that was what a Librarian really was—used to be, a long time ago before most of me'd been born. Someone what could talk direct to a Library, without voders and terminals and uplinks.

And one particular human race had been bred to it.

"No," I said.

And was going to spend the rest of forever paying back for that error in judgment.

"Yet you know my fears before I speak them. And so I ask you, *Alarthme*—if there is any chance that I am right, dare I chance that I am wrong?"

No. Yes. I'd been willing to kill Paladin to stop Archive. Dammit, why couldn't he go pick on somebody else?

"There is not no Library now. I blew it up. It did not eat Baijon's brain before it went to plasma. I was there.

Didn't want to come here, don't want to be here, only came here along of Kennor made me promises which is not getting themselves kept. Baijon done told you who be the Librarian and not even needs his neurons bent to do it. It's Mallorum Archangel, je? Same kiddy what twisted House Dragonflame pere et filldirt and Prettybird *Kore* Winterfire to ice Baijon.''

"*Alarthme,* do you swear this is so?''

"Bai, why bother? You just going to say *chaudatu* is tongueless doorstops and not listen.''

"Then why did you take this book from the logo-otek?''

I'd almost forgot it, pitching my version of reality to the local memory.

He bared his teeth, in the getting-ready-for-dinner hellflower expression that it's stupid to mistake for a smile.

"It was not where it was left. Trackers followed your footsteps there and elsewhere. Some things do not require Imperial technology to understand. Now you will explain.''

We had reached finger-breaking time, and all because I'd been dumb enough to walk back in here instead of doing a beat-feet for the Big Empty with Berathia Note-van when I had the chance.

But then I would of had to leave Baijon. And I didn't want to be the kind of person that did things like that.

So I smiled right back at The Wall That Walks.

"Going for to shop me a Library, bai. Need for to know what you know along of how they work. Archangel lost his last one—think he's stopping there?''

"And could you not ask?''

I laughed at him; I couldn't not. "And just which hell-flower you want me to trust, bai—the ones out to ice me or the ones after Baijon?''

He was wearing a translator, I realized of a sudden, and not trusting to how well he savvied the lingua franca of deep trouble. I guess the stakes was too high for that.

"Then there is no blame, *Kore,* and your courage does you credit. There is nothing you need fear. Your word will be taken, and the People will be forged as a sword against the Machine.''

*   *   *

I hadn't been here long enough to have any kind of feel for the spin alMayne had on its heavyside, but about two hours after every light I could see from my windows was gone somebody came to the door.

Never mind what The Wall said. Leaving was still high on my list of fun things to do in scenic Wailing. The only plan I currently had involved shooting whoever came for me, finding Baijon, and running like hell. I slid my blaster out just as slow as the door opened.

But it weren't nobody but my Imperial cupcake carrying a native handicrafts basket. I put my heat away, wondering if shooting her'd buy me anything at all I wanted.

''I brought you something to eat. I— That is, War-Doctor Firesong told me. I know it's hard to understand, but they are doing you great honor.''

Great honor is usually uncomfortable, inconvenient, and expensive.

She set the basket down and I looked in. Everything was in Quaint Folkways packaging, but I found something that looked familiar and bit into it.

''Maybe you'd like to start from the beginning?'' I said.

So she did. Only a life of training in putting the important things first kept me eating.

ITEM: after our spiffy chat tonight The Wall went to Gruoch with what he thought was a neat solution to all her troubles. They would finish purifying Baijon, adopt me, purify me (painless but tedious both, Berathia said), and then get our signed deposition about what we did on our summer vacation. Then Starborn could knock off those members of Dragonflame who had not already commented on recent events with flashy suicides and go on to a) declare seven-ring vendetta against Mallorum Archangel and b) instruct the Delegate from alMayne, Kennor Starbringer, to bring a formal request from

alMayne to the Office of the Question for a High Book
investigation of Archangel his Nobly-Born self. Yell for
it loud enough, and it'd ruin Archangel socially if it did
nothing else.

That was where things stood at dinner.

Around bedtime Gruoch suggests it will look bad if
House Starbringer is seen promiscuously offering its
shadow about the place. Personhood, says Gruoch, ought
to be harder to come by for your friendly neighborhood
tongueless doorstop.

She comes up with a compromise and rams it down
The Wall's throat—a little hellflower charmer called The
Combat of the Nine Cuts.

"Amrath and Daufin can't stop her. She's well within
her rights as LadyHolder of Wailing to insist on doing it
this way, but The Combat of the Nine Cuts hasn't been
invoked for centuries, and—" Berathia stopped, giving
me time to reflect that if there's anything I hate more
than getting killed it's getting killed in a stupid ritual with
a funny name.

It didn't take much prodding to get the details out of
her: tomorrow The Wall and me was going to walk out
onto the Floor of Honor, the local Starborn frisky business arena, stark naked and with one knife each ready to
fight to the death. His intention was going to be (Berathia
said) to pitch me nine licks in a by-the-book pattern and
not mark me up any other way. I was supposed to put up
as much of a fight as I knew how against something I in
blissful theory wanted. Hellflowers ain't much on passive
resistance.

If I killed him before he finished (fat chance) the result
was the same: Personhood for little Butterfly. Only there
wasn't much way I was going to beat out The Wall, and
after he'd carved me like he meant to, all my insides was
going to be outsides. Even hellflowers didn't do a real
good job of surviving the Whosis of the Nine Whasis,
which's why they'd come up with less messy forms of
adoption.

I had to hand it to Gruoch. Once she got her way she
accomplished three important things.

I'm dead.

Baijon's dead.

And there's nobody to drop the whistle on Archangel.

And I bet Gruoch didn't have any inkling of the last things. She probably thought Baijon-bai just had a few *chaudatu* toys in the attic: purify him, zetz that inconvenient *comites,* and bygones would be Baijon.

"I spoke to Doctor Firesong. He is sorry that you are going to die, but the way he thinks of it, that's just an unfortunate by-product of proving that you're human. From his point of view, it would be far worse to deny you the chance to be human than to kill you tomorrow."

Berathia looked at me with big soulful dark eyes, and I remembered Kennor saying how they paid off the *chaudatu* with money because they had no souls but me he had a special deal for. Another fine and fancy line of country sweet-talk and as half-true as everything else he ever said. For hellflowers honor might be more important than life, but I've always preferred uncertainty and breathing.

"You have to understand how they think," she said. "It is a great honor."

"And what about Baijon?"

Berathia blinked. "Nothing will—oh, his honor. You don't have to worry—they're *honoring* you. Nothing will happen to Valijon."

Which might even be what Gruoch thought too, but I bet I knew my bouncing babby hellflower better than she did. Baijon was going to take this personally. And if he didn't get himself iced declaring vendetta on his own shadow, he was for sure going to be sitting here when Archangel noticed who was yelling Library and did something about it.

"Je. I be real understanding the whole time they's cutting me up alive. A great honor and I be dead."

"I know," Berathia said, staring at the floor. "I've come to get you out."

She said it so casual I didn't quite hear it at first.

"Out? To Baijon?"

"Don't you want to live to see tomorrow's sunrise? Prince Valijon is in the logotek. He's in private vigil—no

one may approach him. My transport is still hidden at
the edge of the plateau; there are ships at the Outport—"

"And what happens to Baijon I just up and kyte?"

"If you. . . ?"

"Kyte—ankle, leave, take the High Jump, be nonfiction, vanish, disappear, *go away*."

For once Berathia didn't have anything to say.

"What happens to Baijon?" I said around a mouthful
of meat-pie. There was a bottle of the local vintage of
hair-raiser in there too, and I put it aside for later. I
didn't see how having it could farce the good numbers
one way or t'other in the morning.

"Your . . . *comites* will be all right. Purification is
serious, but it isn't dangerous—he'll probably be called
upon to perform some distasteful ritual task. If you just
disappear . . ."

Maybe they wouldn't kill him, but Archangel would.

"Didn't you hear me? You can escape. I'll go with
you, and—"

And our little girl was awfully anxious to go zip-
squealing off into the never-never with Yours Truly, putting a serious kink in her amateur standing wherever
hellflowers is sold.

I didn't like it. It was the next best thing to the only
way out, and I didn't like it.

So much for my theory of being half Library. *They*
have a sense of self-preservation.

But I still had to settle with Berathia.

"Oke. I'm convinced. You want to rescue me and save
my life?"

Berathia stood up and started for the door.

"Ne, glitter-bai. Simpler than that. Give me your
shield."

* * *

It was the usual sort; a string of silvery beads about
the size of my thumb spaced out along a length of cord,
most of it charge to keep the field going and at that you
had to change the power-pacs once a day.

Most people wore their shields around their waist or

neck but you didn't have to. To work, a shield just needed to be touching you somewhere; they're designed to key up to your biological electrical grid. You could wear it as a bracelet, or a set of rings, or a hair-comb.

Or you didn't have to *wear* it at all.

Berathia hadn't been too keen on forking it over, but after the lovely line of fantasy she'd handed me about queering her anthro-whatsis by helping me escape she couldn't exactly refuse to do it my way. And for my part, I didn't trust her enough to go walking out of a hellflower cell with her.

It wasn't anything personal. I didn't trust anybody. I'd trusted Paladin oncet, and look where it'd got me. Safer without him, Paladin'd said. Why are people such jerks?

But since I wasn't leaving with her, the only other way out was across the Floor of Honor. And given my druthers, I'd rather do that alive.

Hence the shield.

When I took all the flashcandy off 'Thia's personal shield belt I had a string about a meter long with a generator at both ends and six power-pacs in the middle. The generators was big, but manageable. They'd have to be.

There's this little-known fact of the universe about personal shields, which is if you've got time and too much idle curiosity for your own good, you can actually tune the field to generate itself just beneath the surface of your skin. Miscalculate a silly little millimeter or two and you're dead, of course, because nothing goes through a shield but selected air molecules. Think about it.

Wear it that way long enough and you starve to death, maybe, but I didn't have to. I just had to wear it long enough to cheat my *chaudatu* way through one alMayne trial by combat and screw up their legal system beyond reproach. I got out my inert-blade and a handful of the jewelry I was wearing and got to work.

When I was done the sky was just starting to go light and I hadn't touched the hellflower neurotoxins after all. I held the shield in my hand and turned it on. My teeth and tongue went all fuzzy with the load. I flexed my cyber-hand and was glad to see it still twitched. If the shield farced it someone'd be sure to notice.

I pressed the knife against my real wrist. It sank in a fingernail's-worth and met shield. Perfect.

And I knew for damn sure they wouldn't let me carry it into their arena even if I swore I only carried it for sentimental reasons.

So I swallowed it.

And providing the power-pac didn't fail between now and then I could go on to Step Two of the plan I hadn't come up with yet.

* * *

Full morning dawned bright, shiny, and annoying. The primary was a good distance above the horizon when the hellflower guard of honor came after me, and even then it was just to take me down the way to the bathhouse where I was scrubbed, shaved, oiled, and offered something to drink that I decided not to bother with, thank you all the same. The attendants was placing bets on how long I'd survive.

I wished I had some way to cover that action, but even if I did, how could I collect?

Then they took me where The Wall was.

And I was in trouble.

He was furred and jeweled and trussed up in finest hellflower drag until he looked like an explosion in a joy-house rummage sale.

He did not look like somebody who was going to be after Butterfly St. Cyr's chitlins on the Floor of Honor in just a few minutes.

And that meant somebody else would be.

I hoped it was Gruoch.

But I didn't get a clue from The Wall. He stood in front of a little door that led to the killing ground, and in front of him on a table there was a tray of knives.

"*She* has said that you will choose that which you shall bear. You will choose, and you will pass through the gate, and you will become a Person."

I looked down.

They was from every level of technology the eye could see: The handle of a vibro-blade, just waiting to be switched on. A fixed-crystal assassin's blade from Cadia, unbreakable, deadly sharp, and with the poison reservoir. A filament whip; a blade only by courtesy, but a cutting weapon.

And in amongst them all, a *arthame*.

It didn't look like Baijon's. I've seen his close up: the handle's bone (alMayne bone, but never mind) and carved all over with little tiny scritchy helltongue glyphs, and the butt-end's set with a chunk of black rock.

The blade's pure iron. You melt rocks to get that stuff, you know.

This one didn't have any rocks or runes, just a long gray blade with a little curve on it, too long to be any practical use, and a long straight shank of bone—thighbone, probably, from some noble Starborn ancestor if they was feeling generous.

"You will choose," said The Wall.

Well, hell, I been in this elevator before. I was about to go out there and play duel in the sun with some hellflower and for sure if I wanted to live to grow older I'd pick the vibro or the filament whip, something with some range and power to it. And if I did, I bet sure as back taxes it'd lift some kind of obligation off them and let them cheat.

It didn't matter what I picked, when you came down to it.

So I picked up the unfinished *arthame* out of the box of tricks and bared my teeth at The Wall in the dictybarb expression that is *not* a smile.

*   *   *

The Floor of Honor was white sand, just like all the other arenas I ever seen. Better against the blood, you know—just sift it and play again.

The walls went up higher than I could jump and above them was seats. In about a quarter of the seats was hellflowers. I didn't see Baijon.

Nobody else was down where I was yet. Gruoch was

sitting right above the door my little playmate was due to come through. Amrath King of alMayne was nowhere in sight.

Just how stable *was* the politics on Scenic alMayne, keystone of the Coalition?

I looked around for Berathia and found her. Her spare shield shimmered. I waited for whatever was coming through that door.

They had to slice me and I had to survive it. Fine. And then it was no more Citizen Nice Dicty. Paladin says you should try everything at least oncet to see what works. Now I'd tried being legal and could write it off my list of things to do on rainy days.

The other door opened and a hellflower stepped through.

It was Baijon.

7

Living on the Edge of the Blade

Gruoch's herald stood up and choodled a long screed in formal alMayne—which is just like street helltongue but damnall technical, so's you always know what they're saying but not what it means. *"Today the type-unspecified female will be placed in a situation where environmental factors will aid observers in determining her classification, in conjunction with etcetera-and-tedious-so-forth."*

I looked at Baijon. He was stark, oiled, and carrying his Knife. His hair was skinned back and braided. He hadn't expected to see me.

Berathia had said: some distasteful task. Do it and he was home free. But it was The Wall supposed to do me whiles Baijon just had to take out the garbage forever.

Gruoch could of changed that. With everybody trying to get their hands on the hellflowers and the Coalition hotseat, I bet Kennor'd never oncet thought about all the people that never smiled during Imperial Be Kind to *Chaudatus* Week and'd be just as glad for alMayne to be *out* of the Coalition entirely.

Stupid cow.

Gruoch's herald finished explaining to everybody what most of them knew already and sat down. The only one, seemingly, as found this a lovely shock was Baijon. He backed up. Gruoch'd caught him square between a rock and a hellflower hardplace: duty to his *comites* and duty to his kinfolk. The kind of blithering romance that Thrilling Wonder Talkingbooks likes to run.

"Yo, Baijon-bai, how's tricks?" I said, keeping my voice low.

He raised his Knife and lowered it, and in just about

a minute sure he was going to give Gruoch a double
helping of braincells and get himself iced.

"C'mere, stupid."

He stepped away from the door and into chaffering
distance. He looked worse than I felt.

"Once again I am betrayed: is the honor of the Gentle
People only in their mouths? I swear it will not be so,
Kore; there is redress—"

"Before you go doing something off your own bat just
to be interesting, you try to remember who's sworn to
who around here."

He looked at me and I swear it was hope: that there
was some way out of this that he hadn't seen and I had,
and I made up my mind then there was gonna be.

The peanut gallery was getting restless; they wanted
to see the pony dance.

"You supposed to cut me up along of hellflower nonsense. So do it. Then we kyte when they ain't expecting."

"Never."

He looked up where Gruoch was frowning down and
hefted his Knife. I caught his wrist with the hand that
wouldn't bleed. I hoped nobody was going to mind.

"Baijon. We got to do this. So you cut me now like
they said and don't jump salty. Just do it."

"Your name will be sung forever," Baijon said. I took
a breath to have another go at convincing him and he
took a swipe at me.

I am not never again going to do anything sensible or
reasonable. Every time I do I wind up someplace like
this letting somebody prospect for my chitlins. When I
do it my way at least I'm running too fast to hit.

"I name the LadyHolder Gruoch a thief and a liar, an
eater of corpses!" Baijon shouted. But he did what I'd
told him.

The first of the Nine Cuts runs from the hollow of the
throat all the way down. He wasn't quite close enough to
dig in but I was glad I had the shield all the same. He
saw his Knife not make the cut he expected, and he
smiled.

alMayne house rules included kicking, punching, and

stomping. The shield saved me from some of it. I even got in a lucky foot and thought for a second I was going to ring Baijon's bell and buy me a whole new set of problems, but hellflowers is stubborn. I hit the opposite wall and if the shield hadn't referred the knock all over my corpus delicti that would of been the end of Butterfly St. Cyr's interest in the proceedings, you betcha.

Second and third cuts, under the ribs and down. He got a good hold on me this time and dug in. In some places the shield was farther under my skin than others, but he still didn't punch through like he was expecting.

He rocked back and flung up his head and howled in pure triumph—and came after me again.

Either Baijon was a brainburn or he knew something was up by now. And whatever he knew or thought he knew, he was backing my play with it.

The fourth cut joins the first three to make a triangle cut in half. Coming back for more and staying alive while I did it wasn't any harder than walking into a black gang full of sour goforths and taking double a redline dose of rads to tune them up again. Twenty-seven hours to the nearest fetch-kitchen, and me and Paladin trying every antique prophylactic we had on board while my hair and teeth and fingernails fell out. I lived, and along of later I did it again.

I did this now.

Fifth cut, crossing the midline. Cross and triangle now. I demonstrated to the stands that the *arthame* is not a stabbing weapon. I didn't know if this was enough of a fight by hellflower standards and I'd stopped caring whiles back. But I began to think we might get the whole way through the pandemonium wondershow and wished I'd made a plan for what to do then.

Baijon grabbed my ankle. I kicked him in the face. He held on and began to climb me hand over hand, heading for my throat.

And Berathia's shield failed.

I got advance word of it by the way Baijon's knee sank into my gut. And that was it, I was dead, this bloody-handed bloodyminded innocent was going to kill me and I'd promised him it was going to be oke.

Baijon handed me matched slices on the sides of my face and jumped back just like I was an active threat. The blade grated off my teeth. I got to my knees and then my feet by pure reflex.

Circle and circle and circle . . . There was roaring in my ears and Paladin was shouting at me but I couldn't hear him for the noise and that was when I knew I'd lost it because Paladin wasn't here; just some of his leftover memories abandoned in my head.

Betrayed.

By my—

Library?

Librarian?

I slid so far into weird I came out the other side with the kind of cut-glass clarity that tells you you're about to be sick, unconscious, or dead.

Baijon was facing me. His Knife was wet and red and it was mine, all mine.

"*Kore,*" Baijon whispered at me. "Hold out your hands."

The one thing I always forget in between is how god-lost much pain hurts. *Everything* hurt—to where the sand underfoot felt like red hot gravel.

"Please, *Kore.*"

He had to *cut,* I bet they'd told him that, to prove the Machine hadn't got its lunchhooks anywhere near him. The sweat beaded up on his face and slid down and his whole body shook and he wanted me to stand there flat-foot and take it from him and somebody sometime'd told me never, never to do that.

"I swear to you it is permitted," he said, just a voice hanging on the air and a shadow between me and the sun.

"Hold out your hands. Your hands, *Kore.*"

So I dropped my *arthame* in the sand.

Never bow to a hellflower. He'll kill you.

And I held my hands out to Valijon Starbringer.

And all hell broke loose.

* * *

The door behind me slammed open. I stepped back just in time to get out of the way of six hellflowers and The Wall That Walked.

Baijon made a sound like I'd never heard before.

The Wall was carrying something and it dripped. Up above us 'flowers was scrambling to get out or get closer. Sunlight dazzled on the chrome housings of sidearms and rifles, and just like that I was back in a cheap bolt-hole in a little place called Kiffit, looking at something that used to be human that my partner was going to tell me was a hellflower's way of announcing war.

"The pheon, *or alMayne vendetta wand, is normally only employed among the alMayne, The Gentle People, themselves. The* pheon *may be engraved with from one to seven rings. One ring indicates that the subject of the vendetta is a single individual, seven rings indicates that the subject's entire family to the seventh remove of kinship is to be eliminated. Outside scholars generally agree that the formal initiation of the vendetta occurs when the designated subject sees the* pheon, *which is commonly presented in the ritually-murdered body of a servant or dependent of that subject . . ."*

The Wall dropped the body at where Gruoch's feet would of been if she'd been down here. Gruoch stood up straight like the prow of a sinking ship while that ruined bag of meat leaked into the sand.

It was Ketreis. She had a *arthame* on her belt. She must of just become a grownup and fair game.

Damn all hellflowers forever. For oncet me and Archive agreed on something.

It seemed like forever but I don't think Ketreis'd even hit the ground before Baijon started moving. He grabbed me by the wrist and yanked me out the door The Wall had come in.

Behind us I heard gunfire.

* * *

By meridies me and my *comites* was hiding outside one of the Wailing outbuildings, plotting how to break in and liberate what we needed to go on with.

Was no hope of getting into the castle. Gruoch had it barricaded by then, with Amrath either dead, hostage, or on her side. The Loyal Opposition was using low-yield grenades to break down one of the doors—at least according to the R/T we'd snabbled off a deader, along with his clothes and his battle-aid kit. I had patches over the holes in my face and enough enhancer in my system so I didn't mind the rest too much, but we had to have clothes, food, and weapons.

And a way off the castle plateau, if nobody killed us first.

There was a hellflower warparty camped outside the building I wanted. Some of them was in green—The Wall's colors—and some was in red—the colors of a LessHouse that Baijon seemed to take as a political in-joke. They was just using it as a place to regroup, until they could rejoin the assault on the castle.

Hellflowers at war. It was Gruoch against The Wall That Walked—she'd insulted him because of what she'd done to me, Baijon'd said, so he'd tried to kill her, and she'd (probably by now) killed him, but before that he'd done things up right and declared vendetta against every member of Starborn of her generation.

And he'd used Ketreis to do it.

"My father's sister, the LadyHolder of Wailing, which is the Walls of my House, has insulted me—" Baijon started up again quiet but fierce.

But I didn't want to think about Ketreis right now. Right now I just wanted these guys to ankle, so babby and me could take a shot at the door.

"—she has insulted me; standing on my shadow—"

"And here I thought *I* was your honor, Baijon-che-bai."

He stopped.

"We were to be married," he said finally, and it wasn't Gruoch he meant.

"Why, *Kore*? She had not had one day of Personhood. We kept our vigils together—last night, in the logotek, WarDoctor Firesong permitted us this. *Kore*, he must have taken her as she came from the altarfires with her Knife. . . ."

Because she was Gruoch's daughter. And because two could play the game of more-historical-than-thou. And because Gruoch and The Wall had both loved anything more than people.

"*Kore,* I beseech you. You have said many times that I am of no use to you in this business of darktrading; let me be useless now—"

"And go off and be chop-and-channeled by Gruoch? Ketreis is dead. She won't care, Baijon."

The warparty down below us wasn't moving. Why should that go right for me when nothing else had? In between running and hiding and sneaking, we'd been back by the vehicle pool three or four times, but both sides thought it was a major tactical goodie. To lift anything at all from there we was going to have to liberate a serious distraction from here.

"She will need me in the Land Beside," Baijon finally said in a strangled voice. "*Kore,* I beg you; allow me to—"

"Ne, no, nada-je."

It was common sense to put as much geography between Her Honorability and us as I could, which meant naturally that the hellflower thing to do was wade right back in to what was shaping up to be a prime-class family brawl.

"She'll kill you."

"I do not care, *Kore.*"

I wondered which side of the Wailing walls little Berathia was on and in what condition.

"You my *comites.* You come along me. I'm damned if I did all that rescuing on you just to hand you over to your crazy relatives."

The R/T I was laying on said something in helltalk. Below us the warriors gathered up their weapons and moved off.

* * *

We ditched the skyhorse five kliks from the Zerubavel walls so as not to trigger the sensors. It was about an hour before planetary Lights Out. The rest of a day that'd started too early and went on too long got filled with reaching Zerubavel and getting in.

In case anyone's ever tempted, I do *not* recommend a night stroll on any part of alMayne. If Baijon hadn't liberated a good share of the Wailing armory, we wouldn't of got there.

* * *

The alMayne keep the architecture in the Trade City to their liking by shelling anything built too high, and that meant that Outport was low, sprawling, cramped, and full of Imperials what might any minute think to check the ID Baijon and me hadn't got. Or just hand us back across the Pale into Gruoch's waiting arms.

"*Kore*, I beseech you. The port is easy to reach from here; you may cry *comites* of your Guild."

"Don't work that way, Baijon. Ain't nobody going to stick their ship out for us. And I ain't leaving you to go walkabout."

"They put her into my arms when she was six hours old. Our souls were bound together, the Knives we would bear forged from the same stone. But *Kore*, it is not because of her—not for Ketreis. It is that they lied. The LadyHolder lied. The WarDoctor lied."

Yeah. The whole universe'd promised to be good and had lied. There was a lot of that going around.

We was at the edge of the Outport compound. Trade City proper was awaysaway. I wasn't half as strung out on metabolic enhancers as I'd like to of been, and wearing borrowed alMayne flashwrap that'd used to belong to someone a lot bigger'n I was. It covered all the places I was taped together to let alMayne battle-aid fetch-kitchen do its work, and there wasn't a damn thing to be done about the marks on my face—painted over and medicalled and real noticeable if anybody was looking.

"And now there is nothing left, but I will not live in a world with their lies. You do not want me. You never wanted me. I will leave you, I will betray you. Think what you will, *Kore*, but please—let me go!"

It came to me then what it was he was asking for, even

if he didn't know it. I'd been stupid not to see it earlier. Baijon didn't think he could take Gruoch. He didn't think he could win. What he wanted was to die a hellflower, doing something as made sense to him.

Die purified, free of the taint of the Machine.

Only that was a little harder for hellflowers than for real people.

A long time ago, a kiddy I knew oncet said to me, there was a war. And whiles it was underway, hellflowers was bred to fight the Machine.

Right.

And wrong.

Because before there was hellflowers there was Librarians, who when their proteges went in for genocide decided to turn themselves into a xenophobic race of antitechnological sociopaths.

alMayne.

"*Kore,* I have asked you for much and you have given more—"

"Baijon, how come you think I'm livealive now?"

He knew what I meant. His eyes flickered.

"I cheated. I kicked sand in the face of hellflower honor and right conduct—because if I'd done anything else you'd be dead, and there wouldn't be anybody what somebody had to believe about Archangel and Archive Library, would there?"

"You will tell them."

"Nobody is going to believe me."

"They did not believe *me!*"

"Believed you enough to start a war, ne?"

War.

Why? It was like one of those thingummyites you get when you throw hot glass into water; they look like little teardrop shapes and solid as ever so, but if you just chip the end bit off the tail the whole thing goes to dust. Every time I closed my eyes I could see the whole damn hellflower society disintegrate like a computer simulation: anarchy and blasphemy and is-there-is-or-is-there-ain't-Libraries spreading out from Castle Wailing ground zero while everybody trotted out his own personal honor and declared for one side or t'other of a holy war.

I knew like I'd read it in a book how it was going to
end. The hellflowers was going to decide no more peaceful coexistence with their Imperial good buddies the
tongueless doorstops. They'd raise a fleet up off alMayne
and go looking for the Emperor . . .

—igniting a groundswell of popular support—

—to the total indifference of the other Corporations—

—causing a massive preemptive strike by Throne
against them and other Imperial hotspots like Tortuga—

Leading to . . .

War.

And I'd started it by showing up and asking Gruoch
for a *ship?*

No. It started because anything'd start it. Or nothing.
It was *time* for a war, said the ghost dance in my head,
and there had to be one, like goforths got to high jump
if you power them up.

Glitterborn think about things like this all the time.
And the reason glitterborn don't live to get anymuch older
than they is, is that they think about things like this instead of insuring that no rude strangers lets the air out of
what's doing all that grand choplogic.

Not me. I tapped Baijon's shoulder.

"Street's clear. Let's move. And shut up."

8

Had We but Hell Enough and Time

The Azarine's the merc district, named for the Coalition. It holds everything from sellsword to gallowglass with a short detour through contract assassin, and alMayne's one of the booming markets. I felt more secure once we got there: your uncontracted mercenary's a real peaceful sort. He don't act up for free any more than I run cargo for my health.

I wanted back to that. I was trying not to remember that the last twenty years of my life—my First Ticket, my ship *Firecat,* everything I owned—was in somebody else's pocket in selected locations throughout the Outfar. I looked at Baijon. The one thing I was straight up on was I didn't want him curling up and dropping dead. He was my *friend,* dammit.

Maybe the only one I had left.

Except for what was sorting itself out in my skull. If I ever learned to talk to it. Or became it. And I wouldn't get a chance to turn down doing either one if I didn't get us out of here. I looked around for something I could blend in to.

Most of what was in the street here was hellflowers (it being their planet), a few offworld recruiters in their gaudy uniforms, and one hell of a lot of wigglys.

Hellflowers don't approve of slaves or tronics (or Zerubavel Outport) so all this tidy perfection was being kept up by the wigglys: what the Phoenix Empire in its infinite wisdom calls ''client races,'' although look you, they never got a choice whether to buy Imperial or not. Throne pops a couple starshakers in your sky and you bet what you're going to do is your common or garden rollover.

If we got all the good numbers on our side and nobody a-tall was after us, I figured we could last about thirty hours in the Zerubavel Azarine before putting our foot in it with some heat or t'other. Then we was made, and I was losing count of the people lethally sweet for us on one count or another.

The thing that was going to keep us in the Azarine was the stone impossibility of getting onto the Port without ID or high-powered help.

The reason for wanting to get there was that maybe the ship that'd been in ships-in-port two days ago might still be there and charitable.

If it didn't cost them more'n I had.

My whole plan, such as it wasn't, depended on us staying out of noticeability. So naturally when I saw these three mercs ganging up on this wiggly I took Baijon and we went t'other way.

Right?

Sure.

They was two armored *chaudatu*—Kensey, maybe— and a hellflower. The wiggly fit its skin like an empty watersack. There was lots of things it probably was and one outside chance on what it could be, but the smart money was still on walking the other way.

The hellflower picked it up by its loose skin and started shaking it. It squeaked as it rattled and all kinds glitter-junk fell out of its pouches. The flower dropped it just like you'd bounce a ball, but the wiggly didn't have much bounce in it by then.

"That's mine, you know," I said, walking up.

One of the Kensey turned around. Big, wide, heavy-worlder bones. "Then you want to make good on what it stole, *borio*. True?"

I didn't know what *borio* meant and from his looks I didn't want to. I looked down. The wiggly was a Sibol-ith, I could see now, and sitting in the middle of a bunch of gimcracks: pounce-boxes, inhalers, jewelry, the odd credit piece. It's amazing what you can conceal with a loose flexible inflatable marsupial skin.

The strange hellflower was looking at me. His hair was

cut short like the mercs do and he had wheelknives clipped down the outside of each arm.

"Let her go, my brothers."

Baijon drifted up behind me like radioactive smoke. I wished him or me was dangerous enough to get this re-action out of Brother Gallowglass, but we wasn't. It occurred to me that walking up to him with fresh honor-scars all over my face was not the smartest thing I'd ever done. Story'd be all over Zerubavel by first light. Terrific.

One of the Kensey put one foot on a bit of the wiggly's whatever. Me and Baijon together wouldn't make up one of him. He grinned at me and showed off the new im-proved version of teeth for mercs.

"You don't want us to let him go, *borio*." He prodded the wiggly with his free foot.

I should of been scared. He could ice me, no question. But what I was, was annoyed.

"*Dhu, borio*-bai, you keep him. And me, I let plasma through your armor, you moronic roundheeled *noke-ma'ashki* giving it away free. You got your kick back."

The other Kensey put a hand on the first one's arm and it clanked where the armor met.

"It isn't worth it, Jorum," he said, which proved that all mercs don't get their brains removed at birth.

Jorum didn't look at him. Just when I thought there was going to be trouble he bent down and scooped up the Sibolith one handed and slung it at me. I landed on my tail under X-kilos of wiggly. All my battle-aid tech heaved and hurt.

"She's got it, if she wants it." Jorum laughed and turned away, not even bothering to pick up all that junk he'd been so hot and bothered about a minute ago.

Baijon pulled his *arthame*.

I don't think Jorum'd saw him before that. For sure he hadn't recognized the marks on my face. He looked around for help.

His buddy with the brains looked ticked. The hell-flower folded his arms across his chest.

"This is not my affair unless you make it so, brother," he said to Baijon. "Jorum-*chaudatu* will apologize to your sister. He always does," Brother Flower added with a sigh.

Baijon looked at me. I got up. The Sibolith'd gone limp, but they do that when life gets to be too much for them. It wasn't all puffed out so I knew it wasn't dead.

"If Jorum-*chaudatu* wants to apologize to the wiggly," I said, "ain't nobody standing on anybody else's shadow, right, Baijon-*bai*?"

Baijon grinned; the concept of making somebody else look stupid for fun is both universal and transcendent.

"As my *comites* commands, so is the path of honor," he said with a ghost of his old sass.

Jorum looked at his Kensey buddy.

"Jerk," said his buddy.

Jorum rattled off a line of babble that I decided to take for his apology and the three of them moved off.

"Kore?" said Baijon, looking at their backs.

I waved a hand to shut him up.

"You oke, Tongtip?"

I wasn't real sure, but the right ship was in port and there couldn't be too many Sibolith this dumb.

"Kjhrrr—" The midget green baggie sputtered old burntwine in my face. Tongtip was real fond of burntwine—it's a Proscribed Import to Cibola, and Mother Night only knows what it does to their biochemistry. But Tongtip was real fond of the stuff, and once he got tanked up and it did whatever it did to his nervous system, he'd head out and steal anything as wasn't nailed down.

"Tongtip, you son-of-a-spacewarp, if you ain't you I'm gonna—"

Arms and legs and other things retracted into the pudge and stretched out again.

"Butterfries!" Tongtip choodled, opening big round frog-yellow eyes. "I see my beloved uncle, Butterfries!"

"Kore, do you know this person?" said Baijon like he hoped the answer was no.

"Je. Tong-che-bai, you shipping same *Angelcity* ce Merodach Gentry-legger?"

Angelcity, out of Cibola, and her captain knew me. That was the ship I'd seen in the ships-in-port; stardanc-

er's luck I'd made for myself years ago, coming in to
port when I needed it most.

Tongtip closed his eyes and looked like a very solemn,
very drunk wiggly. "Megaera is captain this trip, Butterfries." He wove extensively to his feet. "I say good-
bye now with profuse thanks."

"Not right now you don't."

I grabbed a good handful of wiggly and slid back into
the shadows. Baijon followed, covering my back without
half a damn idea of what I was up to.

Halfway down a long alley I stopped. The lights from
the street didn't push this far and the alley wasn't lit at
all. I bet hellflowers have better night-sight nor your average citizen, too.

"Tongtip, you going to get me and mine onto port for
to chaffer with Megaera, j'keyn?"

I knelt down beside him and all my fetch-kitchen
pulled, but it was just my skin in ribbons, not anything
underneath. Baijon stood over us, looking both ways,
wanting to be back with his own home and homicide.
And Ketreis.

"But yes! Megaera is glad to see you, uncle, there
being a small matter of wagers owed."

"Yeah, sure."

I didn't have any idea what Megaera Dare, half-captain
of *Angelcity*, Cibola registry, thought I owed her, but
people as thinks you owe them credit is very tender of
your health. And if squaring a fictional debit meant I
could get Baijon and me out of here, I'd pay.

"You won't be telling Megaera about this little mischance, uncle?" Tongtip said hopefully.

"You mean about you sliding off to get elevated and
road-pizzaed, che-bai? Now that depends . . ."

* * *

I remembered Tongtip for an excellent supplier of other
people's goods, and found out that security at the Outport was sloppy to begin with.

In fact, all of Zerubavel Trade City had damn few
legitimates and fewer locks. On the other hand, any hell-

flower what didn't like our looks or our answers was likely to sign us off. Sort of your basic free will love offering legal enforcement.

We walked onto the port in a set of liberated tech coveralls with a hysterical little wiggly telling us in nine kinds of patwa to hurry. Nobody looked twice.

Angelcity was a secondhand Mikasarin G-8 Starhauler shell retrofitted for a crew of thirty, which meant losing a couple holds but paid off in a lot of other ways. Within class they dock by size in Imperial ports, which means all kinds Indies get the raw end of the cubic, but *City* was big enough to be in a good neighborhood; lights and hookups and one of the crew standing to at the open ramp to show the captain's honor, the way you better do on alMayne. He let Tongtip go by and stopped us.

"Got to see captain," I said, "Bidness, j'keyn?"

"No business on ship. And not hiring . . . stardancer."

So much for my disguise, both of them.

"My uncle owes a wager to our captain!" Tongtip peeped up, but the legger had as high a opinion of Tongtip's brains as I did. He waved the wiggly in-ship and didn't stir from out my way.

Tongtip stood pat.

"But it is *true!* My uncle Bu—"

"Button it!" I snapped, not wanting any version of my name wafting over the unmetered air of beautiful downtown Zerubavel Outport.

City's doorman looked at me with new interest.

"Is problem here, stardancer?" he said, real soft.

"Not if me and my bai see half-Captain Megaera."

That fetched him; not everybody knows that joke. She and Mero always said that between them they made up one good captain, and when they finally bought their hull they split duties to match.

"Convince me," said Meggie's crew.

A fool would of offered him valuta. I didn't.

"Is song-ice strike out in the Chullites; Manwarra Directorate claims it but it's far enough away they lease Company ships to guard and freight. Meggie got a Company man drunk oncet as said his cap used to skim the harvest he brought in. So Meggie thought they wouldn't mind a little more split. I flew one of the jaegers she used for that; tell her.''

''Tell her who?'' he said, but not like he disbelieved me.

''Just tell her that.''

He went away on up the ramp, picking up Tongtip as he went. Baijon looked at me.

''You cry her walls, *Kore?*''

''Yeah.''

If she remembered, if it wasn't too much risk, if I could pay up whatever she thought I owed.

Baijon looked back the way we'd come.

''Perhaps they are better than mine.''

* * *

After not-forever the babysitter came back without Tongtip and hand-delivered us in-ship, to a compartment that looked like it was mostly used for making nice with the rich and famous. *Angelcity* was doing well for herself, and I was glad in the same abstract way I hated tariff regs: Mero and Meggie'd been friends of mine once. They'd asked me to come in with them when they was picking crew for *Angelcity,* but I'd said no.

I'd had Paladin.

I sat down and admired all the quiet good taste, and presently Megaera came stomping in from somewhere, pulling off her gloves and looking like she'd been interrupted.

She was tall—had a shot at citizenship once, I heard—and dark, and looked like belonging to any B-pop or none. She'd always been prideful of her hair and she still wore it long; it was banded with ring-money all the way down and dangled below her blasters' muzzles.

''Where's my shirt?'' she said, fixing me with your standard-issue gimlet gaze.

What shirt?

Meggie watched me do a pretty good imitation of the bulkhead and drew a deep breath.

''You swore,'' said Megaera. ''You swore you'd give me the shirt off your back if I babysat that hotload for you back in the Tontine Drift, and then you lit out on me—''

Light dawned.

It was almost fifteen years ago. I'd been running skyjunk in to a sophont who thought he'd rather cash in one of those Class-A warrants that keep my life so interesting than sign my ticket-of-leave, and I couldn't afford to be boarded to make him change his mind. So I called up Meggie and handed the load off to her in mid-tik and she took it on in instead of me.

I was supposed to meet her afterward to split the feoff she collected, but I couldn't let Meggie board my ship either. She was smart; a tech. She'd of seen the Old Fed Library where my navicomp was supposed to be and burned me where I stood.

"Meggie, I had this appointment—"

"—so I babysat. Where's my shirt?"

I looked at her. She was dead serious, and she'd even come out ahead on the money.

It would of made great sense to a hellflower to go around waiting fifteen years to collect a shirt you didn't want and couldn't wear. I wondered if I was the last person in the Empire that thought it was a stupid idea.

I took off the tech coveralls and a jacket and a gun-harness and a vest and got down to the shirt. Then I took it off and handed it to her.

Meggie grabbed it like it was hard credit on payday and let out a whoop.

"Dach-bach, I told you she'd do it! It *is* her! Pay up."

Meggie did a war-dance around the compartment. Merodach came in from where he'd been standing in the corridor; tall like Meggie and a couple shades lighter.

"St. Cyr!" he said, and waltzed me around hard. It didn't do my battle-aid tech any good at all. Mero looked down and noticed the bandages all over sudden and looked penitent.

"Keeping busy, I see?"

So then I sat down and it was just like old times, from back when it was the lot of us hanging around the Never-never Diner, trying to beg buy or borrow the tech to turn our leaky hulls into Mainliners.

But they'd grown up and gone on. And I could of gone with. Instead of sitting here asking favors, I could of been Engineer on *Angelcity*.

It spooled out in front of me like talkingbook might-be-maybes, so real I could damn near take a deep breath and walk into it. The life I could of had. Should of had.

Would of had, except for Paladin.

And Baijon would be dead now, cause nobody but Paladin and me together could of got him out of all that grief Archangel'd dumped him into bye-m-bye.

But I could almost *touch* it—everything I'd ever wanted, cut off from me by one mistake I'd never knew I made until now when it was gone.

"So."

Mero's talking-business voice snapped me back to the here-and-now. Pleasantries was over, and they'd made up their mind to at least listen before showing Baijon and me the air. And I didn't blame them for thinking that way, not with a crew of thirty to think about, too. I'd done the same in my time, for my crew.

I leaned forward. "Need to get off-planet, into Outfar, both of us. No ID."

That told enough and more. Meggie looked at Baijon. Young, maybe she could tell. Not a merc, even with his hair braided back.

"And him?"

Baijon didn't say anything. I kept forgetting I wasn't a *chaudatu* by his lights until we met up with one and he went into his Great Honor Face routine.

"Can pay our freight, Meggie." I emptied out the pockets of my secondhand jacket. No alMayne scrip nor Imperial credits, but plenty of hellflower junk-jewelry, negotiable in any hockshop in the Universe.

"Doesn't he talk?" Meggie said.

"Ne. Mine hellflower-style. *Comites.*"

I wondered if Meggie knew a high-caste hellflower from the sellsword in the street and if the news from Wailing had got out yet and if she knew who Baijon was real and for true.

Meggie stood up from where she'd been sitting and walked over to him. She was in shouting distance, heightwise.

"You. I won't freight honor this tik—you want to come, you leave it down the gravity well and talk like a human person. Now. What's your name?"

He didn't even glance at me.

"Baijon," The Third Person of House Starborn said with a fair imitation of the patwa slur. "I am Baijon Stardust."

After that was all over but Meggie stripping me to my ring-money.

* * * * *

Valijon's Diary:

The WarDoctor Firesong's honor is pure. I wish I did not know this. Because he has slain my chosen, Ketreis, and if he could do that honorably, in honor, then what is honor now?

On Low Mikasa my father told me of his plan: that the accusation against Archangel *Malmakosim* would not come from him or me or any disputable, slayable source, but from the very Walls of alMayne and the assembled throats of the Gentle People.

Such he could not evade. Such he could not kill. Such must even he, honorless, answer.

So my father bid me accuse Archangel to the Memory of Starborn, to the LadyHolder of Wailing, to Amrath Starborn FirstLeader of alMayne.

And I did. The *Kore* bid me come away at once, but I knew she did not mean me to slink away with my message undelivered. So I did as my father said I must.

And my own people delivered me to the Shadow. They set aside those words it is death to treat lightly. In the name of the dead of a hundred suns I begged them to hear me . . . and they did not.

We spoke, in my betrothed's last night in life. She told me that Gruoch-my-aunt had promised that the Outport would cease to be, that *chaudatu* would no longer walk the earth of the Homeplace.

Only Archangel could give that. To promise it, Gruoch must have eaten promises from his hands. Sick with the taint of the Machine, she could not taste truth. She named me mad, knowing that in this one thing even madness did not matter.

Gruoch twisted honor, and so Firesong declared vendetta upon her. But the time for such simplicity is as gone as the time for the Combat of The Nine Cuts. On the Floor of Honor, the *Kore-alarthme* cheated, and did not defame those sands already clotted with treachery.

Is there higher honor than honor? When honor itself twists like a serpent, what shall we prove ourselves against to know we are still human?

Dare we be not human, when the Machine waits for all? I do not know. And there is no one left to ask.

LessHouse Dragonflame conspired against House Starborn, its master, for the tainted *chaudatu* honors my father holds. Honored Alaric sought my life, so that my father must die in battle against the TwiceBorn *chaudatu*—and then the Honored Morido, Alaric's father, would speak for the Gentle People who fight *chaudatu* vendettas.

Now LessHouse Dragonflame fights for the WarDoctor, to bring down the walls of Gruoch-my-aunt. Morido is dead, knowing the taint of the Machine was on him. Alaric must follow.

Honor would say this LessHouse is still my enemy, though they fight as I would fight, if I were free. Gruoch spoke for the Machine and made honor a weapon to serve her ends.

If humans who betray are human no longer, what is honor that is only a tool of kingmakers?

Once honorable kindred fight for scraps from the Empire's table and lose their shadows to the Machine. I am not a child to deny that these things can be.

I only wish to know: what is left?

Betrayal summons vengeance, but if honor dies, can even blood reanimate it?

Archangel must answer me; Archangel who will sell all for the power only the Machine can give.

If the Gentle People are purified and rise against him, will it be in time?

And will it matter at all?

9

The Road to Hell

Baijon and me got to eat and live indoors while *Angelcity* tidied up her bidness on alMayne. They even waited over an extra day on account of passengers that never showed—at least so Mero said.

I didn't care, so long as we got to stay where we was. Inside cabin, no ports, no data-links, and someone to bring our meals on time and not talk much. Meggie was being almost as careful as I would of been. Careful enough would of been not helping at all.

I wondered if Paladin'd ever bothered to look for me in the Washonnet dataweb. I knew him a lot better now. I had a good idea of how time could slide when you're made of light. He might never think to look till I'd died of old age, assuming I lived that long.

I was not stupid enough to think that getting this far solved anything. If the situation Baijon and me was in had made bankable net improvement since we'd docked at Mikasa, it was hard to see how.

I'd made it twenty years out of Market Garden and to the ripe age of thirty-five gsy (galactic standard years) by not being noticed. Everybody I'd ever met lived the same way. Some might be able to stand more looking than others. Nobody could stand up to being looked at by the Second In Line For The Phoenix Throne.

I tried to convince myself Archangel thought we was dead on alMayne. And I couldn't, because looking for us was no bother to him. He just had to give the orders and forget about them and a century later people'd still be looking, diligent in the face of common sense.

That's power, and I didn't have it.

I had other things.

I lay there in my rack on *Angelcity* thinking thoughts I shouldn't of been able to think about things I shouldn't of known and wondered whether and how much I was the person I'd been last year. And the worst of it was, I suspicioned I knew.

And the real bottom-line hell was, it didn't matter.

Me and Baijon was livealive, so we needed a place to be that way. What it was and how fancy was just window-dressing—so, if you wanted to get philosophical, was whether you was alive in a Imp hellhouse or a glitterborn palaceoid.

I knew, just the same like I knew what I wanted for breakfast, that Mallorum Archangel was trying for a war. And if even hellflowers wasn't going to believe in Libraries at the drop of a *arthame* in the first place, it augured badly for the credulity of the solid citizens of the Phoenix Empire.

Yell "Library" on Archangel, and nobody'd listen until it was too late.

Then there'd be war. And Archangel was going to start it and nobody was going to win it because there wasn't going to be anybody left. Fact.

There'd never been a war in the Phoenix Empire. The Empire was built out of the ashes of the war that'd put new constellations in my home sky and converted a slightly larger volume of space than the current Empire occupied to plasma. By the time the Empire had finished putting itself together out of what that war'd left, the habit of banging planets together at twice the speed of light had sort of dropped out of the local population. And maybe Fleet kept its borders with the Hamat and the Sodality and intervened in squabbles between the Directorates, but that wasn't war.

Not like I knew war. Because I knew a lot of things I shouldn't, including how much fun it was to make a sun turn inside-out. Thanks to Archive.

Most of what was in my head was Archive's, I thought now. A little bit was Paladin, but Paladin hadn't known how to do half the things a Library could until he'd met Archive. Paladin'd been broke in the War, and reassembled with my not-too-expert help. So most of what I had was Archive's.

It didn't include the big *"why,"* and I was glad, even if I still wondered about it. Archangel wanted power; I knew from that. But what could a Library want that a organic had, enough to fight about it?

I hoped I'd never find out firsthand.

War, and how to avoid it.

Kennor Starbringer, bless his homicidal heart, only wanted to keep Archangel's hands off the Coalition. He wasn't out to stop a war. He didn't think there'd be one. He just wanted to keep the status well and truly quo and the alMayne in the mercy seat wherever mercenaries are sold.

I had a hunch Archangel's ambitions had gone beyond that, but who'd believe a charter member of the scaff and raff of the Galaxy?

Of course the hellflowers might start it first. And then Archangel could go after the War College logotek, which might not quite be far from his mind. And it would be a little farther to the last act, but not much.

I wondered if Berathia Notevan was who she seemed to be, whoever that was, and if she wasn't, if she worked for Archangel. In which case I hoped she'd got off Wailing safe and warm, and run home to tell him people was blowing the whistle on him.

So when you came down to it, it didn't matter whether I was me, or Paladin, or Mother Night her own self. I was a live thing with Archangel standing square in the way of me and everyone else I might ever meet staying lively.

And I could not think of one useful thing to do about it.

* * *

The day we cleared alMayne gravity, it was Mero brought the breakfast with a smile and asked if we had any objection to working cargo.

"It's Megaera, you see. She has the soul of an Imperial accountant and the thought of experienced crew sitting deadhead is keeping her awake at night."

"So?" I said.

"So she thought you might enjoy the exercise and a

change of pace. There's two places open on the cargo gang. It comes with galley and slop-chest rights.''

"Fine."

It was better than sitting locked up in here watching Baijon tear himself apart over the ''lack of honor'' of his GreatHouse. It was taking him whiles to work it all out to his satisfaction, but he'd settle it in his mind soon or late. I wasn't sure I wanted to be there when he did.

And the only alternative to talking to him was thinking about how people are aggregates of their experience, and since I had a good chunk of Archive's experience now did that make me a Library?

I'd rather shift cargo.

* * *

Mero showed us down to ''A'' Hold—*Angelcity* had six. Tongtip was there, and looked glad to see me, but then Tongtip's glad to see everybody. I didn't let it go to my head.

On one side of ''A'' Hold there was a bunch of big black crates with ominous blinking lights and Intersign glyphs saying about how they was from Barnegat and they was absolutely not to be opened unless and until they reached the planetary surface only of Washonnet 357-II/alMayne.

Lethals.

On the other side there was a pile of knocked down flats of the kind you seal cargo into before putting it into crates slightly less illegal than the ones on the first side.

''There's ten more crates like these when you've finished repacking the first set,'' Mero said.

''You backing a insurrection or what?'' Barnegat's main export is what's alMayne's main import—high-ticket energy weapons.

''With bolts of cloth? You've been out in the starshine too long, St. Cyr.''

''It is not cloth,'' said Baijon flatly. Nobody listened.

''Our next port is Royal—does that tell you anything?'' Merodach said.

"Je, Mero-bai. That you're a damn poor legger shipping cloth there."

*   *   *

Celestial and some Indie ships is families, with a da for captain and everything done his way for love. On the Company ships and in the Fleet the captain is god and has eighty ways to make you wish you died before crossing him.

But on a darktrader—an Indie that's a legger—things run different. They have to. 'Cause you're bending the Pax Imperador every time you lift, and if everyone from the pilot in the mercy seat to the crystal-gazer in the black gang isn't easy in his mind over that, somebody's going to peach to the Teasers and then you ain't got ship nor hull nor anything else worth having.

So a darktrader—a big one anyway—is more of a democracy where the captain's got the veto. Meggie (captain this tik) didn't have to ask her crew's permission to have someone sign Articles (which in point of fact we hadn't, being cargo) but under those same Articles they had the right to petition her to kick anyone off they didn't like.

Things legger crews discuss is not things like whether to have candied chobosh for tea. It's things like what kind of illegal they's willing to get up to. Some ships won't run slaves. Some mindbenders. Some take any cargo. It's all in the Articles—and you better read them before you sign, because that's the only way to tell your legit Indie from your Guild-member darktrader. A tour of cargo gave us the chance to ingratiate ourselves with all and sundry and Mero the chance to get some work out of us.

Now *Angelcity* wouldn't run slaves, because Meggie believed in freedom—a damfool idea in a universe where even air isn't free. But she had no objection to running guns. Neither did the folks back in hellflower heaven.

*   *   *

If you believe the talkingbooks and the credit-dreadfuls, all the illicit behavior that makes the galaxy such a fun place for Our Hero starts bang at the edge of the Outfar. Never in the Core, or the MidWorlds, or even in Directorate Space. And never among sophonts of probity, such as our galactic cousins the alMayne.

Fact: business is business. And as Baijon'd proved to me more'n once, "honorable" and "legal" meet only at meals. alMayne was the legal Destination-of-Record for twenty percent of all the frightfuls manufactured in the Empire. If once it arrived it left for other Directorates where it was strictly on the Proscribed Indicia, that was nobody's problem but the Teasers'.

An Indie as big as *Angelcity* works her run a little different than I did with *Firecat*. My Best Girl was so small I had to get one cargo out of the way before picking up another. It left me more flex, too, but *Angelcity* had her next six downfalls in mind and cargoes picked out to match. All of them legal wherever she'd picked them up, all bound for somewheres they was either illegal or overtaxed, and all on their way to making a tidy profit for Mero and Meggie and their crew.

And the beauty was, since *Angelcity* could show her cargos was legal transactables under autonomous planetary waiver at port of acquisition, even if the Teasers stopped her Meggie'd probably get by with confiscation and a few points on her ticket.

Even if it was guns.

* * *

Three *Angelcitizens* joined Baijon and me, and the five of us spent the next whenever shifting cargo. Tongtip helped—meaning he got underfoot—until he got bored and went off to supervise somebody else. He's Part-Owner of Record for *Angelcity,* which is how she comes by Cibolan registry at a less-than-ruinous rate of fee. There's other ways around the Registry regs than selling two percent of your hull to an indigine, but most of them is dangerous.

I put my mind on my work, juggling a bunch of long pink densepak cylinders that might of contained cloth or chocolate or holy writ from all I knew for sure—except that none of them is prime alMayne export for a ship like this, and when I dropped one and it split I got the confirmation notice. Prime Estel-Shadowmaker bells and whistles, this.

The *Angelcity* gang-boss looked over at me to see how I was taking it, although if Mero'd vouched for me he knew I wasn't a holy innocent.

I pulled it out of the densepak, all chromed vanes and blued ceramic with "Born To Rock'n'Roll" incipient in every line. It fit in between my elbow and my ribs like it was born there.

There was people on Royal waiting for this kick, you betcha.

"You want I should wrap it up again safe and warm?" I asked.

"Je think they going do—refuse delivery for improper packaging, jillybai?"

He held out his hand. I tossed him the rifle. Everybody went back to work.

Guns to Royal.

* * *

There's a war on there, you know: Charlock Corporation against rebel Shareholders, with the Sector Governor taking sides. Area under martial law at the moment, and direct control of the Governor-General. Another of Archangel's little gifts to the galactic peace.

I was starting to develop a plan. It was half wishful thinking, and half hope of divine intervention. It did not have a candle to a stardrive's chance of working. Still, it was mine, and I thought Baijon'd like it when it was old enough to stand company. Meanwhile I fiddled it around my head with the thing that wasn't Paladin and—might-be-maybe—wasn't Archive.

Three stops after Royal *Angelcity* would be stopping at a Free Port. You don't need ID to move around a Free Port. Meggie was willing to take us as far as there, I hoped. Our places on the cargo gang said she was.

If we could stay out of the way of bounty hunters we'd be fine. Just give me a chance to pick up new ID in the wondertown and Baijon and me could start getting *really* lost.

I wondered how Kennor'd take the news.

* * *

"*Kore,* what is the right? You are my *comites;* my father gave me to you. What do I do?"

We was lying in our racks in the dark. Three days out from alMayne, seven to Royal.

I'd settled back into the shipside drill, and Baijon picked it up like he'd never been anywhere else and it wasn't beneath his glitterborn self. He wasn't dumb—just literal and bloodyminded. Between them, Gruoch and The Wall had pretty well done for his damned self-confidence.

I wasn't sure if I liked what there was going to be left.

"Depends, bai, on what you want to do," I said after whiles.

"I want to go home," Baijon said.

I took a deep breath and blew it out again.

"Can't do that."

"I know." He sounded miserable. "It isn't there anymore."

I sat and listened to the dark. Lies are the devil, but true-tell'll get you every time.

"Yeah," I said. "Well."

"So what must I do, *comites*? I have thought . . . I think I must kill Mallorum Archangel." He sounded shy about it, like he was worried he'd upset me.

"You'll never get near him. You know that."

I'd always used to thought that being alive was worth damn near anything. But the more I thought about it, the less things there was on the list I'd do without a blink to keep breathing.

"I must try, *Kore.* Is that not the course of—" he hesitated just a tik in the dark "—Right Conduct?"

"You got to do what's right, bai. But it's better if you win."

Bending Baijon to suit my fancy was coming on for being one of them.

"My *Kore-alarthme* and *comites* will tell me, then,

what I must do to do this,'' Baijon said, with what he was using for a sense of humor. ''Once before we prevailed, when our walls were weakest.''

That'd been a cakewalk next to this.

''Well you can't just walk up and shoot him. Somebody'd object.'' And I wasn't really sure it'd stop the war, just give it a different set of players.

''I want him brought low, ground in the dust, stripped of his titles and honors and wealth, alone, helpless, naked to his enemies, inutterably dismayed!''

See ''Harm'' in the logodex of your choice.

''I'll think about it,'' I told him. ''When I come up with something, I'll let you know.''

''You are my *comites, Kore.* In that I may still believe.''

I should of known better. He believed it. He fell asleep. I stayed awake, giving his problem serious thought.

Kill the third most expensive sophont in the Empire. Sounded good to me. How?

Simple, really. Cry Library.

How? We'd tried on alMayne and nobody listened.

But Kennor'd said Archangel had enemies as high-up as he was. They'd listen.

If there was a big enough noise to listen to.

Like the noise the Delegate from alMayne'd make. Kennor'd believed Baijon. Right?

So he'd gone and dropped heat at the Office of the Question. Right?

Had he?

Did I want to bet my life on it?

No, as a matter of fact. I'd got used to taking the larger perspective on things these days. And from that vantage place, it was clear that Kennor Starbringer couldn't hold the whip-hand over Mallorum Archangel if the rap was out in sight for Archangel to beat.

So Kennor (who was maybe out to kill Baijon and frame me and maybe not by now) wasn't going to be the boy who cried ''Library.''

Depending, of course, on what the news from home was these days. A couple zillion hellflowers can't be wrong. Or shuffled under the rug when they was crying for Archangel's chitlins.

And maybe—just maybe—Kennor'd told us the truth in the first place. Maybe all we had to do was wait while bad luck caught up with our boy Archangel.

The trick, of course, was getting through the waiting alive.

In around all this thinking, what I didn't give a second thought to was *Angelcity's* too-convenient placement on alMayne. Then, anyway.

* * *

Time passed. Baijon'n me both gave up the clothes we was wearing in favor of looking like everyone else. Baijon cut his hair to look more like the 'flower in the street. It made him look funny. *Angelcity's* fetch-kitchen got rid of everything on me that said Souvenir of Castle Wailing except the marks on my face. They was dark and raised and left matching ridges on the inside of my mouth and *Angelcity's* med-tech wasn't up to dealing with them. I didn't care. Nobody'd seen me with them before, so nobody was looking for me with them now.

Shipboard was nice and quiet and Baijon started looking less haunted and I wished it could go on forever but a day out of Royal *Angelcity* made Transit to realspace to let the engines cool out and to give everybody a last chance to tuck away anything that might not be strictly legal upright and moral on Royal's heavyside.

We was within range of the Travelers' Advisory beacon at the edge of Royal system and I talked Meggie into tapping it.

"Why? You trying to find out how your fleet did on its last Riis-run, St. Cyr?"

"I put good money on a bad actor, Meggie, I swear I never knew you was his mother. Give me a break."

She looked me over and made up her mind.

"Je. But why you care where Company high-iron goes—"

"I don't. I care where it don't go. Truth."

And it was, but not in a flavor that was likely to be of any use to the Captain of *Angelcity*.

Travelers' Advisories is for the tourist trade: bulletins

originating in the Imperial Bureau of Interstellar Shipping and Transport. They're usually half a lifetime out of date and full of things I never wanted to know.

This one wasn't. Washonnet Sector, it said, was Absolutely Shut. Don't go there unless you are dropping off Washonnet/alMayne citizens and can prove it. All alMayne are ordered home. All provable fare costs for transport guaranteed by the Starborn Corporation.

The message repeated once and then went on to a notice that Tortuga Sector was under heavy manners and the Roaq was closed to visitors.

"You knew," said Meggie. She unfolded her feet from the table, but didn't get up, quite.

We'd tapped the beacon from the Captain's Cabin; most of the bridge systems referred the late-breaking news here.

"If I knew, I wouldn't of asked you to pull it for me, would I?"

"Would you?" said Meggie, who is sometimes almost as suspicious as I am. "*How* did you know—don't tell me," she added, because I'd been going to.

"Well you aren't there now, so don't shop *me* your troublekick," I said.

"Is Baijon going home?"

Meggie'd got fond of our boy, seemingly.

"No." Which told her some things if she wanted to know them. Maybe even true ones.

"Oke." Meggie stood up. "Tomorrow we hit Royal. See a man about a kick. I need some flash and comedy by me. You and Stardust're elected. After, you sign Articles here to your Free Port, part-shares and wages. Suits?"

"*Ea*, jillybai. Or maybe I just want my shirt back, ne?"

"You've got Destiny's own chance of getting it," said Meggie. She'd made up her mind to something, plain and certain.

I should of stood home. If I'd been smart, I would of. But if I had, I'd be dead.

10

How to Exceed
in Darktrading
Without Really Trying

As a planet and a biosphere, there is nothing wrong with Royal. It is capital of the Tortuga Sector so it has a Imperial Governor's mansion, and seat of the Charlock Corporation (which makes Tortuga Sector the Charlock Directorate instead of the Tortuga Directorate, but these things happen) so it has a Corporate Headquarters. It has big blue oceans, fluffy white clouds, lots of chlorophyll and vitamins, and an attractive location relative to shipping and handling.

Probably it used to be some high-glitterborn's home-away-from, hence the name, but the hub of galactic commerce had since moved west, and now Tortuga Sector was Outer MidWorlds only by courtesy.

But it had a downside port, a lunar port, three inhabited planets in its capital system, a asteroid belt full of miners, full weather control, and visits from the Governor-General's pet navy whenever he was in town.

The war it also had, had started like this:

Once upon a time Royal was corporate headquarters of the Brightlaw Corporation, holders of all developmental patents for the next best thing to Libraries, and don't think they didn't walk pretty soft indeed staying on the sunny side of that line. *Angelcity* her own self had a Brightlaw Corporation brain in her hull; damn near anything that needed to think used their tech.

Well and good. But a sad mischance had carried off every single member of the ruling Brightlaw Corporation members except little Shareholder Damaris. Very sad, Uncle Charlock called in to form a new Corporation, administer the Brightlaw patents, and (in the fullness of time) marry little Damaris off to his son Hakon, after which everything'd be all in the family, so to speak.

Too bad little Damaris hadn't thought so. A couple years back she slipped her leash and started a revolt, with the aim of forming a new corporation of one. Things reached the point that Uncle Charlock appealed to Throne, whereupon the Governor-General (my old buddy Archangel) took the Azarine Coalition mercenaries out of the warpool by slipping in a couple divisions of Fleet on the Charlock side and declaring martial law.

This was supposed to make everybody shut up, but Damaris' partisans hadn't stopped their side of the war just because they lost their professionals. Now Archangel was down a couple divisions of crack mediators and Tortuga Sector was a boom market for artillery.

Paladin once said that the Codex Imperador was the greatest argument for solipsism he'd ever seen. Archangel had superseded the Sector Governor. He had loaned troops to Charlock, forcing the Coalition troops out of the arena. He'd even declared martial law so the Space Angels could arm their weapons and no Company ship would enter the Sector. But still officially it was Damaris Brightlaw versus Chairman Charlock and a private family war, and neutrals that could duck fast enough could come and go with impunity.

It strikes me as a damn roundabout way to collect taxes.

But while there was a war on there was bidness to be done, and where we was going to do it was Port Mantow on Royal, where Meggie would hand over an ample sufficiency of street-lethals to someone best unnamed (the valuta was on its being Damaris' side), the captaincy to Merodach, and *Angelcity*'d be nonfiction on its wayaway.

At least, that was how it was supposed to work.

*   *   *

It was half-past meridies and on its way to being dark when Meggie, Baijon, and me left *Angelcity* to meet the sophont as was eventually going to give us her money.

It was summer in Port Mantow. The crete was giving up stored solar radiation in waves and the air shimmered. Archangel's Best was flying formations overhead, zinging back and forth like black bat knights and making me scairt they was going to drop one of those overcoked high-heat flitterbyes on my head.

I wondered where His Nobly-Bornness was, and how he was keeping care of nights with all alMayne fighting the question of was he a Librarian back and forth big and noisy and public.

Two Imperial Space Marines, well-armored as home-grown starships and twice as temperamental, ran us through scanners and checked our tickets at the gate. None of us'd bothered to try to go out armed; Meggie'd peace-sealed Baijon's *arthame* back at the ship and the Marines passed it.

They looked twice at me, but they always do; it's why I stay in the Outfar. But they passed all three of us and we got off the port facility and into the teeming downside, which it wasn't much at the moment.

"I just hope we can get this settled before they lock us up for curfew violation," Meggie muttered.

We had four hours till then and the streets was empty even now. Archangel's Finest was coming down hard, and probably the only reason this wasn't an Official Imperial Action was Archangel couldn't come down hard in too many places at once without he had the warmbodies to do it, and his warmbodies of choice was all locked up in the Azarine Coalition.

We got to where Meggie's contact supposed to was and went in. She'd told me she'd got two-thirds up front—S.O.P. when the legger's got to shell out to buy the goods—and now she wanted the small change and whatever ideas the buyer had on taking delivery. It wasn't impossible he'd be taking the stuff right off *Angelcity* in port—there's things you can do with the right squeeze to the right groundcrew.

It was a place called Warped Space; good entrance, good exits.

"Table in back, by the door," Meggie told me.

I motioned Baijon to close up. There was a divider

running out from the wall. It hid a bench and part of the table; you could see without being seen.

We came round it, Meggie first. Her contact was waiting for us.

It was Errol Lightfoot.

Errol Lightfoot had been last seen running Old Fed Illegals into the Roaq for Mallorum Archangel's front-lizard, Kroon'Vannet, what I'd dropped a proton grenade on. Errol shouldn't of been alive.

He was one of the few people that could finger me for a High Book rap. He'd been one of the people who'd brought Archive back to life. He sold me as a slave when I was fourteen. And besides, I plain didn't like him. Some people just take you that way.

He took Baijon that way, too. Didn't even try to clear his *arthame;* he just knocked Meggie flat and dove for Errol. Probably he saved her life.

There was something bent about Errol's showing up here but I didn't have time to reason it out right now. I had just time to remember that fair was fair and I had after all promised Baijon Errol's life next time he came acrost him when two Space Angels popped up from behind the bar and started shooting.

I grabbed the nearest thing handy and chucked it in the direction of the blaster-bolts. Meggie was rolling to her feet and pulling the hideout she'd managed to slip past Debarkation Control, and the Angels was yelling for reinforcements; I *knew* it.

Was explosion out in the street and the front of Warped Space went warped for sure.

Errol sliced Baijon with something. Meggie shot back at the Angels and hit some technology behind the bar that blew up and sprayed us with molten goo.

"Go!" I shouted.

I shoved her at the back door and hoped we was just not important enough to waste any more Angels on.

Baijon was sitting on Errol. He had one hand wrapped around Errol's throat and was hauling at his *arthame* with the other. He also had a gen-u-ine hellflower bloodstain spreading across his gaudy shirt where Errol'd tagged him. I saw this in the instant it took me to grab Errol's blaster and use it to discourage the local boys in black from raising their heads up. We had to get our heads out of here. And Baijon's hair wasn't long enough to grab him by any more, dammit.

"Come on, come *on!*" I yelled without looking. I snapped off another shot. The A-grav transport full of reinforcement landed in the street. Out of the corner of my eye I saw the flash as Baijon finally got his *arthame* free.

He looked at me.

"Come on or we're dead."

Baijon let go of Errol and started to his feet. Errol made to do something he never finished because the *arthame* flickered like summer lightning and cut Errol Lightfoot's throat from ear to ear. Errol fell back in a splash of blood that looked on its way to being real permanent-like and Baijon and me went out the back way as more Angels was coming in the front.

Welcome to Royal.

* * *

"This way."

Baijon seemed awfully damn sure of where he was going, but I didn't necessarily have any better ideas. Behind us there was yelling and shooting and all the sorts of noises I generally go the other way from.

Meggie was nowhere in sight.

I had to run to keep up with Baijon; when he saw I was he went faster, and nevermind he was leaking. We switchbacked roundabout until the ruckus behind us Dopplered off and I couldn't of said which way the port was for any credit.

The city got bigger and I got lost. You couldn't see the port towers any more for the buildings and floaters in the way, and the things I did see belonged in a talkingbook, not reality.

We went in somewhere, and then up a bounce-shaft, and then we was out on a roof.

Stardancers have to have a head for heights. When you're in a suit hanging outside your ship with nothing between your boots but so much down that you could fall forever and not get there you'd better not get too excited about it.

I'd never cared about the fall before.

This was different.

It wasn't just the gravity, or the air-mass trying to push both of us over the edge of what wasn't a dropshaft. It wasn't even that we was up so high that I could see for kliks and kliks.

It was *what* I could see. As far as I looked there was city—nothing green, nothing wasted, just city going on and on forever like a puzzle-box, or a machine.

And Royal wasn't even really big. The talkingbooks called it "gently rural," whatever that meant.

On and on and on.

"*Kore,*" said Baijon.

I turned away from being dazzled by the light. Baijon was crouched in the middle of the roof, hand over his side in a gesture more hopeful than useful.

"Let me see that." I was still holding somebody's blaster from back at the Warped Space. I set it down and hoped the wind would leave it there.

I ripped his shirt out of his belt. It came away easy on account of he was still bleeding.

"Can't you keep your skin in one piece together for five minutes? Every time I stop to scratch I'm kitchening you up again."

It was wide and gaudy but it wouldn't kill him except maybe for bloodloss, and there wasn't a damn thing handy to my hand to cork him with.

"I am all right," Baijon said. He put a hand back over the leak and winced.

"Sure you are, bai."

"I wished to take the head of the *chaudatu* Lightfoot. It was mine," Baijon said wistfully.

"Sure it was, babby," So Errol Lightfoot, Fenshee slaver and all-round antidote to the work ethic, was dead. It probably should of left a bigger hole in my life, but I was all took up with wondering if Meggie was all right, or laid up somewheres with a serious case of being dead. I knew what was up with *Angelcity*.

If Mero'd been fast she was buttoned up and the heat had her wrapped in tractors and was trying to starve her out. If he hadn't been fast enough, him and all her crew was off somewheres in a box with locks, waiting out the merciful and reasonable justice of the Empire.

"Where are we, anyways?"

"I do not know. We have a little time here, at least."

Baijon pulled off his shirt and vest and ripped the shirt into a passable bandage. He looked at me for whatever great plan I'd spontaneously come up with and then went back to his patch job. I held the pad in place while he tied it down.

"The port is that way," he offered, pointing with his chin.

"And how do *you* know?"

"We came from there," he said, and shrugged.

I thought over all our options on Royal for a real long time—maybe a kilo-second.

"Well we better get back there." Because like it or not, Port Mantow was our only way out of Royal's killing box.

* * *

I would of holed up in Port Mantow if I thought ID that named *Angelcity* as our ship would be a ticket to anything but free Imperial room and board for as long as Archangel didn't know who we was. Baijon and me both had credit, but not enough to fox ID or bribe a lift even as far as Royal's moon.

And I didn't think that the late Errol Lightfoot's being the one to meet Meggie was as much of a coincidence as it ought to be.

But it *had* to be, right? Because Mother Night her own self hadn't known me and Baijon was going to be on that ship.

There was something that still bothered me a whole lot about Errol, but I put that thought out of my mind for later prospecting. Might-be-maybes is for when you're safe, not running for your life.

* * *

Curfew fell whilst we tried to find a way back that
didn't include Space Angels. If I'd thought it out I would
of gone for the fastest route and never mind the Angels,
because Archangel's Finest don't work overtime.

Something else does.

The wartoy caught up to us within sight of the port.

Taller'n me, taller'n Baijon, taller'n The Wall That
Walked back on sunny alMayne where I couldn't imagine
why I'd wanted to leave it just now. It lurched out in
front of us and started spieling the warning that some
cratty back on Throne a thousand lights away probably
thought was cute: all about how this area was under the
direct control of the Nobly-Born Mallorum Archangel and
I should just be tickled to death at the fact.

To death was maybe right. The wartoy was big and
wide and covered with enough hostile artifacts to remind
you that breaking curfew was a automatic Class D warrant. I had a feeling it probably wasn't going to be any
too gentle tagging a innocent passerby for later pick up.

"Run," I suggested.

Baijon skittered back, trying to square common sense
and honor and do it on his feet. The wartoy trundled
forward. I raised my stolen blaster.

I saw its launch-arm come up and I had sense enough
to throw the heat away from me. I threw myself the other
way and the tronic blew Errol's hand-cannon out of the
ether. Then it missed me with something long and ugly
that writhed like a brokebacked snake, looking for something to wrap around and squeeze. Baijon wrenched a
holosim exciter off the side of a building and chucked it
at the critter next.

I rolled into the gutter and wondered if I could make
it down the maintenance access and knew the answer.
There was a snap as ports in the wartoy's little metal
waterline popped open and something heavy, oily, and
yellow started vaporing out.

Then the top of its head exploded.

* * *

"Dammit—I thought you two were with the Rebellion!"

Tronics from all over was converging on the smoking ruin Meggie'd blasted the wartoy into with a rifle she'd persuaded some altruistic Angel to donate—and we was converging the other way.

"That's why I took you with me—we were supposed to pick up a Brightlaw courier on alMayne but whoever it was never showed up—and then you go and shoot my contact!"

"And six-dozen Space Angels! Saved your livealive, Meggie-bai; was Errol Lightfoot, first class trouble."

There was some more silence whiles we hotfooted it down deserted streets where every part of reality was machined like a high-ticket blaster. Civilization.

"It's lucky those damn things're so stupid," she said after whiles. "I'd wanted to shoot one anyway to draw the others off. Thought I was going to have to rig the rifle to overload. Look, are you sure you're not with the Rebellion? We could use the help about now."

"Meggie, don't you think if we was wanting to join up with a bunch of idealistic brainburn cases on Royal we'd of told you?"

"No." That from Baijon. I looked at him.

"Right. Here we are."

She stopped in front of one of the buildings that ringed the port. There was a regular touchpad lock on the side, and if you had a suspicious mind you could see there was a door there. Beyond the building was a blank space, then the fence—and paradise and freedom if we could get there.

"Access tunnel to the port," Meggie said, and pulled a shimcrib out of her boot.

"Remind me to go walking with you sometime when you're well-armed," I said.

She just grinned and put the card over the plate.

"*Kore*, are we breaking the law yet?"

"Since about you jumped Errol-peril, bai," I told him.

And Errol the ex-Peril'd broke it first. An older law, about not selling out your own side.

"Good," my hellflower said, real satisfied. "I wished to be sure."

The access tunnel opened and we went in.

* * *

The three of us went down the tunnel to the first branch. Meggie stopped and leaned against the curved wall, and sat down.

"As good a place to wait as any," she said.

"For what?" Baijon was puzzled enough to ask, and I had a bad feeling I knew.

"Inspiration. Or did you think I had a plan, both of you? Funny; I hoped you did—I just hope *Angelcity's* oke and Mero can put the fix in to get us off. It's a good thing he buttoned her up tight when we left."

Meggie looked up and down the tunnel. She could figure odds as well as I could; these weren't good.

"Probably all they wanted was the guns. And I could prove we didn't have them."

"Wrong," I said.

"But," said Meggie, like it was a whole sentence. Like: *But what an t'hell do you mean? You been holding out on me, St. Cyr, maybe?*

"You remember I done told you one-time about Fenshee slaver hight Errol Lightfoot."

She nodded; Meggie and me go back to where I was still figuring angles on how to find and ice our boy Errol.

"Last seen walking into Mallorum Archangel's pocket out in the Roaq in a Chapter 5 rig, trust me. I was there. Selling all sides against middle, likely. He'd of found your guns, Meggie. And anyway, he knows your rep. Wouldn't even bother to look. Just gig the lot."

"And his life was mine, and I have taken it—but I wished to have his head as well," Baijon said, plaintive.

"It'd look great in your hopechest, bai."

"So what about my ship?" Meggie said.

The only one as didn't know the answer to that might be Baijon.

"It's only guns!" said Meggie, opening and closing

her hand like she wanted something to shoot. "Just a fine."

No. Not even if me and Baijon hadn't been along; not even if Meggie'd walked right into Errol's arms and then into Imperial lockup swearing all the way she'd never *seen* a starship. There was the scent of Example To Others about Royal, and we all smelled it.

"So you tell me my life-story and I'll tell you yours," I said. Meggie shrugged. What else did we have to do with our time?

"Guns are steady profit, if you have the hold space to waste on enough of them. alMayne's one of our regular stops, every two hundred days or so. Hawkharrow and Estel-Shadowmaker rigs from Barnegat; one of the Starborn LessHouses buys them for us. What else can we do—Indies can't compete with the Company anywhere in Directorate Space; they'll ship free rather than lose a cargo to one of us."

"Cut to the chase," I told her, even if it's true about Company ships.

"We were on Diapason, in Harmony. A cut-out offered us the job; standard split and a meet-cute in Port Mantow. We had the contacts, the money was good—it had to be the Brightlaws—"

"Chairman Charlock not having too much trouble arming his troops these days," I put in.

"So we hit alMayne and made our deal for the mixture as before. It usually takes them a couple few days to put a deal together, but it's not a bad port to lie-up in—"

She was rambling all over the story, was Meggie, wondering what was happening to *Angelcity* and thinking she maybe knew. I let myself wish that Paladin was here; I'd been in the own cousin of this scrape a dozen times and he'd always got me out. Reality is what your computer tells you it is, and computers believed anything Paladin told them.

"—so we were waiting and someone with a conduct from never-you-mind came and booked two passages to Royal for whoever showed up and said the magic word before we left. I wondered for a while if it was you, but I guess you would of said, right? They never showed.

Left something for them I've still got in my lockbox. And this just isn't *fair!*''

No it wasn't. And for once it wasn't my fault.

But it was my problem.

What is reality? I felt the pushing feeling at the back of my mind that I'd used to get when I was about to be brilliant and got these days when somebody else's mindset was yelling for attention. Or maybe it was mine—how would I know?

What is reality?

Is it what we can drag in through the natural receptors of a piece of protoplasm? If it is, then the world is a small place. But we don't like small. We build new senses to gather reality. And if what our made senses tell us is different from what our bodies see, which do we believe?

The wrong one, usually.

Our problem was reality-based. We couldn't do damn-all about the problem, so there was just one thing left.

Do something about the reality.

I thought about Errol's head, and how I really couldn't think why Baijon shouldn't have it if he wanted it. I thought about how Mero and Meggie deserved enough luck to get upside with *Angelcity*.

I thought about most of the things you think about in the dead of night whiles you're listening to your mind disintegrate.

"I want you to do me a thing, Meggie. I get you out of here, we got a deal, deal?"

Meggie looked at me, more suspicious than hopeful.

"Nobody can get us out of here—unless they're drawing to an inside straight."

"I get you out, I get *Angelcity* up, you do me a thing, je?"

"St. Cyr, you get us out of here and I'll marry you."

"You don't get off that easy. It's like this. Washonnet's at war because the hellflowers've heard Mallorum Archangel's a Librarian."

Meggie made a editorial noise.

"I get you out of here, you say they're right. You tell everybody: he's *Malmakosim*, he's riding High Book."

"The point of the exercise, St. Cyr, is supposed to be an improvement on how things are now."

"Did I say you got to stand around and wait for the late-breaking reviews? Don't put your name on it. Just pass the word."

"Are you sure about this, St. Cyr? About Archangel?"

"You telling me you *care*, Meggie-bai? Ask hellflowers for true-tell; me, I just asked you favor."

"There's no way you can pull this off."

"Then we all be dead and you got nothing to pay."

Meggie looked at me like she thought I was crazy. Silly frail; I *knew* I was. No harm in it. Some of my best friends is crazy.

And besides, there was one of Paladin's old tricks with the Imperial dataweb I wanted to try. Only I didn't have his advantages. I had to get tó a terminal.

"Do I have a choice?" Meggie said.

None at all.

* * *

The Power Tower is a tower even when it's a bunker underground—it's the building on any port that handles in/out traffic.

Usually it's big enough so there's a place where the Trade Customs & Commerce Officer updates the ships-in-port registry and arranges to search any ships flagged there; lockups for confiscated contraband; places to handle fees licenses registration and all the other ways the Empire scrapes credit off you for trying to make a living with a ship.

But it doesn't have to have any of those things. All it needs is one room with a DataNet hookup for the songbirds to juggle the incoming and outgoing traffic on.

It was the dataweb I wanted, and I didn't see any reason to walk in uplevel amongst the *legitimates* and ask for it. Not with the connects running right down into the maintenance tunnels where we was and with an access terminal here for systems checks.

I didn't know if this was going to work. What I had

was the stone bankable belief that it would—but then I also thought I was a Old Federation Library Archive, or sort of.

Paladin had done it. I knew that from the outside and remembered it from the inside if I wasn't crazy.

It was simple to do.

If you was made out of light and magic.

But I was flesh and bone—mostly. I couldn't walk into a computer and think its thoughts for it.

"What are you going to do?" Meggie came up beside me. I looked at her and shrugged.

We was both following Baijon. Not only was he growing more larcenous by the tik, he *always* knew where we was relative to *Angelcity* and the main port gate. Without that we could of been lost slightly longer than forever down here; starved to death and been found by the housekeeping tronics.

Better'n what Errol's playmates had planned for us, but how much was that saying, really?

"This way." Baijon came back from where he was scouting and waved us on.

"Going to go into the DataNet and change the file on *Angelcity* so's you've got Clearance-to-Lift," I told Meggie.

"Oh, what a relief. For a moment there I thought you had a plan."

*   *   *

Around bedtime Meggie's variable-generating compkey did shimcrib on one last gate, and we was in the downdeep underneath the Power Tower.

I like knowing how things is put together. Always have. With the net result I know a lot of pretty damn useless things, 'cause when is a girl like I going to be underneath the Power Tower messing with its main computer?

Now, is when.

"Now what?" said Meggie.

I looked around. It wasn't really a room at all, just the place where a vertical pipe intersected a horizontal one. There was a row of hand and foot holds going up the wall—to guide you when the dropshaft was on and use alone when it wasn't. They led up to things like light and air and *legitimates*.

The touchpad was right where it belonged to be, sticking out from the cable going from up to down like a afterthought. A tech pulling maintenance on the dataweb would jack a separate brain in here, not to mention a display; piggyback it on the main DataNet access to check for lumps, bumps, and strange foreign logic.

Which meant there was a way to plug in.

Meggie was carrying enough toys for me to pop the housing easy and quick. Inside it looked like every other piece of partytech ever hatched, except cleaner. The jacks for the peripherals was bundled in place.

I pulled off my gloves and ran my fingers over the pad, and I knew I could do it.

"Baijon, you loan me your Knife, one-time."

Because whatever I was now, I was just not-human enough to get myself killed real spectacular.

"St. Cyr?" Meggie said again.

I shook my head to clear it of the series of access codes ringing in my brain. The way wayaway into the part of the Royal planetary brain that controlled all the port functions was so clear and open I could walk it—and only existed as pulses of light.

I took a deep breath.

"Now you go back *Angelcity*, Meggie. Three minutes, then up and into the building. Nobody stop you, specially if they don't see you."

Meggie stared at me, weighing all the other things she could maybe do and coming up with the same answer I did. Finally she nodded.

I looked at Baijon. He shook his head. I wasn't surprised. He was staying with me, faithful for the next fifty-six galactic standard years, or until he figured out I had *Malmakos* on the brain.

"And maybe we see you again and you remember this. And maybe not."

"You don't have to do this, Butterfly," Meggie said, although since she couldn't think I was going to jack

myself in series with the planetary core I don't know
what she thought I was going to do.

"There ain't no other way, Meggie. Now go on and
let me get to cases."

She kissed me and hugged Baijon and went. And there
we was.

Three minutes.

It wasn't me, I kept telling myself, which I'd believed
all along until it was time to cut it. I knew it wasn't going
to hurt. High-class cyber-work has a cut-out to keep its
dainty patrons from feeling stress and unease. I took Baijon's Knife and slit the fake skin on my arm.

I peeled it back and dug through the padding and insulation until I could see the glass bones underneath.
This was part of me; this was what jumped when my
brain said hell and high.

Two minutes.

There was a bunch of color-coded leads running back
and forth: silver for power, purple for memory, and a
couple others that spent their time datagathering and then
tricking my brain into thinking it felt something. Those
were the ones I wanted.

I slid the *arthame*-blade under one. Baijon watched me
intent like I was doing it to him. I twisted the blade,
hoping it would shear through.

White light exploded in my skull as the sensors mailed
everything home at once. I staggered, and Baijon held
me up. Two yellow wires curled up out of my arm and
for the first time I could feel the prosthesis as something
not part of me. I flexed its fingers. They opened and
closed just like always, but a little heavier.

And now I could plug the computer right into my brain
and play Library.

I didn't want to. And I did. Ultimate risk. The wildest
ride that ever was, and not even needing a ship to take
it. Pure fun.

I wrapped the dataweb jacks around my sensory-lead
and the world went away.

One minute. I keyed the touchpad with my free hand.

At first I was just fooling about, feeling my way into
the net. There wasn't the holotank that would of shown

me the computer's answers in Intersign glyphs, but I didn't need it. What I was doing was like remembering a dream, only I wasn't remembering anything. I was making it real.

Or I was lying to myself.

It was simple to dump memory from the sensors uplevel without saving it somewhere for Security to see it. I followed Meggie out of the building by the scanners she tripped, but everything they had to tell they told just me, and I wiped it.

There was a stasis field around *Angelcity*. I couldn't turn it off or cancel it without setting off alarms, but I could move it to some other ship. So I did.

That's when they started to notice. I knew they would, but they wasn't quite sure yet. They didn't know what and they didn't know how—just something where and (pretty soon) who.

I was finished with the Port computers; I'd done all I could with them. What I wanted now was in to the planetary core where they kept laws and facts and suchlike.

It's supposed to be impossible. Paladin did it all the time, silk-sailing. For me it was somewhere in between— and it took time, which I didn't have much of.

"*Kore*, they are coming," Baijon said, strained.

I knew it. But I was close, so close, almost in, and it was so damn awkward making my fingers do what my mind could see, and the touchpad ports was so *slow* . . .

Code, and wait, and code, and wait-wait-wait, like a lag-time between thoughts and how could anybody *think* this slow? And me never sure I was hearing the computer right, or my fantasies was playing me false, or maybe Baijon'd figure there was something not-quite-right enough to make real trouble.

Waiting . . .

Now I could hear what he'd heard—rattle and rumpus and *legitimates* out in the tunnel looking for to find their way in.

Like I was in. I had the whole world in my hands, and anything I wrote was truth.

There was no warrant for Megaera Dare.

There was no hold order on the Independent Ship *Angelcity*.

The ship had immediate clearance.

I told the DataNet that and it believed me, and after that, any other truths didn't matter. I was dazzled watching new truth write itself in unreality for anyone who wanted to check it to believe.

The port computers and orbital data-catchers told me *Angelcity* was gone: real truth, not virtual truth.

"*Kore*—" The footsteps was close now: men in armor.

"You was the best friend I ever had, Baijon-bai. Fact."

But it was too late for Baijon and me to go anywhere at all.

11

Tainted Love

The cell was like all other cells. There was plenty time to think whiles you was in, and plenty things to rather not think about. Partly I thought about Charlock Corporation's werewolves taking Baijon. They'd took him somewheres away from me when they found us. I wondered if he was still alive.

What I thought about mostly was how Baijon and me was maybe not the galaxy's best team, somewise. Oh, he was cute and fast and ready with a blaster and I've got my points, but wasn't neither of us temperamentally suited to say "whoa" when t'other one came up with a fun new way to get killed.

I'd always counted on Paladin for that. Only he wasn't here now to tell me my notions was damfool; what there was, was a starry-eyed kid who thought I was god's older sister.

One of us was going to have to learn to be—what was Pally's word for it?—*reasonable*.

If we got out of here I promised to start working on that. Tomorrow.

Not that there was going to be one. Fake ID, curfew violation, trespassing—we was spare parts. At least I was.

I was debating the musical question of whether it would do Baijon any serious net life good if the *legitimates* knew who he was when they gave him back.

It'd took four of them to carry him here and they didn't try to set him down any gentle—they *threw* him. He bounced right back and started trying to claw his way through the shut door.

Eventually even a hellflower had to give it up. He slid

down to the floor in a huddle of misery and finally saw me.

"They have taken my Knife, *Kore*," he said. Then he clung to me and wept like they'd cut out his heart.

Ever wonder why it is you got no hellflower trouble under the Pax Imperador? They all come hardwired with a built-in hostage to fortune, is why. The Knife. It isn't something they own. It's *them*. A hellflower's going to leave his *arthame* behind about the time I shoot myself in the head for recreation. Whoever's got the Knife's got the owner. And that makes a hellflower real vulnerable.

And now the *legitimates* had Baijon's.

Finally he quieted some and looked at me. Some kindly soul had bandaged him up all legit and official, which he had made serious renovations on trying to walk through a locked wall, and lifted his Knife whiles they was doing it. And I didn't think he was cute, or funny, or any other such condescending thing. He'd put everything he had on the line for me time and again when I was doing things that was just as stupid and nonsense to him as grieving over a damn knife was to me. I owed him.

"First you tell me, Baijon. Then we kill all of them and get it back."

It wasn't really important that we was both on the same side of a locked door, neither. Or that I had about as much chance of making good on that promise as I did of being elected Emperor. I meant it, and that was all Baijon cared about.

"They are *not* human beings, *Kore*—they are animals, breaking even their own law. The *chaudatu* laws say they cannot touch it—do they doubt the word of one of the Gentle People, the vow that it will not be used in battle against them?"

Well *I* would, and so would anyone with any sense. But that wasn't the point.

"They be just wanting to nail you somewise, bai, and make you tell them things." Like who you are, and who your da is, and what we two was doing with their computer, and how. I flexed my fingers and watched the cybereisis bells and whistles move back and forth in the open part.

"Never." Interphon didn't have enough flavor for him—he repeated it in helltongue where it really does mean that: *never, forever, and I really do know the difference between never and not-now.*

"Yeah, bai. Never-ever-forever. And we get out of here and crottle their greeps, sure. But we got to wait for it."

Baijon rocked back on his haunches, ready to wait at top speed. He looked at me, suspicious I didn't quite understand his point of view.

"They are not human, *Kore*. They are less than animals—they could have been human, and forswore humanity. Thus they endanger humans by their example. They are *wrong*."

"Sure, bai. I know." He might of had a point, but it was too damn pretty and theoretical for me. And they already made me mad enough to agree with Baijon whether he was right or not. Because he couldn't of hurt them with his damn Knife—and if they was scared of it they could just of glued it shut. But they took it.

Why?

Not a bad question, when you came right down to the hard-and-sharpies.

Because until we was definitely criminal, the *legitimates* had to play by the rules, and the rules was, Baijon got to keep his *arthame* until after he was dead. Even on Wanderweb Free Port, they'd only took it after they said he was guilty and condemned, and Free Ports don't follow the Pax Imperador.

But the people who'd took it here had medicalled Baijon—which meant he was valuable enough that they surely wouldn't risk him icing himself over getting his Knife took away.

Right?

Unfortunately the empirical evidence was against it.

* * *

Baijon and me was left alone for the optimal period some paid expert sometime told the heat was the right length of time to soften up members of the criminal element with trepidation and remorse. Then a couple Size

Large werewolves in Space Angel black came looking for
us.

Baijon looked at me. *Wait for it,* I 'signed at him. But
we wasn't going to wait one tik past where his Knife was
in sight. I owed him that, and I wasn't putting it aside
for some "greater good," neither. Fair is fair.

Darktraders pay their debts.

So we walked meek down the corridor between the
heat, me looking for an angle I could use.

I had been in this situation lots and lots and I'd never
been in it before. I'd been in some trouble, sure, but
mostly I'd *almost* been in trouble if somebody was to
notice what I was doing.

And I'd never been in Directorate space, let alone got
in trouble here, because any basic medical scan'd reveal
me for what I was—an Interdicted Barbarian, illegal im-
migrant from someplace as had paid the Empire good
money to throw away the key. I'd heard rumors, and
stands to reason more people'n me'd tried it, but I'd never
met anyone else from one of the dicty-worlds in Tahelangone Sector. They don't send you home when they catch
you out here, neither. They shoot you.

It was a pretty good bet I'd been scanned in the cell.
So looking at it from that angle, wasn't nothing logistical
standing in the way of me helping Baijon turn the place
inside out going after his Knife. I had nothing left to lose.

We was still somewheres in the Power Tower—at least,
all the time I'd been conscious we hadn't gone anywheres
that could be outside it unless the *legitimates* was playing
pharmaceutical headgames with my reality. We went to
a lift, and up, and then we was on a level with windows—
fancy nonsense when holosims'd work better but *I* like
'em—and I could see there was still port outside, coming
on along of dawn.

I knew every ship down there, origin-destination-
dockage-tonnage-stowage-and-rating. I knew who they
was and where they was. *Everything* from the ships-in-
port directory.

I was drowning in raw memory.

Whoever "I" was.

When the shivaree in my skull had died down and I

could pay attention to the real world again we was in very important sophont land, and we picked up four more little helpers—all glittering armor this time and armed to the high-heat. Baijon fluffed up a little when he saw them, but he went on waiting.

My head hurt. Only slightly worse than that second-hand chaos and old night was the absolute conviction that somewhere in that mass of undigested data I shouldn't never have been able to get off a touchpad keyboard even with a hotwire straight to my brain was guaranteed luck and a way out.

If I could find it in time.

We went through a last set of doors into the kind of stone lux place they bring you to tell you to kill yourself somewheres else and save them the fuss. The kind of place every bully has if he can swing it, from nighttime man to pimp to king. Business as usual, really. It was impressive, but it was supposed to be impressive. So I wasn't impressed.

There was another short-order of Space Angels there, and someone else. And I knew we was in real trouble. Fact.

You couldn't look at him. Very slick: holosim augmentation and subsonics and maybe pheromones. No matter what you did you couldn't look at him straight on.

So I didn't even try. I looked out the window at the ships left out on the field. I could see a little of him out of the corner of my eye: silk that ate light and glitterflash so damn expensive I'd only read descriptions of the stones.

"Welcome to Port Mantow. I am delighted to be able to greet you properly at last—Valijon Starbringer and Butterflies-are-free Peace Sincere."

His voice had a distorter on it, too: fear and command and other stuff that made it so you couldn't get your attention off him. Not too useful for long chats, I bet, but then Mallorum Archangel didn't have to have too many long conversations.

"You have my leave to speak," Archangel said, and Baijon ripped out a sentence of pure, double-distilled, helltongue treason. It settled my mind considerable—

there wasn't no way either of us was going to get out of
the room alive after that.

"Trite," Archangel said. "But children don't know
any better—and you, foolish boy, are unlikely to have
time to learn. You can be of some small use to me to
make up for the small inconvenience you have been. You
will do all that is within your power to please me because
you have nothing left to bargain with—while I continue
to have the opportunity to grant . . . concessions."

Archangel said it all unruffled like Baijon hadn't called
him seventy-seven kinds of bad name. He gestured, and
his hand came clear a minute when it got outside the
distorter field. And I saw what Archangel was holding.
Baijon's Knife.

Baijon saw it too, and the two Space Angels clamped
down on him quick. Their armor rattled as he lunged,
but he couldn't move them. Archangel probably smiled,
and Baijon's *arthame* vanished back into the field.

"Concessions, as I said. You have no idea what a great
pleasure it is to see you again so that we may have this
conversation. Now. Where is it?"

I don't think Baijon heard him, but I did. All the distorter harmonics making every word His Nobility uttered
the most important there ever was, and what I heard was
Archangel asking the wrong question.

"You brought it here from alMayne. You used it beneath the Port. I am not interested in a long seduction.
Where is it?" Archangel said.

Not *"Who are you?"* or even *"Aha, I have you now,
Fillintheblank."*

"Where is it?"

The TwiceBorn Lord Prince, the Nobly-Born Lord
Mallorum Archangel, Governor-General of the Phoenix
Empire wanted some*thing* out of us, even knowing who
we was—and whatever it was, we didn't have it.

I heard the servos in the Angels' armor whine as Baijon fought them. I just stood there, flatfoot and stupid
while shimmering evil looked us over and decided which
one to take first.

"You *will* tell me," he said to either of us or none,
and only twenty years of habit kept my mouth shut.

So a Space Angel tuned me up some—not bad, just enough to remind me how much pain could hurt. If I'd been on my own turf and they'd been serious, they'd of followed it up with taking off a finger or doing something else permanent to indicate their sincere displeasure. But they didn't.

The next thing I remembered was coming back from being kicked in the face, felt like, and seeing three Angels holding Baijon front and center of Archangel whiles another one offered Archangel a little black box.

Little black boxes never have anything in them you want.

I must of moved, because there was enough Angels at large to haul me up and shake me.

The pain felt like it was something very important to somebody who wasn't me. Visual focus went on and off in flashes of light and I dripped on the carpet, but I could see.

The black box went on a side table and got its two halves yanked apart. Then it got turned on.

A beam of light ran between the two terminals that'd been in the halves of the box; dark red, the beam was, and all along the surface it sparked where the motes of dust touched it and made the conversion to energy.

A molecular debonder. The small kind, for tidy security in home and office. And I bet I knew what was going into that beam, one piece at a time.

But I was wrong. They hustled me up close all right, but just to watch.

"If you actually think that I am unaware of your father's pathetic ambitions as kingbreaker, little prince, think twice. Your revered and moral father was my hound to flush out those who wish my Empire to be less than tidy, and now the time has come to whip him to kennel. You will be the lash. For love of you Kennor Starbringer will beg on his knees to serve me in any way I choose. But you'll do it first. I want the Brightlaw Prototype—the one you were attempting to bring to the insurgents under cover of an arms delivery."

Oh, *that* Brightlaw Prototype.

Baijon snarled, too far gone to talk any kind of words at all.

Archangel held out his hand. Light and music rippled all over him from the distorter fields and I had to look away. Out of the corner of my eye I saw Baijon's *arthame* flash red in the light from the debonder.

"Where is it?" Archangel said, all silk. "You can't deny it. You used it against the port computers to help the gunrunner escape. The 'honor' of the alMayne—it has doomed you and your creature and gained nothing. The ship never left the system."

"No," I said, before I could help it.

"Yes." I got Archangel's undivided attention for a instant and wished I hadn't. "Tell me, Prince Valijon, which do you value more: this tribal totem, or . . ."

"Librarian," snarled Baijon. *"Malmakosim."*

Even here it got a little attention—you just don't call someone, anyone, a Librarian and go back to what you was doing the minute before. But the six-pack of Angels'd heard it before, or maybe they just didn't care.

"It was *your* Library," snarled Baijon, "and all the Gentle People know your shame, eater of—"

One of the Angels holding Baijon smacked him a short business-like wallop with a truncheon, which put an effective end to discussion of Imperial hot cuisine.

Archangel turned the *arthame* and the blade flashed red in the light.

"Do you actually think anyone will believe that? This is the nine-hundred and ninety-second Year of Imperial Grace, Prince Valijon, not the dark ages. Your hellflower kindred know what they want—and it isn't a holy war."

"The Gentle People—"

"Will do what is prudent, expedient, and politic. As *you* will do what I want, my darling hotspur—for this. In the end, the alMayne is not so different from the *chau-datu* he despises, is he?"

Flash, the blade in the light. I tried to move, but my pet Angels wasn't having any. Any more folding from them and the cybereisis was just going to shear loose of what was left of my original collarbone.

"I don't want it," Baijon said, flat. His voice was hard, and there weren't no kinchin-bai left in it at all.

"Very well." Archangel opened his hand. The Knife slid through his fingers into the debonder beam. When it hit it warped every way at once with a sound like hot grease poured into water. Then it was gone, and just a couple flakes of carbon was left.

Baijon went gray and made the kind of sound you hear in nightmares. He hung boneless between the two Angels, and now they was holding him up not back. There was a flicker from behind the distorter, and they pushed Baijon down to his knees. His head hung, limp.

"Pretty princeling," said Archangel. "Strength of character prevails only in the talkingbooks. Now you've forced me to question your little friend—again."

Then Mallorum Archangel turned off his distorter and I could see him plain.

The shocks came in sequence. Each one hit separate, giving me time to feel them all.

Clothes more expensive than anything I could make up. Half armor that was mostly a joke and the rest valuta made solid. Human as me, or Baijon.

His hair was short, dusted with something that glittered. Brown hair. Eyes would probably be dark. Fenshee breeding population, by the genetic markers.

Then he turned away from Baijon and toward me. He smiled.

"Hiya, sweetheart, how's tricks?"

It was Errol Lightfoot. But Errol was dead back in that dockside bar.

Then his expression changed, and now the face went with the clothes: arrogant and inhuman, a face to go with all the stories the Patriarchs had ever told back home about hellgods.

"Don't ever confuse playacting with reality, *'Sweetheart.'* "

"You're dead," I said, probably only to me.

He turned away and knelt by Baijon. Archangel made every bad dream I ever had seem like a walk in the sunlight.

"You belong to me now, little Valijon." He put a hand

under Baijon's chin and lifted, and looked down into Baijon's eyes.

"You leave him lonealone, bai." I wanted to look around for who'd said it, but I had a awful feeling I knew.

"All right."

He came toward me, and now when it was no damn use at all I remembered what'd bothered me about Errol back at the Warped Space.

Errol's eyes were black. Always had been.

But the Errol that'd been waiting for us'd had purple eyes, same as this Errol here.

Only this Errol was Mallorum Archangel. And his eyes were the deep drowned violet of lethal radiation. They seemed to pulse, a spiral song sucking me in like a Old Fed warpgate. He smiled, and the look was pure predator.

He left Baijon alone.

But he came after me.

"Hold her still," he said while I tried to kick him. I felt the buzz of his personal shield and my foot slid off. The Angels dug into the nerves on my arms, but the left one didn't have any and they couldn't hurt me enough anyway to make me let Archangel touch me.

"Oh, little Butterfly," he said. "I am going to *enjoy* this."

But he did get his hands on me. The barbs on his gloves slid into my skin and ripped, and I didn't feel that either. The only thing in the world was those eyes, and when Archangel was finished enjoying himself wasn't going to be nothing left.

Then something slid by me in my skull on its way to someone else and left me alone. There was a jangle of raw synesthesia that part of me was trying to sort to find out if it was me being hurt, and Archangel shrieked.

"She's a cyborg! *It's in the cyborg!*" He hit me across the face and then turned on one of the Angels holding me, mad somewise beyond reason.

And the Angel let go.

I didn't stop to gawk. I didn't even know what I was going to do until both hands closed around one terminal of the debonder.

Three of my cybereisis fingers slid into the beam and vanished.

And I threw the box.

I didn't care if I killed him, but killing him wouldn't be good enough. What I wanted was what I got—the matter-eater beam hit Archangel's personal shield, tried to suck energy, and blew lunch all over the room.

And then it was just like with bullies the galaxy over. Everybody lost all the careful common sense they'd been saving for a special occasion. They'd go for Archangel first instead of hanging on to us—a chance, if we could use it.

Baijon heaved up and flung one of the Space Angels at the Governor-General. The other one was dead already. I grabbed Baijon and ran.

* * *

There was a dropshaft at the end of the hall and we took it without waiting to inquire whether it was powered or not. It dropped us two levels down in a place that was obviously where people went to wait for the high-heat to whistle them every day but today. Today it was stone empty, which meant no one between us and the next dropshaft.

If I stopped to think about what'd happened back there I'd go mad. Mallorum Archangel was . . . something . . . that was very bad indeed. And that mindbender'd called me a cyborg.

And destroyed Baijon's Knife.

"*Kore, Kore*—" said Baijon, sounding desperate scared.

"S'okay, babby. I got a plan."

"We can't. I can't. I have *killed* him, *Kore;* wherefore does he live? And he had killed me—how will I find Ketreis without— *Kore*—!" Baijon was starting to fold up again now that the first rush was past and I couldn't let him do that.

"Bai, you want him to have you?"

Baijon stopped dithering like I'd kicked him. He'd run into something worse than hell and death and hellflower honor, and he'd listen to a Library if it'd tell him the way away.

Good thing.

"No," said Baijon, and we got our bearings and ran again.

Eventually we came to a dropshaft that was locked.

"Damn!" I slammed off the wall and back against Baijon.

"We are running?" he said, like we hadn't already had this conversation. He looked like a sophont as had gotten his death-wound. But he was moving.

"We is tactically retreating so's we can blow the son-abitch to hell. C'mon, bai, don't clock out on me now. I need you."

I grabbed his arm before he could think of a argument and pulled. Baijon came with the pull, like a proton grenade just waiting to happen.

We'd been running blind, we'd been running *away*, and if it hadn't done anything else for us it'd put enough time between us and Archangel or whoever he was that I could think around the edges of him and plan.

Plan what? There was nothing left but running.

And if I could reach it, something that would give us the longest run of all.

12

Dressed to Kill

I didn't know what level we was on, or how long we'd been running, but I did know that wherever we was we was sealed in with no way out until they came for us. My hands started to shake. I watched them with interest—one born, one made, nothing much to choose between. The made one was missing fingers. The sheared ovals of glass bone glittered. Behind me Baijon was opening doors like he'd found a new mission in life, but there wasn't going to be any way out behind any of them.

"Kore," he said. I turned around. Baijon was standing in a doorway.

And he was holding a gun.

One of the things the Empire does best is impound contraband. Since contraband comes in through port, the pound is at the port—usually somewhere in the Power Tower—at least for the small expensive illegal stuff.

"Illegal Stuff" was what the Intersign glyphs on the door said, and it was—everything small, cute, and liftable the Empire'd taken off passing ships in the last never-you-mind. Food, perfumes, furs, raw gems, made jewelry, tapes and holos and talkingbooks. My onetime stock in trade.

And weapons.

Enough to get us a death quick and certain, and I might of took that way out except after seeing Archangel up close I wasn't sure it'd be *final* enough. If minds could live in webs of starlight and flit from skull to skull on air, just how safe was being dead, anyway?

Not very. I knew Archangel. Just like I knew Errol. And I didn't want to think about either one just now.

So I went for the heat. There was crates and crates,

laid out like mayhem's dreamshop, all the way up to a plasma catapult somebody'd shagged off from an Imperial Armory and hadn't got quite wayaway with.

And there was salvation.

I don't know where the original legger got them, and Royal should of scrapped them instead of stashing them here. They've got no resale value, after all.

But I ripped the cover off the first crate and there it was, truth in advertising made flesh.

A suit of Imperial Hoplite Armor.

It stood taller'n a man and not so wide as a starship—the powered armor Fleet'd decommissioned as being too dangerous. For Fleet, they meant. The incidence of fragging went way up when every man-jack of the cannon-fodder'd been issued what amounted to his own portable starship. So they dished the armor.

There was six suits of it here.

"Prob'ly no good," I told Baijon, and broke a nail prying open the chest carapace.

He stared at me like I was crazy and he was in a position to judge, and probably he was right; wasting my time on outlaw tech when a whole rathskeller of frightful was sitting here waiting to be scooped up and primed. But the power-pacs was all there: a double row of big silver buttons just like I slap into my blaster.

"Armor," said Baijon, when he figured it out. "Powered armor."

"Yeah, right. Help me get it out. And hope I remember how to hook it up before they get here."

* * *

Paladin always used to say I wasn't interested in learning. That isn't true. Knowledge is stuff that isn't of any practical use. I've got lots of that.

I bought a maintenance manual for the atmosphere suit I had to put together oncet so my ship *Firecat* could pass inspection. It covered all kinds bulgers, including powered armor. There was a chapter on the Hoplite stuff—it was new when the book was animated. I knew there wasn't any Hoplite armor anymore, but I audited that part anyway. And I guessed what I remembered of it wasn't real knowledge, because it sure came in handy now.

Hoplite armor comes all in one piece: you open up the chest and climb in. It doesn't have any built-in weapons—although a man wearing one can use a plasma-catapult like a blaster—it just makes you bigger, faster, and stronger than anything remotely human. What you do need to do with it, to get ready to rock'n'roll, is hook up all the connections between the inner and outer layers of the suit and make sure all the secondary charge accumulators is working.

Anybody sealed up in a working suit of Hoplite armor would be set to walk right through anything Archangel had to throw. Anything.

Tools and extra power-pacs was in the crate, and I could almost hear, through the ghost-dance in my head, Paladin whispering to me: ground-level and below-ground access was sealed, the top floor was secured, then the next, and the next . . .

We was in Fifth Floor Storage, in case anybody wanted to know, Fifth Floor being the cutoff between the working stiffs and the power elite, signified by being full of stuff neither side much wanted.

Baijon was a extra set of hands and I hoped he was learning lots. I was clumsier than I thought without half my left hand, and the armor'd fit him but not me in the time I had to trick with it.

I sealed the last of the leads back behind their foam.

"Do it," I said, and Baijon punched the power switch.

The armor spasmed; we both jumped back. Then it just lay there purring to itself. Waiting for someone to come and tell it what to do.

Maybe I'd hooked it up wrong. Maybe it'd mince Baijon to chitlins when he got in. Yeah. And maybe Archangel's personal guard wasn't six inches from finding us.

No choices left. Baijon stripped down to his bandages and slithered in. I settled the neck brace on him and closed the chest. It went down most of the way for my shoving and then stuck. The suit systems came on and pulled it the rest of the way closed with a snap.

The suit sat up. I backed up. Faint keening like go-forths going sour came from it. Baijon moved like he was drunk—big sloppy swinging moves, a little bit fatal if he connected. I backed up again.

He tried to stand and went over with a crash. The sound went on too long, and that was because the door'd went, too. Six Angels in full powered armor: black and silver and looking lightweight next to the Hoplite armor.

"Too bad it didn't work," the captain said. His voice was stripped out flat by the voder. "Where's the prince?"

The armor on the floor sunfished again and nobody needed to draw Mallorum's Angel a picture. He raised his magnetic uncoupler and pointed it at Baijon until the room temperature went up twelve degrees and sparks was jumping between every point on the armor they could.

"There. That should—"

But it didn't. The armor thrashed one more time and stood, and then belted the chief Angel out of the way. He didn't fly far, but he went fast.

They was professionals, they was armed and used to people making trouble, and they was outclassed. Two of them dropped and started firing and the other three scattered. Baijon went right over the two in the doorway. Their armor shattered like cheap formfit and their blasters could of been shooting oxygen for all the good they did.

Baijon didn't need a blaster. All he had to do was walk up and hit them.

"*Kore!*" His voice was all warped and distorted through the voder. I scooped up the nearest blaster—another Class B warrant, possession of a military sidearm—and chased after him.

Right into the tangle field.

They work the same way a tractor-pressor combo does: push-pull until whatever's grabbed moves only where you want it to. Fine for starships.

Lousy for people.

Cause my feet was *stopped*. The thing was set to prohibit lateral motion only—I could jump straight up, if I could, and it wouldn't stop me. But it wouldn't let me move forward, and if I got unlucky it could kill me. I could fall and twist joints out of their sockets trying to fold me up the way my original designer intended. And if I fell real wrong and made breathing a lateral motion, I'd be dead.

But I didn't have time to fall. It was like running into a wall, and I yelped, and Baijon whipped back around and lifted me straight up out of the field. The suit's whine was loud, but even louder was the sound of the max-field shorting out from a suit of Imperial Hoplite Armor being dragged through it.

Someday I'm going to get me a set.

The main power net blew and probably took Port Mantow with it. The secondary generators didn't have enough power to run the tangler, and Baijon set me down. We was somewhere in the Port Authority Building with too much high-heat between us and anything that could get us off this rock.

"Now we go back," Baijon said. The Power Tower systems kept coming up and crashing as something else blew. A ten-second cycle: disorienting.

"You're kidding, right?"

"We must . . . *Kore, how* can Mallorum Archangel be Errol Lightfoot?"

"You saw it too, right?"

I couldn't see anything but my own face reflected in the Hoplite helmet. I knew what Baijon was thinking anyway. He'd seen it. It *was* Archangel.

And it was Errol, too—I'd bet anything I had left on that.

"We must kill him," Baijon said, thinking it out careful-like. "Both of him. Again."

"Terrific—but wouldn't you like to be a success at it this time?"

Baijon considered that, too, whiles I picked up a belly-and-back and a night-helmet from a Angel what didn't need them anymore, and started putting them on.

"What must I do?" he said finally.

"Why don't we start with escaping, j'keyn?" I pointed at the wall and waggled my remaining fingers until Baijon caught on.

* * *

Cubic is cheap, downside. There was meters of waste space in every wall of the Power Tower and between floors, too; used for power-cables or insulation or nothing. If you was wearing full powered armor, you could make use of a fact like that.

The plastic stretched, then split, then tore like taffy. Baijon started peeling it off its structural supports. Real soon there was a big enough hole for even the armor to crawl through. He smoothed out the edges with one big bluesilver gauntlet like a child tidying mudpies.

"First we escape. Then we slay," Baijon said firmly.

"Sure, bai."

I followed him into the wall.

* * *

I didn't know why they hadn't used gas yet. There was no one alive to report that it'd be fifty percent useless, and it wasn't because they didn't have it—Royal was at war. The only thing I could think of was that maybe Archangel wanted things done his way, and like all damnfool glitterborn he was clueless.

I wanted to believe that.

I really did.

But I didn't, because I knew who Archangel really was, and it didn't make any sense. No sense at all—

The next level we reached was sealed too, but all that meant was nobody was shooting at us whilst Baijon dug a hole through the floor this time and we went through that to what we found out was Level Three.

After that the home team got annoyed.

We found Charlock troops on Level Three. They shot at us and we ran—all same to Baijon and me, 'cause we wanted to go the way they was chasing us anyway.

What we didn't want to do was run into a barricade with a molecular debonder—a disintegrator ray—big enough to planetoform a star attached.

Baijon recognized it—you show me a wartoy a hellflower doesn't. He backed up two lumping steps. I used him for cover and snapped off a couple of shots as might discourage the Angels coming up behind us.

Trapped. Neat, sweet, and thorough.

"Run," suggested Baijon. "I will hold them here."

So I did.

* * *

I didn't know what orders Archangel had given about who was to be taken alive and who got to be an example to others, but Valijon was a big noticeable target in almost impenetrable armor and I was small, harmless, and helpless.

I hoped they thought.

Because that molecular debonder of theirs was a fierce toy for sure, but it was also too big to run on a powerpac. That meant grid power, and you could turn off grid power.

Just ask any DataNet terminal.

I set one toggle on my rifle for "Continuous" and the other for "Dispersed" and swept myself a way past the Angels before the rifle turned to warm plastic in my hands. That bought me a minute alone in a corridor.

Nobody was supposed to be up here in the Power Tower without authorization anyway, so all the keycodes on the doors was simple—about the level of keeping Techie A out of Techie B's lunchbox. And everybody knows you can't get onto the Imperial dataweb without permits stretching nineteen ways from Night.

My Angel babysitters was a half-jump behind me when I slid into the first promising cubie. I had the door shut again before they was in line of sight, and kicked up the doorspeaker to hear them go galumphing past. Everybody knows it takes time to crack even a simple keycode, after all.

Everybody knows.

There was a damn sight too much blithe assumption going on in this legger's Empire, and I had the horrible feeling I might be among the chief assumpters. But I didn't have time to change my ways just now; about the time the Boys in Black got tired of playing Bullies-and-Blasters and brought some high-tech to bear on the problem of little Butterfly, Yours Truly would be nonfiction.

And Baijon would be plasma.

How long to wind the debonder up to rock'n'roll? Would it stop him? Would he run without me—and was there any place anymore, really, to run to? Audit the next exciting issue of *Thrilling Wonder Talkingbooks* for these and other unanswered questions.

I grabbed the touchpad on the desk and felt my way in to the system. There wasn't time or tools to jack it through what was left of my cybereisis, but this time there was a screen, and the wondershow was strictly between my ears anyway, down another imaginary set of not-really corridors one of which would lead to my idea of a black gang so I could shut down the spaceport grid.

I needed my miracle too much to jump salty for it, but somewhere in the back of my skull was storing up nightmares out of what I was doing now.

And the worst of it was, I wasn't good enough.

I could glitch their powersuck, but I couldn't stop it. The things I needed to grab slid out of my hands like skeins of hyperspace. I was too slow, too clumsy, too damn human still to do the only friend I had left any good at all.

It hadn't taken me a kilo-second to find out I had a great career as a failure—plenty of time left to dodge back out and watch them turn Baijon into smoke and ice. The debonder started to cycle up—it pulled enough power from the grid to make my corner of the dataweb go all wobbly. Everything was snow and stars and static, and me imagining I was running down a nonexistent corridor to find a room that wasn't there.

"Butterfly?" Paladin said. "What are you doing?"

His voice was thin and vague and hashed up with ground noise, and me not knowing if it was in my head or real.

"Shut it down, Pally—*shut everything down!*" I hammered the keypad, but it was too little and too late and I knew it.

"You're having fun again." might-be Paladin said dis-approvingly, and everything went black.

Everything.

* * *

The emergency exits crashed open behind the holosim screens and so did the door to the room. It was full day out and no lights, no holos, no moving tronics in sight.

"*Paladin!* Come back here!"

But if he'd ever been there at all, he was gone now. The DataNet Access Port was dead. Everything that ate power on Royal was dead. And I only had time to worry about one thing.

Baijon.

There was a crash from the corridor. I ran.

* * *

Pitch-black, and my friendly helpful backbrain trying to remind me how similar this was to being marooned in a powerless derelict drifting randomly in space. I found the door by the flashes of light coming through it and Baijon by the fact that he was the only thing lit up. The Hoplite armor sent beams in all directions illuminating a scene sure to be playing on select hollyvids everywhere Real Soon Now: Desperados of the Outfar.

They must of tried to fire the debonder. And they couldn't, or not enough to do any good, but by the time they'd figured that out they'd got Baijon Stardust and a full suit of Imperial Hoplite Armor really, really mad.

He'd picked up x-thousand kilos of debonder by the muzzle and swung it. It glittered at the far edge of the armor's watchlights, and the corridor looked like a mine had exploded. There wasn't even anything left that looked human enough to get sick over.

The big blue gauntlet came up in a slow hail. Valijon Starbringer'd just delivered the first installment on pay-back to his enemies.

"Come, *Kore*," Baijon said. He waved down the empty, unopposed, and dead silent corridor. Everybody

Archangel had available to go after us must of been at the debonder.

"Not that way." My mind was infinitely subdivisible, and the only part I was on speaking terms with now was only interested in the best way out. "We got to go how they don't expect. Power's down all over the port. C'mon."

Power was down over one hell of a lot more than the port. Whatever'd shut things down—me, my shadow, or a Library I used to know—had done one hell of a job.

We'd left ship *Angelcity* with Meggie last night just before curfew. We'd broke back into the port well into the dark part of the night, and Baijon and me'd spent serious hours under the Power Tower after that. We'd been rousted out to dance with Archangel just about dawn, and with one thing and another it was probably within shouting distance of light meredies now. Time for all good grubbers to be out running the economy, right?

Wrong.

A ship is a closed system, all of a piece. Shut it down and you'll kill all the crew, soon or late, but that's all. Power her up again and she's ready to rock.

A city's different. Turn it off and it *breaks*.

Through the open third floor window of the Power Tower I could see most of Port Mantow and a good chunk of the city. Nothing flew, nothing moved, nothing changed colors. Every computer in the Net, every computer swapping data with the Net, was wiped clean as a fake ID.

Baijon clomped over to the window and looked down. He put both hands against the window and pushed, and the thin sheet of plastic bowed then warped then popped free and skimmed off on the air like a sheet of thermofax, leaving an unsafe hole in the wall.

It was quiet enough I heard the first sirens go off—something with a discrete power-pac, or something else not tied into the Net. I tried not to think of how many deaders there was if even only one percent of the population'd bought real estate. Mantow City holds ten million. I saw.

"Now, *Kore*, we will jump out the window, and prove

to the gods of the Gentle People . . ." He stopped in the middle of what he was going to say. Archangel'd burned his soul back there. By hellflower rules, Baijon wasn't a hellflower no more.

"Yeah. Right. Just we get out of here, oke? We paid enough for the damned ticket."

I hung on for sweet life and an early retirement to the grabhandles on the shoulders of the Hoplite armor. Baijon took a running jump at the hole in the wall and that took care of getting us down the last three floors. He left two big craters in the crete and walked away. I've had worse landings.

"Now—" Baijon said. But I knew where I wanted to go.

Even with war, curfew, quarantine, and disaster, there was about a thousand ships down in Port Mantow. I knew. I'd counted them. And in all the high-iron on the heavyside, there was one ship with full inventories that only needed a solo pilot, had heavyweight personal armament and engines to match, and was where she could get upside without port tronics to help.

That was our ticket—if we could reach her.

Port Mantow was a big busy Directorate Capital port. It was slightly less busy than High Mikasa at teatime on any day but today. There was ships in rings, ships in bays, ships as said they wasn't going anywhere real soon racked in cybernetic cradles in the Port's bottom levels. There should have been people on the field—the ship's crews if nothing else—but there weren't.

Archangel'd done something with them, maybe. I tried to imagine having enough power to hand grief to that many Guilds at once, and couldn't.

He had so much power, what did he want with any more?

I looked around. There was ships and ships, but nothing was what I was looking for—the ship in a cradle slotted into long-term storage in the north/northwest (by planetary orientation) corner of the Port.

I looked down at the grid coordinates stamped into the crete and the credit-bit dropped. I'd misread the diagram I wasn't supposed to be able to access in the first place.

If the ship I was looking for was here, there should be a zillion levels above us.

But there wasn't. Because we wasn't on the bottom layer of Port Mantow where the ship was.

We was on the top.

"No," I said, and stopped. The downside version of the Big Empty was all around me, and a dozen more like it underfoot—a couple klicks of down that without power and light Baijon and me stood a dicty's chance of getting to.

I couldn't even turn the power back on.

I'd fixed us real good.

I stood there and thought about it, and slow-like it sunk in that the sound I'd thought was the ships' engines wasn't.

"Why do you stop?" Baijon asked, but I wasn't listening to him.

It was a sound that might be a riot and might be something else and might just be the sound of several million people I'd never met finding themselves in a world of hurt. Port Mantow City looked like a war-zone for sure. And I'd done it.

For being sloppy, for panicking. Shut everything down, I said, so something did.

"*Kore* San'Cyr?"

Fun was fun, and I didn't want me nor Baijon in Archangel's hands noway, but that last cheap trick'd put me over the line that separated Butterfly St. Cyr, doing what she had to to get by, and Lord Prince Mallorum Archangel, gazetted evilspeak. There was no difference between what he did and what I'd done.

Except, maybe, that doing it bothered me.

The noise from the city built to a dull roar of pure ugly. Somewhere something was burning.

"They are fools to build cities that will kill them," Baijon said calmly. Morning sunlight gleamed off the Hoplite armor's blue-and-orange. He stood there waiting for me like he had all the time in the world.

I didn't say anything. City power didn't fail the way this one's had. It *couldn't*.

Not by itself, anyway.

"They will head for the port soon. The Imperial Armory is at the port. They will want weapons to defend themselves. We must be gone before that happens," Baijon said.

They'd riot, and the Empire'd come down with both boots. Tortuga Sector was already under martial law. Riot was treason.

"Space Angels be having something to say about that, bai." My voice felt antique. I'd trapped us here on the surface of Royal. Our only way off was as far away as if it was on the moon.

"Without orders?" Baijon said like it was a joke. "Their only orders are obedience—with no one to obey they are craven."

"Archangel ain't dead. They'll listen to him." Archangel wasn't dead. Archangel wasn't never going to be dead. Archangel was. . . .

Never mind that now. Archangel wasn't dead, and he had as much proof as a walking nightmare like him cared for that me and/or Baijon was something that he wanted, and the ship that was our best chance of getting out of here was buried out of reach.

"Archangel also has orders, but we will not be here to know them. This way, *Kore*," said Baijon, and ankled toward a lock that headed downunder. The right way, as it happened, but how did *he* know?

Plastic shrilled as he twisted the access hatch off its moorings and crumpled it between his gloves like a piece of thermofax. He tossed it away. It made a dull sound on the crete and the armor's watchlights flared on, lighting the back of the shaft and making the numbers and warning signs reflect.

However he knew, it didn't seem important right now. I followed the Hoplite armor into the dark.

* * *

There was no power. There was no light. It was hot in the underport without technology to smooth the way, and the air was already less than prime cut. Without my eight-foot flashlight I never could of found anything but slow starvation. We went down the dropshafts using handholds with Baijon to light the way, and after whiles I just let the Hoplite armor do all the work.

"We go this way, do we not? To your ship?" He'd stopped the 'sponder's volume all the way down to a buzzy whisper, but Baijon's amped voice still echoed flat in the tunnel.

"Turn around; I can't see."

He did, and the spotlight on his chest showed off the wall glyphs for Level and Section in big bright Intersign glyphs. I ran my fingers through my hair and tried to reconcile what I was seeing with what I knew.

"440/A, North," said Baijon happily, and tripped off.

He was right, too. Again. But how the hell did *he* know?

* * *

Docking bay 440/A North was . . . well, think of a cube made up of about a quarter of a million smaller cubes. 440/A was on the outside bottom. Not useful for getting out, except for one thing.

Port Mantow was built at the edge of one of Royal's oceans. The other side of the docking bay wall was nothing between us and the never-never but water.

We got to 440 and I was damn glad neither of us'd been stupid enough to lose the armor. The bay door was shut, and locked, and I knew the keycode but I couldn't use it without power.

That was why the Libraries had lost.

It must be the bad air making me sick. I didn't want to be thinking about Old Fed Tech, about what it could do and couldn't do and had done.

About how easy it was to make it helpless.

Without power—and things that power could move—Libraries was nothing.

About how easy it was to be helpless.

I'd never wanted to be helpless. I'd spent the last twenty years getting shut of it, getting to a place where I'd always have a weapon and a bolt-hole, where nobody could push.

All gone now.

I felt the wall slide up my back as I sat down. All gone, and the odds shortening into the negative numbers. Running another escape just out of habit and watching everything I touched dissolve into entropy and old night.

"Kore?" Baijon said.

"Whaddya want?" I was tired and probably breathing everything but air.

"Now we must enter the docking bay and steal the ship," he prompted.

"Yeah? And how you going to get the door open?"

Baijon put his hands on the door. His gauntlets scraped over the surface with a high faint squeal that put my teeth on edge.

"No."

Maybe he could rip it out of the wall—although I was betting that it was proof against even a Hoplite's best shot—but we had to be able to seal the door behind us again, or else when we ruptured the wall we'd drown every ship in the port. The weight of the water'd mangle everything that was left, too, providing there was anyone left to care.

Did I care? I hoped so, but it was like hoping you'd win the lottery or get the good numbers on your next downfall; nothing to do with anything real.

And if I—or whatever I was—was going to lose it, let it wait until we got far enough out of here for Baijon to have even chances.

"Give me . . . you better hope that suit's got jumper-leads, bai, or we picked one hell of a garden spot to vacation."

* * *

Every other suit of powered armor I ever read about had a basic tech-kit as part of it, and this one was no exception. It had tools to lever the face off the doorlock, and cables to hook the suit up to the door. It was easy but not quick to power up the door, code it, open it, and get through. Baijon yanked the leads and the door rolled shut behind him, deadweight and sealed. Wasn't no way now we could get it open from this side.

But that didn't matter.

She was long and low and sleek and made any other ship I'd ever seen look like old news. She stretched from end to end of the bay like darkness visible and her plane surfaces swooped and soared like the wings of night. She was black crystal decadence nose to tail and I could see myself reflected in her hull.

She'd been a Gift Transfer to my old buddy Errol Lightfoot about the time me and Baijon'd been setting foot on Low Mikasa. For services rendered, the file'd said.

Only there wasn't no such person as Errol Lightfoot, was there? And a Gift Transfer between Errol and Mallorum Archangel was just pure fantasy, wasn't it?

Baijon's suit-lights put a galaxy into her hull. I went closer, and I was there too, pale and distorted in smoke and mirrors, with hellflower scars like a matched set of curses and Archangel's fingerprints bloody all over my face. I touched the hull.

Mallorum Archangel was Errol Lightfoot. And that didn't make no sense a-tall.

Errol Lightfoot was a cheap smuggler. Errol Lightfoot was the man who was known from one side of the Outfar to the other as causing hullplating to rust just by walking by. He named every ship he had *Light Lady* because otherwise they fell apart so fast under his maintenance he couldn't remember their names. Errol Lightfoot bought into any kick that gave honest darktrading a bad name.

He couldn't be all that and the second in line for the Phoenix Throne.

Could he?

But he was.

Baijon lowered his gauntlet to my shoulder like a ten-ton snowflake.

"*Kore*. We must enter the ship, *Kore*."

If Mallorum Archangel was Errol Lightfoot I just hoped he'd had somebody else pull maintenance on this ship. I turned away from my reflection and toward the air lock.

I was betting our lives he had.

* * *

Her security lock was lit. You can get them keyed to your hand or retinal print—but anybody can get those away from you. Or you can get your security lock keyed to your gene-scan, which is really secure but real expensive, and then you're the only one that can get your ship open, and someone slips you one dose of Mutabis can fix that real quick.

But TwiceBorn don't like to do for theyselves what they can get somebody else to do, and besides, they like to run on their rep. Is everybody supposed to be too damn intimidated to kyte from them's the way it goes. So this high-ticket yacht had a plain old keycode just like the last ship I'd owned, and I knew what it was.

The outside lock split four ways, breathing out light, heat, and oxygen. It tried the air outside and told me the inner door wouldn't open until the outer door was closed, so Baijon had to wait outside whiles I cycled through into Receiving Room One.

The first deep breath I took made me all silly with excess oxygen and damped down a headache I hadn't noticed into old news. The Receiving Lounge was cool and clean and looked right out of the factory-box, dripping with naturally-occurring organic materials on every available surface.

I flipped switches to let Baijon come inboard. A tasteful shipvoice informed me in hushed embarrassed tones that powered weapons were being brought through the lock scanners and did I want it to initiate security procedures?

"No."

"Keycode operator acknowledged," it whinged, and went off wherever computer generated voices go.

Baijon louted low through the lock, the armor's shoulders scraping both sides. The hatch buttoned up behind him.

"And now?" he said.

"Now we go."

* * *

The ship had a standard four-place cockpit—mercy seat, worry seat, songbird and numbercruncher. Worry seat had the weapons console, but it could be shifted over to let the first pilot run it.

I slid down into the seat, grubby in my overused bloody *Angelcity* rags, and heard it purr whilst it adjusted itself to me. Telltales and displays came awake all over the place, telling me everything I ever wanted to know about fuel and power and light and air, date of last supplies onload and (I swear it) inventories of everything down to how many boxes of wine there was in the galley. The only lights not lit was on the astrogator.

It was on, so I turned it off. Then I turned it back on and got the string of gibberish that means there's nothing in there for your computer to chew on.

I knew what I'd find, but I checked the automatic ship's log anyway. And I was right.

Whoever'd been in the mercy seat last'd done what I'd of done; what anybody'd do. He'd left the ship tapped in to the port computers for updates and to get messages and like that.

So every computer on the ship'd been sucked blank when the port tower went down. The rest of them reloaded from the ship's main memory core, but the navicomputer couldn't. Right now this ship was about as smart as I was. Literally.

I sat back in the seat and put my boot up where it made a nasty black mark on the white suede that some maniac'd upholstered all the control panels in. No navicomp, no numbers.

No numbers, no way out.

Oh, I could get the ship to orbit and hang her there. I could pull enough numbers off the sensors to land her, too, anywhere you liked.

I even remembered the numbers for the basic Transit to Hyperspace in the vicinity of a planet of standard mass or less, but that's a riddle problem they learn you in Famous Starpilot's School so's you'll know why you have to have a computer to suck sensor-web and spit out what you need.

How you go in tells where you'll come out with angeltown. Guess wrong and you're plasma. Your astrogator knows every star, comet, and ball of rock in fifty lights and can sign paper for information on the rest. Give it the where you are and the where you're going and it does the rest—all you have to do is pull the stick.

Some "all."

The manuals call it the Hyperjump Interlock. Everybody I ever met calls it the angelstick, 'cause it's what makes angels out of more pilots than anything else. The Jump *distorts* you, someways—oh, it won't do it through a stasis field, but you're not in a stasis field, you can't be—you're right out there on the same side of never as your sensors, and there's always that one chance in howgood's-your-maintenance that you won't make it this time, just stay Intertransitional until you die.

There's pilots who aren't—pilots I mean. I knew one oncet until he died—just woke up one morning and decided he couldn't pull the angelstick for one more Drop. You lose your nerve, I guess.

I hadn't lost mine—not for that, not yet. I could even get us up and at go with the textbook numbers and then pull the stick.

Of course, we'd never come out anywhere.

No place to run after all.

The cockpit hatch opened and Baijon stumbled in. He'd took time to shuck the clown-suit. He was bruised and galled all over from where the armor hadn't fit. His face was hagged. I caught myself looking for what wasn't there and stopped before I said anything. No Knife. He saw me looking at him and grinned; feral and tired. He sat down.

"And do you go now, *Kore*, in this your enemy's ship?"

You go. Not *we* go.

No Knife, no soul. No hellflower. Dead man walking.

No. We wasn't going to do it that way. Not and give Archangel—or Errol—what he wanted. Not no matter what I had to do.

"*We* go, j'keyn?"

Baijon didn't answer. There was no point in sitting here fretting about it now. So I powered everything up and blew out the wall.

*   *   *

The wall blew back in a nanosecond later as the advance-solid for a wall of water. According to the external sensors the ship flipped over and hit a couple of walls and ceilings. Inside, all comps and gravities on, we didn't feel a thing.

I looked at Baijon. He was sitting there like he had all the time in a world or two, and only one ending.

I put my hand on the power throttles and stopped. Stardancer's superstition; bad luck to take a ship up unnamed. Archangel might of named her once. But was only one name she could have now.

"*Ghost Dance*," I said, and goosed the lifters.

She rose up silly and slow in the water, but all that water was just another kind of atmosphere to move through. Royal's ocean had tore loose everything that wasn't nailed down; *Dance* sailed out a wide-open port into murk.

Sensors told me there was nothing above; we slid up slow through the water. It went black to glassy, then bright, then gone.

Image jerked on the pick-ups as we floated on water. Sensor-sweeps said there was nothing in range. I firewalled the lifters and *Ghost Dance* raged to heaven on a column of steam.

She was almost worth dying for. She didn't have to be babied, she didn't have to be coaxed. Anything I asked her for she gave me, and she'd give until her goforths cracked. I tumbled her through atmosphere for the just-being-able-to of it, and I wished I'd met her while I still had a life.

Then we hung in the sky above Port Mantow, free in orbit with only the little matter of no astrogator between us and escape. Every gauge I could see sat low in the green, except the only one that counted right now. The navicomp's "Not Ready" light was steady on red.

"I've done it. I've really done it," I said out loud.

I was ready for the talkingbooks. Illegal takeoff from an Imperial Port, with no clearance, in a stolen ship, without a pilot's license, and having sassed Lord Mallorum Archangel to his face and iced all his prettyboys.

I'd finally done it. I could not possibly be in any more trouble than I was now, even if you handed me two Old Fed Libraries for bookends.

There was a certain job satisfaction to that.

"Told you we'd commit every crime in the Calendar, you come along with me, Baijon-bai," I said, turning around to eyeball him.

"We did, while we lived," he said finally. "But there will be no songs, *Kore,* nor anyone to sing them of us now that—"

He stopped, and leaned forward in the songbird seat, and anything that'd make a de-Knifed hellflower interrupt his own death-aria to goggle was something I wanted to look at, too.

I thought.

I spun around. I was staring down the tonsils of five of the Empire's biggest and best. Jagranathas. Starshakers.

* * *

They're actually more portable planets than starships— no self-respecting starship *I* know has a port facility— and they provide Fleet with nice handy dangerous bases for operation—or would if Fleet ever got into a war. Nobody knew quite how many Throne had, but two were posted permanently at Grand Central and how many could the high-heat possibly need, anyway?

I now knew for a fact that our Glorious Emperor (gods bless and keep him far away from me) had at least seven.

Then *Dance* stepped down the magnification and said that the ships had been identified as Imperial military vessels and did I want to tap their message beacons and hail them?

"Hell, no!"

The day someone invents artificial *intelligence* I'll buy stock in the company.

"*Kore*, what are they doing here? Five of them?" At least Baijon sounded interested in something besides being dead.

"That information is not available at this time. Do you wish to trigger their—"

"Shut up," I told the ship, at which one thing I had lots of practice. "Five shakers?" I said at Baijon.

"Jagranathas," said Baijon, like I didn't know their right name. "But Royal isn't that important."

Errol/Archangel's goddamn noisy ship started to mouth off again but I found the volume control in time. I could disable the thing if I lived to get older.

"They don't see us," I hoped very much, because even Prince Mallorum's own personal battle-yacht which this probably wasn't couldn't outrun or outfight a planet.

I cut the goforths back from pre-Jump and started sliding down the curve of the planet like your friendly neighborhood chunk of space debris. If I could get the planet between us and them I could do something about getting out of their sight for sure. Hell, I could even land.

Bad idea.

The shakers pulled in closer over Royal, to where their shields was putting a lightshow over I bet any whole hemisphere of the planet you cared to choose and the induction howl our sensors picked up was like to deafen us. It gave me a nice warm feeling to know they'd probably farced their own sensors to the point where I could of landed *Dance* on one of their hulls without notice. Something that big isn't meant to go into atmosphere, although in blissful theory a shaker could, in fact, land— and warp the topsoil off half the continent getting upside again.

Whiles we watched, something came up off the heavyside to join them—one alternative mode of transport leaving the planet Royal with a real torqued Governor-General Archangel inside, odds was. It slid up close to one of the jags and vanished—docking, was my guess. And once it had, the jags started to move.

They was close in and looking like a star gone nova when parts of them started to drop off, deep enough down the gravity well to fall on the heavyside. And if I could see them at all, those little bits of light must be about the size of the Port Authority Building, each.

"They are bombs," said Baijon, and I wanted someone to tell him he had fusion for brains, but I couldn't. Because right then the surface of Royal started to boil.

In less than a kilo-second blue water, brown land, and white clouds had all mushed together into this sick shimmering gray as far out as gravity held atmosphere. I looked at Baijon. It'd took him outta hisself, all right. He might even know what made Royal look like that. I shouldn't. But I did.

And if our timing had been just a little more off, we could of been down there.

I gave *Dance* the numbers she could turn into a nice slow slide out toward the big empty, away from the attention of five starshakers where they shouldn't be what'd dropped what they shouldn't of had on Royal. I didn't risk another sensor scan, and when I looked back by eyeball the Fleet shakers was just a clump of overbright stars hanging over the curve of Royal.

Pale, glowing Royal.

I didn't want to think about that, but I did.

There's this drug called Mutabis, which isn't as beside the point as it might be. It's illegal, and for once is something you wouldn't even want; it shuffles your internal blueprint into any number of exciting new designer combinations, so that the next time you go to patch a bit of hangnail you read it off the new specs and not the old. Mutabis usually kills you, but not outright and not quick.

And it's got this long registry number what isn't anything like Mutabis at all, but why it's called Mutabis in the nightworld is because it's named after a bad dream most everyone else's forgot.

Paladin'd never told me about it. I'd just lately learned to remember it special.

Once upon a long time ago there was a bomb. It didn't do anything so vulgar as blow something up. No. This handy-dandy little hostility took what you may call your

basic building blocks of matter and unhooked them from
one combination and shuffled them into another without
liberating too much in the way of nasty atomic glitterflash. It could damp down after wiping out a few cubic
kilometers. Or if you used enough the reaction went on
until there was nothing left but a lump of about the same
mass you started with, and nothing else the same.

The Libraries used them in the war—or maybe it was
the humans, because they'd kill a Library just as dead
if they caught it planetside. Archive knew how to build
them.

They're simple to make, really. And Archive must of
told Archangel how, damn his piezoelectric eyes.

And Archangel'd used them. On Royal. Unbound dust,
now, and me and Baijon five minutes shy from having
joined it.

Not the kind of thing that called for witnesses.

A moon, two space-stations, an asteroid belt full of
miners. That was Royal System. Archangel must be planning to do them all and leave nobody to tell on him.
Moons don't run very fast.

But starships do.

I got Royal's moon between me and the jagranathas
and made *Dance* pick up her feet out toward the Big
Dark. Most of Royal System's planets were on the other
side of her primary. This way the traffic'd be thin, just
some ice and rock making its rounds and the odd satel-
lite. I watched the indicators edge up through percentage
of lights. Babby's top real-world speed could get us out
into the Big Dark in a matter of hours, and wasn't nobody going to be looking for a ship slogging through
realspace there.

Of course, we'd be dead of old age before we reached
the next star.

The dark was friendly and didn't ask much out of my
life. Eventually I noticed that the ship's systems indicators was sliding into amber, and then on to red, but it
didn't really matter.

Shock, said a part of my mind. *Play for time.*

I mulled that one around for a while before I reached
out and shut off the goforths. *Dance* seemed to sigh with

relief and the numbers dropped right back into green. The estimated probable adjusted speed we were going didn't change.

I thought about what was going on back at Royal now: traffic coming in and trying to put down, maybe, if the system wasn't closed. Had Archangel left anything behind that could broadcast a warning? Or was the whole system just a whirligig of remanufactured matter, and nothing left to tell anybody its name but the spectrograph of its star? Would the Mutabis reaction take the first ships that downfalled, or would it have stopped by then?

I stared at the dark.

There's some things, they just have to happen around you, not even to you, and you can feel them make you over no matter what you do. I'd used to pretend there wasn't things like that, even whiles they was happening to me.

Royal was one. It was such a big thing that part of my mind kept trying to say it hadn't happened while the other half insisted I do something about it right now.

Made for headaches.

Because there wasn't nothing I could do. Except tell, and wouldn't nobody need me for that. Royal wasn't there no more. Soon or late somebody'd notice, and get to pointing fingers and naming names. Archangel's had to be one.

Didn't it?

I made myself concentrate on what I knew. I set *Dance* up to run in realspace by herself: proximity klaxons and shields at full charge and a couple basic evasive routines laid by. She'd go on long past the time she ran out of air and food and water. A ghost ship on a ghost dance, all alone in the never-never.

A nice bolt-hole to die in.

I got up and walked back to the songbird seat. Baijon was just sitting, staring out into the dark that looked empty and wasn't. His eyes was open, but he looked relaxed as a sleeper and no more older nor he was.

"Baijon-che-bai?"

He blinked and looked up at me, vague around the eyes to where I wondered if he'd looked into the same empty I had and wasn't coming back.

"If we tell of this, *Kore*, is there anyone who will listen?

He sounded scared and defeated and young and I didn't blame him. I touched his shoulder and he grabbed my hand like I could do him some good.

"Somebody's going to notice soon or late, che-bai."

Baijon looked at me. "It will be as you say, *Kore*," he said, and neither of us could tell if it was a question or not.

"Sure it will."

Sure. I had a naggy creeping paranoia that somewhere Throne if it even knew and particularly Archangel his own self was going to find a scapegoat for this Mutabis rap and walk off having shifted the heat, and if that was all they would be going to do I wouldn't mind so much, but I didn't think it'd stop there, somehow. There wasn't any profit in just doing that, and if there was one thing I knew, it was finding the profit.

Butterfly St. Cyr, Savior of the Universe. Sure.

"So, bai, why don't you turn out and roust this crib? We going to be here whiles. Need fly-vines and fetch-kitchen, forbye—and food, maybe."

Not according to my stomach, but it always was a liar. And where there was food there might even be more useful things, like something you'd want.

"Still—still I serve you, my *comites*," Baijon said, and we didn't hear any more about singing ourselfs to death, neither.

One thing's sure, a little holocaust can help you forget your own problems.

Or some of them. I waited until Baijon'd gone off, and sat back down in the mercy seat. My beautiful lady of the never-never, and where could I take her?

Errol/Archangel'd called me a cyborg.

And normally I wouldn't mind, 'cause everybody's got a right to be wrong, but he'd been trying to do something to my head at the time when he ran into something that made him stop.

Cyborg. And he'd thought I was the one carrying the Yegg McGuffin that Brightlaw was trying to smuggle into its own home town. The Brightlaw Prototype. Whatever that was.

I wondered if Baijon knew.

We made a fine set of partners, him and me: Baijon'd been kicked out of the hellflower fan club, and I was turning into something he'd probably be obliged to shoot anyway, hellflower or no. Tainted with Library Science, and stuck on a ship with no computer when my condign knack was for breaking into them, the galaxy against us. . . .

Why?

Self-interest is a wonderful cure for the larger issues of life. Never mind Royal-the-ex-planet. What did all this have to do with *me?*

One time somebody'd closed down a entire Free Port to keep me from getting off it, a kind of overkill that should of warned me at the time there was something salty jumping, 'cause I wasn't worth that flavor trouble.

I hadn't took the hint then. But I can learn from my mistakes. In our last exciting episode, Fleet had closed down Royal in the permanent-most kind of way, using I-bet-banned Library Science which somebody in this so-phont's galaxy was going to notice the fingerprints of Real Soon Now.

And since I still didn't think I was worth that kind of trouble, the question that I had to ask was: just what had there been on Royal that Fleet wanted to keep there enough to put a two-billion-taxpayer hole in the Emperor's budget?

I could not immediately think of much. Not, certain and for truth, the moronic Brightlaw Rebellion. It just wasn't that important in the greater galactic scheme of things, even if alMayne had a hotwired interest in little Damaris winning. Past tense.

But what if it wasn't to keep somebody there? What if how Royal was now wasn't the means to a, but an end in itself?

Something cold slid into the pit of my stomach and started trying to burrow out. Question: what did you get if you showed the Empire a Royal System destroyed by Library Science?

Three guesses. And that it was a soforth destroyed by etcetera would be vouched for—hell, it'd be rammed down people's throats—by those galactic arbiters of honor and the lazy-fair, the alMayne. Everybody knew they knew more about Libraries than god's older sister.

But thanks to my boy Baijon they'd nail it right to Archangel's shadow, which he couldn't want.

Another good theory shot to hell.

But Archangel knew the hellflowers'd blame him for Royal. He knew Baijon'd seen him at Rialla with Archive Library. He knew Baijon'd gone home and told. And he for sure knew there was civil tiff in Washonnet Sector.

But he'd still Mutabis'd Royal, even knowing all this.

What if Archangel meant to frame the *hellflowers* for it?

Sure.

And he'd almost had his proof. Baijon Starbringer, gazetted prince, courier legging something into the system for Brightlaw—which alMayne was still backing in defiance of Galactic Statute Number fillintheblank.

Baijon could deny everything. Archangel could say he didn't know what Baijon'd brought in for sure. People'd believe what Archangel wanted them to.

Bottom line: it didn't matter if Baijon's mythical darktrade kick even existed. Royal'd retired from the planet business courtesy of a weapon only a Library could build, and the alMayne would be sure to say so just in time to be told that one of their own had dropped it.

And then Archangel could put all Washonnet on Proscription for collusion to commit High Book and take in the Tech Police that nightworld gossip said was his bought hardboys to pry loose everything he'd ever wanted in the way of Libraries and Library Science, of which they had so much there on sunny Washonnet 357-II.

It would of been possible, that was to say, if Washonnet wasn't throwing its own private little war. Every hellflower in known space had gone home to choose up sides, no amateurs allowed. They was used to fighting wars. Nobody'd get hurt—until they settled their family spat and took on the rest of the Empire. The only thing an Imp incursion would do would be settle the war on alMayne faster.

I had the frustrating feeling of being almost half right but missing too many pieces, and thinking about Royal just made me feel sick—and glad in a rotten way, because what Fleet'd done covered up what I'd did and made it seem damn near harmless.

Paladin would ask: *"Who benefits?"*—which is a fancy way of wanting to know who ends up standing and with all the credit after the smoke clears. And the same question applied to Royal: who got to spin credit if it wasn't there no more?

It sort of made a girl wonder what Kennor Starbringer had actually been after.

Paranoia's a wonderful drug: I wanted my brain to shut up but it wouldn't, and all that left for me was watching it swoop like a bat after dragonflies. Everything fell into place like a well-oiled domino theory.

Maybe those assassins back on *Circle of Stars*'d been Kennor Starbringer's and maybe they hadn't, but for damn sure they'd put paid to my plans to win a billion credits and debark early. That landed us right in the middle of alMayne where Kennor's kid sister Gruoch was all set to have my guts for garters and Baijon had to say the one thing that'd start civil war on alMayne faster than Badhb's your uncle and put "paid" to Archangel's hopes of landing troops there any time soon.

Was Kennor actually unaware of Gruoch's little xenophobic quirk?

Had he thought Baijon was *not* going to tell everybody back home that the person at the top of his personal *chaudatu* hit parade was a Librarian and therefore an open season target of opportunity for everything that carried a *arthame*?

Was I actually as stupid as Kennor seemed to think I was?

If the answer was "no" to the first three, then that meant I knew the real truth—not this fake truth Kennor'd already tried to sell me twicet.

Kennor'd wanted alMayne to blow up the way it had.

Just as soon as he'd known Brother Mallorum had his hand in the Old Fed Tech cookie jar it'd be obvious to

anyone with more brains than I had that the next place
Archangel was going was the largest and only legit cache
of Old Fed Tech inside the Empire's borders—the Logotek of the War College at Wailing on alMayne.

So Kennor'd arranged for alMayne to go up like a
roaming candle—a perfect alibi, among other things. And
as for the ship he'd promised me . . .

I bet I'd got it.

I wondered if Meggie and Mero'd made it out of Tortuga.
Archangel said they hadn't, but that was just business as
usual in the hardboy trade. Maybe they was all right.

I hoped so.

But meanwhile:

Archangel—in the guise of darktrader and trafficker in
dicty-toys and Old Fed Tech, Errol-the-Peril Lightfoot,
a stone truth that I still found damn near impossible to
swallow—had been waiting at Port Mantow to gig Meggie when she showed up to meet the receiver for her kick.

Why? Archangel didn't give a damn about the guns
Angelcity'd been picking up to run to Royal. He'd already
arranged to put a guaranteed end to the Brightlaw Rebellion; it didn't matter who offloaded how much heat.

But Meggie'd been expecting to take on a load at
alMayne she never got: two no-questions-asked couriers
to drop on Royal, for whom she was holding ID and
valuta and a package. She'd thought we might be them.

What if we *had* been them?

No proof, but I almost believed it. Who'd sold Mero
and Meggie the guns in the first place, after all? A
LessHouse of Starborn—or House Starborn its own self
? Kennor'd know *Angelcity's* schedule; he was that sort.
And had Baijon and me been meant all along to disappear, not die, in House Starborn's private little war, and
be smuggled off alMayne in a load of heat run by a darktrader beholden to Kennor?

And by Berathia Notevan, who due to a sudden case
of *chaudatu* fever on Gruoch's part, had been under house
arrest when she was supposed to be meeting the shuttle
from *Circle of Stars* at Zerubavel Outport. She could of
walked us right across the crete and knocked on *Angelcity's* door. If she'd been there.

But then Baijon wouldn't of got to deliver his message. Kennor had to know Gruoch well enough to know what she'd do—step on Berathia's tail long enough for Baijon to deliver his message, then get one or both of us out when the shooting started.

Or had Kennor expected any shooting at all? He hadn't expected Winterfire to sell him out.

No data. I went back to following out the lines of what I knew.

Meggie'd been supposed to take her live freight to Royal and I was pretty sure it was us. Berathia's part in all that (and it had to be her; Meggie would of said if her courier was a hellflower) had been to dump the package on *Angelcity* for later pickup. Anything else she'd been told was probably another one of Kennor's double-dealing fantasies. But we'd been meant to go to Royal, I bet.

Was there a godlost Brightlaw Prototype after all? And what was it? And if there was, why should the Prexy of the Azarine Coalition have it? For that matter, why should hellflowers back rebels? Or the Coalition back them, even if they was paying customers? Or even Kennor his own self be interested in a bunch of *chaudatu* dweebs?

My train of thought derailed before I could come up with a satisfactory reason-why link between Kennor Starbringer, head of the Azarine Coalition, and a Tortugan Political Action Committee.

I knew that Kennor wanted there to be war on alMayne to seal it off from Archangel's lackeys. Therefore, Archangel had every reason to try to frame alMayne for Library Science.

But what reason did alMayne have for actually being guilty?

All of a sudden all that space outside the ports was too big and too cold. With no questions answered I got up out of the mercy seat and went off after Baijon.

* * * * *

Valijon's Diary:

Now I am dead. And I am afraid. There is no Right Conduct now; I cannot choose good from evil—to act, even, is heresy, and should I speak, none of the Gentle People would hear my words.

I do not hear theirs. I reject them. Even a show of honor in Archangel's shadow is better than nothing. That act of mine was true.

I did not think it would be so hard.

I have seen, and I do not understand. The *chaudatu* reiver Errol Lightfoot whose life was promised me I have killed. I know this to be true: even the war-medicine of the Gentle People could not have saved him from the wound that I in honor dealt him.

How, then, is he resurrected as the *Malmakosim* Archangel?

I do not know. I do not know that it matters. I am kept from my death, and the *Kore* will not understand that it is needful. She understands so little, and yet has great wisdom.

At least so I once thought. But if everything else I have ever believed in has been found to be falsehood, perhaps the *Kore,* too, is false.

I cut her upon the Floor of Honor and she did not die. I would say that for that she might be a goddess, but the Tongueless Ones have no gods.

I think it more likely that she cheated.

But I do not know *how* she cheated, and thus is her cunning proven to be great. Having such cunning, is it not possible my death is being withheld as part of a larger plan?

Does that matter? Am I so cowardly that I will grasp at life as tool to a *chaudatu* plan rather than choose a clean and honorable death?

Yet she is not *chaudatu*. She is *alarthme* at least—only a Loremaster could say if she, bearing honorable scars and surviving, is now one of the Gentle People.

And I reject the teaching of the Loremasters, for it is lies.

What must I do? Three things I know: *Malmakos* walks once again, slaying planets—and seeing this, the *Kore* speaks to me of food. Archangel-who-is-also-Errol-Lightfoot must be killed—yet we flee him.

And I am dead, and have no more part in these matters, yet I still breathe, at the behest of my *comites*.

All is not well. All may never be well again. And how will I find Ketreis in the Land Beside without my Knife? Without my *arthame,* how will we know each other?

Perhaps the *Kore* will know. Perhaps she will tell me. I may not disobey her, yet she orders me into dishonor. Dishonored, I must save her from further dishonor, yet, *al-ne-alarthme,* it is not my place to act. Can I, honorless, judge honor?

Does the *Kore* have any honor?

Is she even human?

I wish I were not alive. My thoughts are tongueless, yet I hear them.

I witnessed to the Gentle People that the Machine was among us again.

They called me liar and oathbreaker.

I saw the face of the *Malmakosim* Archangel and he was the *chaudatu* reiver Errol Lightfoot, whom I had already killed. I swore his death again. Yet he killed me, and now we are both alive.

The *Kore* proved honor and humanity and her right to be heard on the Floor of Honor that lay between my own walls.

Yet . . .

I will not think of that. I will think of nothing.

The Machine is manifest, and I am afraid.

13

The Theory and Practice of Hell

I found Baijon down in the galley. There was probably a dining room somewhere on this flying indulgence, but the galley was rigged so the crew could eat here and we was the crew now.

Baijon'd left out minor details like clothes and medicalling, and he'd gone at the supplies the way Gruoch'd took Wailing. It was distributed even-handed-like over all the flat surfaces in sight and food was only made for one.

"You living on air, now, Baijon-bai?"

He wouldn't look at me.

"You got to keep your strength up, bai."

"For what, *Kore*?" He looked up at me and looked like a man dying. "It is true, *Kore*, that you have been served with dishonor by the Gentle People, and that they in their dishonor are not worthy of your love. Yet you have said— You have said—"

I knew where this was going and it wasn't no place I wanted to visit. "It wasn't your fault about your Knife, bai! If it was somebody's fault it was mine, oke—"

"*That does not matter!* If a thing is so, *Kore*, does blame matter? I have no *arthame*. I have no shadow. If I go on alive, I will become . . . less than human." He hung his head. "I am afraid of that, *Kore*. You have said you cared for me in the way *chaudatu* do. If that is so, let me go."

He was my *servites*. He had to have my permission to die.

And then I'd be here and all alone.

There was choices, even now. I could blow up *Dance*, for maybes, or wait out here a kilo-hour or so then go back to Tortuga System and see if someone was there. If

I had the luck of the damned there would be, and he'd be a legger willing to download his astrogator for a price. There was still running to do.

And I could even mount my own one-sided crusade against Archangel. With enough luck I could be real trouble. Baijon could be more. I could sucker him into that, I bet. Promise him enough murder, he'd stay on top for it.

I could.

I would.

"You do me one thing first, kinchin-bai. Won't take long. Then you do what you got to. I let you go."

But that was what I said instead.

* * *

"This is a auxiliary Jump interlock. You pull it, you make Transit to hyperspace. It's to override the pilot, in case everything's ready to go and he won't either kick it back down off redline or pull the stick."

"Yes," said Baijon, cautious.

"It's for when the thing *is* ready to go—that means numbers in the numbercruncher, which we don't got. You crank it up and kick out the jams now, I guess we wouldn't be anywhere any more."

Ghost Dance's black gang was a thing of beauty: no less than fifteen plates of goforth, rated hyper-Main and all turned out like a techno's dream. It didn't need anybody to keep after it any more than I needed somebody to watch out for my heartbeat. If you wanted someone down there for maintenance or show, there was a little *geoffreis* hole all lined in banks of gauges and dials which I was showing Baijon now.

"*This* is the goforths cut-out. When the engines are at Jump standby, you pull this, they cycle down to rest. You got that?"

"I understand."

"Baijon, you *sure* you can tell them apart?"

I stared at him. He looked back. Eyes too blue to be human back where I came from; mark of the hellgods.

"I promise you, *Kore*, I will know them. One turns off the engines. The other destroys the ship."

"Just keep them straight, oke?"

In the back of my skull there was a wild dissenting vote with regards to my current plan. Just like back on Wailing, only then I'd been the one what hadn't liked my plan, I thought. This time I liked it just fine. I guessed.

And it was fair. That was what mattered. It was payback, and it was fair.

"You said you would release me," Baijon prompted.

"Je. This is how it goes."

I turned to one of the consoles and slapped switches. Goforths came up on line and I braided them together, a silent song of power that rang through the ship, making the air tremble. *Ghost Dance* strained, waiting the office to Jump.

"I tell you some stuff and ask you some stuff. And then you pick one of the switches to pull."

The light was green and red and gold and orange; a spotted rainbow.

"Is this a game, *Kore*?"

"Depends on how you look at it. Do you have some particular objection to death by plasma-conversion?"

Baijon thought about it while the goforths shook frustration into my bones.

"No. That is acceptable."

"Oke. Now."

I took a deep breath. What'd happened at Royal made this easier. It still didn't make it easy.

"Baijon-bai," I said. "You tell me: how you learn yourself you going for to trust someone?"

He translated the question back into Interphon and probably from Interphon into helltongue. Then he thought about it.

Of course, the goforths might just overload and ice us whiles he was thinking. I kept my back to the read-outs that would tell me about it.

"At . . ." *home*, Baijon was going to say, and didn't. "On alMayne this is not a question that can be asked. You know, *Kore*, that they are your people, and hold the same things holy that you do."

"Like cutting up cranky with vendetta, and like that."

"Ah, *Kore,* that is not a matter of trust. That is a matter of honor. A dishonorable man may not be trusted. He is not human." He was giving me as much of a honest answer as he knew how, and it was still back to Square One. No help.

"But you got friends, maybe. How do you decide who they is?"

Baijon looked blank; I guess maybe it wasn't the sort of question a young hellflower of means was used to being asked.

"You befriend those within your House, *Kore,* perhaps even within your GreatHouse."

alMayne GreatHouses is big—passels of LessHouses all can owe fealty to the same GreatHouse. Maybe even millions of people. Too many to all be friends with.

"Je, che-bai, but which ones?"

"The ones you *like, Kore.*" He was starting to get frustrated now, me keeping him from the Long Orbit with this nidderling triviality.

"So how do you decide who you like? And do you trust everyone you like?"

"Often." Baijon had a look as indicated he had fond memories of liking some pretty untrustworthy people. "More often you . . . *Kore,* it may be that you trust someone unquestioningly, and respect them. But you do not like them very much."

"But people you like—and trust—they're your friends?" I didn't ask if I was one of them.

"Yes."

"I had a friend oncet." Now we got to the good part. I put my hands flat on the front of my thighs, flat, awkward, and helpless.

"He wasn't a person. I trusted him anyway."

I concentrated on staying where I was, keeping my hands where they was.

"He lived in a box."

Baijon was fast. And strong. He could break my neck with his bare hands, even without the help I was giving him. I just hoped he'd remember which godlost lever to pull afterward.

"He was a Library. His name was Paladin."

Baijon didn't move. The only thing changed was his eyes; big and dark and dilated. Most people can't control that reflex. But I wasn't really sure he'd heard.

"I'm a Librarian."

He'd done give up his Knife for me. I owed him everything, including his life if he could take it back out of this.

He still didn't move. One hand was braced against a wall. The other one hung loose. I'd never really noticed Baijon's hands before. Nails cut back short, calluses from cargo work. Not glitterborn paws. Not any more.

What gives anybody the right to change anybody else? Or is rights just a joke, and all there is is what we take from somebody else?

"Baijon?" I said real soft.

"There is no Library. I saw it die. I saw it *die, Kore.*"

"You saw one die. But there wasn't one Library at Rialla. There was two. The other one was my friend. He was just a person. Like anyone. He made the other Library—Vannet's Library—so it couldn't hurt anybody no more. He was my friend." And that was a damn poor explanation. Nothing—and everything.

"You are wrong. There was no Library." He looked at me, pleading.

"I'm a Librarian. My Library's name was Paladin. We was together twenty years, bai, and that's how come I want to know about being friends, because maybe you can turn it off and not be friends no more, right?"

"A Library." Baijon's voice was flat. No clues in it at all. "You—*had*—a Library."

His *comites* wouldn't lie to him. Sure I wouldn't. But he believed it, just like he believed in hellflower honor, and now he got to choose between believing I was a liar and believing I was the worst thing a hellflower could think of.

"You know I'm dicty. You know why we ain't supposed to leave home. We don't get the Inappropriate Technology indoctrination that makes all you fellahim so scared of Old Fed Tech. I didn't even know what a tronic was when I left home—you think I'd of got told about

Libraries? I didn't know what Paladin was when I found him. And when I did know, he wasn't a thing any more. He was my friend.

"He was my friend," I repeated lamely. "You don't sell out your friends."

There was a long pause while Baijon tried to think about something so damn obvious he'd never wasted one brain cell on it before.

"It was a *Library, Kore*. You say you have not been schooled—you do not know what they have done—"

"*I know.*"

That stopped him a minute.

"I know. I was there. You think what happened at Royal was bad? It's a joke. Party games. Stick with me, bai, I lay you out a war that make you wish you was back on Royal in the before-time. Think I could build some of the weapons the Libraries used, I bet. Know I could build what they used on Royal. Where do you think Archangel found out how? Library Archive told him and what Archive knew, I've got it all in my head. Archive—Vannet's Library—did something to me when I went to kill it. What your buddy the WarDoctor Wall That Walked knew about. He thought it was you, maybe, that Archive'd got to, but it wasn't. It was me.

"You talk along of not being human. I guess I'm not, any more. I didn't think you could put a Library in someone's head. Paladin never said. But I remember what Archive remembered, some. I know why people is still hunting Libraries a thousand years later."

I could see the cords standing out on Baijon's neck, and sharp reflections of the lights all over his skin. It looked like it'd been oiled. He was sweating like somebody was roasting him alive.

"I know about Libraries. But Paladin wasn't—isn't—like that. Paladin wasn't like Archive. He was my friend. Same way you make friends—by learning them, how they are. So he told me he wouldn't hurt anybody, or let Archive hurt anybody, and I believed him. I knew him half my life. He was my friend."

"*Kore*," said Baijon, all full of sorrow. Sorry I'd been took in, sorry I'd told him, sorry for a thousand things.

"He went away to get me not burned for a Librarian. But he didn't know what Archive'd done to me. I was thinking to go find him. That was my plan for after Royal. don't got no plans now. Letting you go, too. Your choices, now, bai.

"So now you do what you got to; I'm done."

I walked out past him, He didn't touch me.

Halfway up the ladder I started to shake so hard I just had to stop and hold on. But that was just chemicals in my blood; nothing personal. Every bone in my body hurt. I'd been sure I'd be dead by now.

Now someone knew. The thing I couldn't never tell, the thing I had to die to keep anyone from finding. Someone knew. And what happened next wasn't anything of my making. What happened next was set a thousand years ago, when organic life created the alMayne out of their leftover Librarians to be the human answer to Archive. Hellflowers and hellgods.

I didn't bother with going to the cockpit or the drive room. There didn't seem much point. I'd shot my bolt. If Baijon wanted to be live or dead or express his opinion on which I should be, he was going to get his chance.

I found a cabin and went in. The bunk was stripped, but I curled up on it anyway.

Funny; Paladin'd left me so I wouldn't be alone no more. And I wasn't; I had half a Library in my skull trying to eat its way out. But still no one anywhere I could touch.

The drive didn't explode. I guessed Baijon'd shut it down.

Too bad.

*   *   *   *   *

Valijon's Diary:

It would be easy to do as the songs instruct. But so many of them have been wrong; what if this instruction, too, is wrong? I am no longer one of the Gentle People. My soul is destroyed, and my *devoir* is clear. As my soul has gone, so must go my body.

But if this is so, and my first duty is self-destruction, it follows that there is no responsibility I must discharge before that. And afterward, I am dead.

If I am dead, I cannot then kill the Librarian.

So logic teaches, but I am a man alone and know that logic lies. I live. If it is proper to kill the Librarian, no consideration of antecedent honorable suicide would intervene.

What is right?

Do I die here, then what I might do against Archangel remains undone. Do I kill the Librarian, what she might do, too, to foil Archangel remains undone.

I named her honorable, and my father swore to me that honor is that which cannot be held by beasts or machines. My father, too, named her Worthy-of-a-Knife, as did the Memory of Starborn.

If all these are wrong, then honor itself is a lie. And if there is no honor, then my acts or lack of them, too, are meaningless.

And, does she lie to me, my power to harm is small.

A paradox: I am so useless that what I do does not matter, yet so worthy that I must fight on, in hope that mine will be the hand to slay the Enemy.

The *Kore* would say this is a situation with no downside.

But I do not think it has a topside, either.

There is no one left to trust. Everyone and everything I have believed in has broken in my hand. Even honor.

There is only one choice left.

* * * * *

I wanted to be asleep, or dead, or anything else that involved not thinking any more, but my brain refused to cooperate.

Not surprising: how much of it was still mine? I was dying by inches, sure as if I'd been poisoned, and no remedy in sight.

Things like this is lots more fun when they's happening to someone else in the talkingbooks.

Item: all this was Archive's fault, because most of this was Archive's memories and all of it was Archive's doing. And having Archive's memories would of been bad enough, but memories wasn't all he'd dumped down me when it came time to kiss and part. The old reliable Butterfly St. Cyr-as-was could never of walked into a protected memory core through a dumb terminal and shut down all the power on a planet.

Ex-planet.

But I hadn't done that, had I? I'd just run into Paladin, and *he'd* done it, right?

No. It wasn't that easy.

Because no matter what he'd done to me going off like he had back on dear old RoaqMhone, no matter how I was sure now I'd never really understood him, Paladin wouldn't of done something that stupid. Not shut down the power in all of Port Mantow like a tronic with no interlocks. Paladin would of got me out of there without.

Wouldn't he?

If it had been Paladin shutting down the planet, why had he done it like that?

If it hadn't been Paladin, who?

Or what?

But whoever it was it wasn't me, I tried to tell myself. Not Butterflies-are-Free Peace Sincere, ethical arbiter of the spaceways and all-round stand-up sophont. I saved Baijon's life several times at considerable personal sacrifice. I couldn't be the kind of person who'd trash a bunch of harmless innocents just to save my neck.

But I was. And I had, whether I'd pushed the final button or not. And I hadn't even thought twice.

My head hurt. And after that, telling Baijon all about Paladin made a weird kind of sense, because I really wasn't sure what I was going to do next. The real problem was, I didn't know how much longer there was going to be a *me* at all.

Megalomania, Paladin'd say, and for once I didn't have to ask what the words meant. If I was all that dangerous that I needed a keeper, I wouldn't be trapped on a nowhere ship in the Outfar feeling so helpless against whatever Archangel was going to do next.

Whiles later I realized I had to be asleep, because Paladin was there with me. He was trying to explain where he'd been and what he was doing and what it was I should and shouldn't do. And it was real good, real urgent advice that'd save my bones if I could just make it make sense. I wanted to. He wanted to help. But I just couldn't wake up enough to hear.

But I tried. And made it.

Baijon was standing over me like grim talkingbook death. Hollow cheeks and burning eyes, and he'd found himself a blaster somewheres on *Ghost Dance* to point at me.

He was still alive.

"Why did you tell me?"

I took a moment to be glad I wasn't lying in the direction of anything important; when he shot me he wouldn't scramble too many ship's systems.

"Why?" The blaster jerked.

"If it was something going to make a difference in your plans, Baijon, after you was dead weren't any time to tell you."

"Librarian," he said, but he still didn't pull the trigger.

I sat up, careful like I cared.

"You come to gloat or complain? Told you: Paladin was my friend. That was a accident. He fixed it. Gone now."

"Yet you *glory* in it."

"Didn't you never have friends, bai?"

We glared at each other for whiles, or close to it as either of us had energy or inclination for. Baijon looked tired. I wanted to tell him was everything golden, that we was partners, that there was some way out.

I was tired of lying, among other things.

"Did you *want* me to kill you?" Baijon asked finally. "Are you afraid to take your own life? A . . . coward?" His voice dropped on the last word like he expected to be struck by lightning.

"Sure, if you want. Whatever you want." I rubbed my eyes. "We's in a broken starship with no place to go. Archangel's just blown up Royal with a Old Fed weapon and's probably looking to hang the rap on us. All your hellflower relatives is mad at you, and you done lost your Knife, and—"

"And so you thought that *now* would be a good time to tell me you are a Librarian," Baijon finished.

What he sounded was more exasperated than anything else. Like Paladin used to when I'd get up to didoes.

"Or a Library. I . . . Look. I give up, oke? All I ever wanted was a starship. Paladin never hurt anybody in his life. Archive's gone. Maybe Paladin could fix what it did to me. Maybe not. But it seems to me if you got a Better Dead list, you should maybe put Archangel at the top of it, not me."

"Maybe." Baijon bared his teeth at me. "And maybe I should start with what is within the reach of my arm."

"Go for it. Who the hell cares?"

"You do," Baijon pointed out.

"What do you care what I care?"

"You have made it my business, *Ko*—San'Cyr. You told me what you are. Did you think I would do nothing?"

"Maybe I just thought Mallorum Archangel deserved trouble more than I do, bai."

"So I am to ally myself with a Library—and spare you—because I fear my foe possesses one. In such escalation of weapons what place will remain for people?"

He was right, Archive's memories told me—and wrong.

"I know Paladin. I trust Paladin."

Baijon bared his teeth. "And do you trust yourself, San'Cyr?"

He looked at me. I looked away. We both knew the answer to that, after Royal. I'd just been looking for someone else to tell it to me.

"The Machine killed billions," Baijon said in a low voice. "Gone as Royal is gone—a thousand billion people. A thousand suns. There was no mercy. There was no compromise possible. They would not listen."

And now Baijon couldn't afford to listen either. He was right. But something else died in that war that deserved to be remembered.

"Je, babby, I guess you got to do it for what's in my head. But Paladin was a Library, too, and he'd likely talk you to death, but he wouldn't fold up your sun. I remem-

ber the war. And maybe all the Libraries didn't agree to
have it, but ain't nobody left to say their side. People can
come in boxes. And not-people in flesh-and-blood.
Archangel dropped the dime on Royal. I'd pick him over
a Library if I only got to shoot one.''

There was a pause. That wasn't what I meant to say,
dammit—I meant for Baijon to shoot me, because I might
trust Paladin to the end of the numbers but I didn't trust
me.

''Pull the trigger, will you, babby? You're wasting my
time.''

''And is Archangel, then, to fly free? No one else can
stop him.''

''Neither can we. Stop farcing yourself.''

''But we can try, San'Cyr. If success belongs to others, then the assay is what we keep for ourselves. We
must try, San'Cyr. If my death is to have meaning, it
must be used for this. It is the last service I can render
to my father and my House.''

Baijon'd said it one-time, whiles back. About how you
can't let people get away with things like that. Even if it
kills you. Even if it ain't happening right to you. Even if
what you do won't make any difference.

You got to *care*. Because being people ain't just what
you are. It's what you do.

''You got any bright ideas on how we going to do that,
you glitterborn moron? We got no navicomp. No navicomp, no Jump. The only place we can go is back to
Royal sublight. And say we do that—get back to Royal
system and pirate a navicomp? Where do we go? We can
get to Archangel, sure—coked, wrapped, and in chains.''

I thought about those eyes, purple and glowing and
ready to turn a brain inside out.

''I don't think I want to do that, bai.''

Baijon nodded, sober.

''I have a better plan. I will seek out Archangel and
challenge him to an honorable death-dance. With my
Knife. In honor, he will accept.''

It took me a minute to figure out Baijon was making a
joke.

''There is a way. You will find it, with the *Malmakos*

that is in you. If I can survive my death and embrace what I am not, so can you. Archangel made us. He must pay. We will make a new plan, San'Cyr. As . . . equals.''

The galaxy trembled, I bet. But I felt fine.

''And what about when—if—when Archive Library takes me all the way over?''

''Ah, San'Cyr—*then* I will kill you.''

He tossed the blaster on the bunk beside me. The safety interlock was still on.

14

The Maltese Prototype

Saying we had a plan was the easy part. Our plan was to ice Mallorum Archangel, whoever he was this week. And whatever color his eyes was.

How to get to Brother Mallorum while in a condition to sign the lease on his real estate was the tricky part.

"If we had something he wants—bad enough—he'd deal, right?"

"He dealt with a Library, San'Cyr. I do not think Mallorum Archangel is overly fastidious."

Dealt with a Library, dealt with a Library. . . . It went round and round in my head, like it was trying to do me some good.

"Archangel tricked with High Book—why?"

"Because he is evil, San'Cyr," Baijon said patiently.

"Yeah, I know that. But why go to all the trouble of finding a Library—which ain't all that thick on the ground—if he could get what he wanted some other way?"

"Because he could not get it some other way. The Brightlaw Prototype *was* only a prototype, and it was not certain that—"

"Waitaminnit. We was supposed to be losing that kick at Royal. Archangel thought we had it. And you know what it is?"

"All the Empire knows what it is," Baijon said primly. "It is an abomination." And then he told me what it was that everyone else all knew.

What it was, for less biased observers, was AI. Artificial Intelligence. *"A machine hellishly forged in the likeness of a human mind,"* as they say in the talkingbooks. Illegal as hell, proscribed six ways from galactic north. . . .

A Library.

The real heartbreaker with Proscribed Tech in the Empire is that it's so damn useful. Take your basic Library. A computer only two-thirds as complex as a Library could provide instantaneous error-free communication from one side of the Empire to the other—if anybody was allowed to build it.

The Imperial DataNet is slow, it's balky, it's restricted access, and can barely handle the traffic it has. Its limitations means the Empire has an Outfar where information-handling is one step up from flatcopy, lucky for me and anyone else that wants to hide between the lines.

But my being able to do that means the Empire loses revenue, a thing on which Empires are not notoriously big. The Empire wants what Libraries could give it—and doesn't dare go after it.

Enter the Brightlaw Prototype. Brightlaw had been building—or trying to—a computer with the capabilities of a Library, but safe for people to use. When Charlock had taken over the Brightlaw Corporation the Prototype and development notes had vanished.

There was no reason for Charlock to of either destroyed or hidden them. Charlock had been backed by Archangel, even then. And it was a safe bet that Archangel had no interest in running Brightlaw's AI Prototype past the Technology Police, the Office of the Question, or the Imperial Censor.

"And Archangel thought I had it." I looked at my left hand. Streamlined, like one of those functional claws they fit tronics with. Human looking up to where it stopped.

Cyborg with a Library chaser.

And if it was true. . . .

"I can get us out of here, bai. And I can get us Archangel."

*   *   *

"If my father had not been who he was, I would have been the next Memory of Starborn. It was to go to our line next, but there was no one of suitable age and rank to bear it.''

"Is this supposed to mean something to me? Hand me the plasma torch.''

He did, and I slid it up into *Ghost Dance*'s insides where she was not accustomed to rude mechanicals mucking with her computer systems.

"It means I know more about Libraries than you do,'' Baijon said smugly.

"You and the rest of the Empire.''

I didn't need the navicomp.

That was what dream-Paladin'd been trying to tell me.

That was what I'd stumbled over. Baijon'd called me *Malmakosim* until my ears rang with it—but in helltongue it doesn't mean "Librarian.'' Not quite.

It means "the Machine that takes human form.''

That was what had worried the hellflowers all along. Not an interstellar super-computer that could crash their datawebs. They could live without datawebs.

But under the right—or almost-right—conditions, a Library (Baijon said) could mindwipe a organic and pour a Library into its skull in place. They could do it because humans built the first Libraries, and modeled them on the only thinking architecture they had handy.

So if a brain and a computer are pretty similar—

And if the major difference is that a computer holds more stuff more reliably longer—

And if you've got a human brain stuffed full of the sort of stuff usually found in a Library—

—or a computer—

—or even the Brightlaw AI Prototype—

Then why not see if along with all the rest of it there might not be something useful in there?

I could be the ship's computer. I'd been in the Port Mantow computers. I knew everything I needed to.

I hoped.

"Now hand me the *noke-ma'ashki* cable, che-bai.''

Baijon passed me a curl of stuff we'd cannibalized from what was almost certainly some kind of entertainment center in the master cabin. He was damn useful—in another life I could of made a for-sure first-class darktrader out of him. Pilot, smuggler, and all-round techlegger. *Ghost Dance* was proof. Now the cable that used to run between the navicomp and the Jump-brain ran from the Jump-brain to a touchpad keyboard all set for me to use. I wouldn't pull the numbers off the navicomp anymore. I'd make them up.

The only reason for doing this—other than the known hellflower fondness for suicide missions—was that it gave us slightly better odds than trying to pirate a ship in Royal system. Archangel—or his sisters and cousins and aunts— was almost probably still there, making tidy.

On the other hand, if everything in my head since alMayne was all just a long delusional setup, we was both dead.

There was only one way to find out.

"Oke, that's it." I unwound myself from under the seat and propped the fairings back in place. You could see every fingerprint and scratch I'd put on it, not to mention the slots I cut to feed the leads through.

Pity.

I sat in the mercy seat and looked out at nothing. There was one star brighter than the others in sight: Royal's sun, severalmany light-hours away.

Baijon was looking at me. Hopeful. Eager. All I had to do was relax and let the numbers come up. Every trip my mind made down the brainstem to where Archive'd left its get-well present made the next trip easier to make. And bye-m-bye wouldn't be no more trips to make, because what it knew would be what I was, and nothing left to lose.

We had to have a plan, Baijon'd said.

Now we had one.

I didn't think he was going to like it.

The good numbers was right there in my hands. I pulled the angelstick and *Ghost Dance* Jumped sidewise into nowhere.

15

Hellraisers

Ghost Dance made Transit to realspace over a blinding blue-white ball of ice. Probably it'd been warmer once— there was still atmosphere, thanks to an ocean with enough salt in it to be liquid. I didn't look for traffic controllers or beacons. There wasn't any.

"So we will land your ship, San'Cyr. And then?"

"Then we ask babby real nice one time for what we want."

I didn't bother to mention that the possibility Oob'd cooperate was right up there with me getting a full Imperial Pardon for everything I'd done this year.

"And then?"

"Then we take it."

* * *

About a lifetime ago, this was my home base; a little place called Coldwater on the cutting edge of the never-never. My nighttime man was a wiggly called Oob who told me what to kyte and where to kyte it, and didn't mind if I picked up a few side-jobs on my own.

It'd been a good working arrangement. I was sorry I was going to have to see him again.

But there was one thing Baijon and me needed in order to live to get older, and in a ship this hot the only place I could get it was a place that wasn't there. And Coldwater had the only trip-tik.

It's like this. Our glorious Phoenix Empire, the con-catenative brains of which I was doubting more with each passing moment, has got a number of little monopolies, and one that's a real killer: all ports everywhere is Imperial ports.

Even on Closed Worlds like Riisfal or Restricted Worlds like alMayne, the port is a Imperial port and when you're on it it's just like you was standing on Grand Central its own self.

Any port not built, owned, operated—and policed—by the Empire is illegal. Illegal ports is fair game for your Fleet and mine to blow up, and there's no way to hide something that, at its crudest, is a square klik of big flat place with a traffic control computer and a sensor suite.

But Coldwater is a *abandoned* port. All closed down, the *legitimates* packed up and pulled out, no licit traffic in and out ever more. Who'd want a place where the temperature only goes above freezing point of water at high noon of local summer?

Any enterprising crimelord as wanted a port—that's who. And the Empire wouldn't look twice—because it *knew* it was there, and it *knew* it was closed.

There was an Imperial DataNet terminal on Coldwater.

* * *

You'd think I'd of had enough of the DataNet, and you'd be right. But what I was after now hadn't been in the port computer on Royal-as-was. Besides, there was one segment of the galactic power elite I hadn't ticked off.

Yet.

Ghost Dance fell out of the sky sweet as you please and right into my old docking ring. The external temperature sensors wobbled alive and sank right down into the negative numbers. The main ship's computer probably ached to tell me to wear my woolies, but I'd ripped out its voder along with doing the rest of my custom chop-channel.

I shut down the boards but left her hot. I wasn't worried she'd go walking off. Nothing human can handle the fourspace maths to fly a ship without a navicomp and I'd set her so she had to have Jump coordinates before she'd lift.

Nothing human.

Baijon and me went back to the hotlocker and I put on my party clothes. There'd been time on the way here to assemble a kit of fly-vines that should impress even Oob, and no lack of raw material. It even covered up what was left of my left hand, so nobody'd know I was borged. I was saving that for a surprise.

Meanwhile, the rest of it was the prettiest blaster-harness I'd ever owned; I looked like a high-ticket version of a talkingbook space-pirate and with the rating of the heat I was packing I didn't even need to hit what I aimed at to cause it serious personal distress.

"You remember how we planned it?"

"San'Cyr, I still think the danger should be mine."

"*The* danger? Bai, I hope you don't think any part of this is safe."

* * *

The wind hit me first thing out of the hatch. I leaned into it, heading for the converted bunker at the edge of the field. For a minute I spun me the fantasy that every-thing'd gone reet with my last run a half-year back: I'd dropped the bookleg at Wanderweb Free Port, lifted ro-keach and gems to Kiffit, and from there to Orili-neesy, to Maichar, to Dusk, and back home again, to pass gos-sip, pull maintenance, and see what Oob wanted me to do next. It was a depressing commentary on the current state of affairs that my previous life looked inviting.

* * *

What used to be the Port Authority Building was dug down into the permafrost and held Coldwater's entire population. There was only one bar, and it didn't have a name. I pushed open the door and went in.

"Hey, St. Cyr," somebody said when I pushed my hood back. There was pilots for the two other ships I'd seen on the field and the usual gang of mechs, techs, and sophonts as thought this was a good place to be. If it mattered, I was the only human there.

"Heard about your ship," said the tender, reaching under the bar. "Bad luck."

"Worse luck if you finish that move, bai."

He stopped and regarded the blaster. I'd come in with the advantage. I was expecting trouble.

I made a smile I didn't mean and waggled my right-hand heat at him. I took the time to unship the other one, just like a talkingbook space pirate. A little slow with the half hand that was left inside the glove, but the fingers I had left didn't feel the cold.

"You dead, you know that, Gentrymort?" the tender said.

"Sure. And anybody wants to join me can stay right where he is. Everybody else can ankle."

One time I just would of shot them. Or lobbed a grenade through the door before I come in and walked through what's left after you do something like that. None of them'd be any loss.

But I wasn't in the mood today, and wasn't no way this could be a lightning raid like in the talkingbooks anyway. I stood there and gave Oob all the time he wanted to get ready and set while the patrons of the Nameless Bar & Grill shuffled themselves out into the snow.

I dogged the door shut behind them. I knew where I was going, so I went on in.

It was a long narrow hallway that probably used to run to a outbuilding and now was the only way in to Oob's front parlor. By now I'd got warm enough to be cold.

Oob don't like heat; his B-pop isn't rigged for it. But if I'd been him I could of thought of a more comfortable way to arrange things. Oob ran a good slice of the Outfar nightworld. Pandora to Tangervel; a chunk of cubic running all the way out to the edge of the Hamati Confederacy. He had power. I'd seen it. Not power like Archangel had or was reaching for, but if he stepped on you there wouldn't be nothing left to argue the difference.

Did having power like that make living in a freezing hellpit like this tolerable? Or did wanting power mean you didn't care about nothing else?

I pushed open the door to my boss's private office. It

wasn't locked. Why bother: nobody sane'd come all the way out here to cross him.

Never mind what that made Baijon and me. I went in.

Oob was behind his desk; he always is. A thousand kilos of wool, gristle, and blubber in colors not meant to be seen in daylight don't shift too well under one Imperial Standard G. He could rig the gravity, but he's never bothered. Hanging behind him like I expected was a state-of-the-art wartoy in ready-to-rock mode. I had reason to know all of Oob's security measures real well. I just hoped he hadn't changed them.

"Captain St. Cyr," the voder on the desk said. I jogged a blaster at him.

"Refrain from immature acts," the voder said. Somebody'd programmed it one time in Imperial Standard, I guess, and Oob'd never bothered to fix it. "Do you actually contemplate that my security systems are incapable of anticipating your every move?"

"Well," I said, about the time the back wall of Oob's hardsite went away.

I've never anywhere seen something what tells the lifting capability of Hoplite armor. I do know that lifting anything needs a handle to grab and a place to stand.

Baijon'd made both. The wall came up in pieces.

And Oob's first line of offense turned on him.

I fired on it. I didn't make a damn bit of difference but I didn't need to. The wartoy hesitated with being hit two ways at once and yelled for help. Baijon came the rest of the way through the wall and battered the input out of it.

"Question, che-bai, isn't who shoots first or last, but who's left standing, je?"

The temperature was dropping like an innuendo and the wind was taking a chance on anything mobile. Soon enough Baijon was going to be the only one really comfortable.

"I forgot to tell you. I picked up a partner last tik."

Oob looked at Baijon and back at me and blinked; three sets of eyelids sliding over eyes I could see myself in. His throatsack bulged; the voder spoke again.

"You will cease to exist. The Smuggler's Guild will disavow you. Whatever mode of transport you arrived in will become mine. I will return you to the slave-pits, barbarian.''

He was pretending we'd won, which was awfully sweet of him.

"Not impressed. You want a piece of me, babby, you got a long line to stand on. I come to do bidness.''

"What do you want? Letters of Transit to the Confederacy? A wise choice, but costly. Deactivate your armaments and we will discuss it.''

"Place I want's inside the Empire, not out. Toystore. You tell me how to get there. I check it through the dataweb. Me and my friend leave. And before you get any efficient ideas—" I opened my jacket to show him the rows of grenades wired on the deadman's switch. "My heart stops beating, we all dead.''

And I'd be dead anywhere in the Outfar the minute I set foot outside this room, no matter whether Oob was dead or livealive. I was closing, sure and for certain, the last possible bolt-hole.

"I suppose your companion is equally willing to accept the hazard of premature demise?''

"He's hellflower.''

"Hellflowers are crazy. The galaxy knows that,'' Baijon said. We'd fixed the voder; he sounded like him now; sing-songy and pretty with the hellflower lilt in his voice. He bent down and ripped a limb off the wartoy and hefted it.

Good act, if it was. Baijon looked seriously crazy. Not like he didn't care if he lived or died. Like he couldn't tell the difference.

"You tell me, we go, boss; you don't never see me no more. What've you got to lose? *I* got nothing to lose, bai, you know that already, people talking about what happened along of me in the Roaq.''

"Very well.'' A mechannikin what Oob used for hands minced across the desk and dipped into a drawer.

And whiles we was all supposed to be looking at it, Oob's back-up wartoy came up through the dropshaft in the floor.

There was a blast of light and sound as Baijon swung up what'd looked like a bit of fancywork on his armor.

Half-blinded me ready or not even though I'd been expecting it. Over the echoes you could hear a teeth-setting whine as the wartoy's safety fields overloaded from damping its own explosion in order to save its master's life. Touching.

Baijon lowered his gauntlet and shucked off the half-melted fairing. What we'd rigged for the armor would only fire once. I hadn't really been sure it'd fire at all.

A couple of kilocredits of expensive hostility dropped to the floor, having retired from the adversary business. One for use and one for show—that was what Oob'd always had.

I smole a small smile at my ex-boss. Twenty years in bidness along of him, I'd learned my way into his little quirks.

"Wartoys make my partner nervous," I explained. "I guess his finger must of slipped. Now, you was getting me that trip-tik?"

Oob didn't say anything for a real long time. If he ever got his hands on me now, there wouldn't be enough left to shop to the bodysnatchers.

"All your posturing is futile. I am not intimidated. I refuse to aid you."

The Hoplite armor sang as Baijon prepared to settle in for some plain and fancy intimidation.

"Don't bother," I said to him.

I walked around to Oob's side of the console. I didn't know his setup, but I pushed buttons until something happened.

The back wall slid open, and there was the DataNet terminal and all its works; a sideshow to impress the rubes they was getting what they'd fronted for. The terminal was a commercial port model; it was fitted with limbic jacks. I walked over to it whiles Baijon stood over my boss. Ex-boss.

"That will avail you nothing," the voder said.

"Shut up."

I didn't want to do this. I didn't want to be a borg, with hellgod metal mutating under my skin until I turned into a *thing*.

I didn't want to be here.

I wanted to go home.

But Baijon wanted to go home too, and he wouldn't never get the chance. All those solid citizens on Royal wanted to live as much as I did.

If you aren't part of the solution, you're part of the precipitate.

I pulled off my glove and then pulled back my skin and shook my wrist until the plugs dropped out from between glass and cybereisis bones and dangled. I'd put them in back on the *Dance*. Universal connectors. You could jack anything up to them, and I did. I felt Oob watching me, and Baijon not watching me. Borg. Hellgod. *Malmako-sim*. Your friendly neighborhood darktrader, Butterfly St. Cyr.

This time wasn't like either time at Royal. Something knew what it was doing—something I could hitch on like making the Jump to angeltown without a ship and follow down to what I needed.

Cyborgs' brains is buffered to take the input. Mine was still under renovation. But I'd had some practice and I was getting more.

Paladin, are you out here? Can you hear me? Answer me, bai. You owe me, dammit.

Nothing. Paladin wasn't there. Not this time. But everything else was. And I got what I wanted.

"We got to thank you for hospitality and say it's been a real pleasure we don't hope to repeat."

The trip-tik cassette full of information came up out of its slot. I plucked it and flipped it to Baijon. The armor caught it without looking.

"And before we go—just in case you think to be unfriendly-like, bai—we got one thing more for you." I yanked my brain loose from the computer's and gave it the office to run.

Coldwater wasn't like Royal. When I shut down everything the computer could reach, only the terminal went dead.

Then we left.

*   *   *

The storm we'd landed in was a blizzard when we left. I pumped a covering fire around us just for grins, but I knew the clientele. They wasn't the type to jump us on the heavyside.

Baijon slapped open both locks, and *Dance*'s air came smoking out.

And the lights on the other two ships on the field came up.

"She's pretty, but can she fly?"

The over-amp made the pilot's voice wof and yabber. There was a flash. We was sprayed with boiling water while somebody's top-cannon tried to find a range.

Then I was in, with Baijon in all his glory landed on top of me in the hushed presence of great valuta acquired by unlawful means. If we was taking any hits, *Dance* was too much of a lady to let on.

I beat Baijon to the bridge by not-much, and slammed the cassette in for the Jump-brain to chew on while he squirmed out of the armor. All we had to do to use it was get to Transfer Point alive.

"St. Cyr, you in there? Pop your locks, jillybai, I'll make it quick," my commo said. I wondered who he was, but not very hard.

There was another spray of wet mud across the external pick-ups. Baijon slammed into a seat and pulled his straps down. I grabbed a handful of lifters and pulled.

And watched *Ghost Dance* tell me she was doing her best against a hundred gravities of discouragement.

Tractors.

"San'Cyr?" Baijon, wondering why we was hanging around.

"Mother's got problems just now, babby-bai."

Two ships on the field, leggers and pirates equipped with the standard box of tricks. Tractors to lock them on to a ship or free-floating cargo, guns that could angle to protect a ship on the ground. And a nasty sense of civic duty.

Dance's guns were fixed, with damn few degrees of arc. In space you turn the whole ship, je?

They was going to hold us on the heavyside and hammer us to death.

They hoped.

I gave her all the go-devils in the inventory, to where I was sure something was going to cut loose and blow. She started pulling away, and the view-screens went fade-to-black as the darktraders on the field gunned their engines to hold her.

I opened a wide channel. Both of them would hear it.

"This is *Ghost Dance*. We got fifteen plates of goforth and nothing to lose. You boys want to be serious nonfiction you just hang on; I guarantee to wrap you around the first lamppost in angeltown."

No answer. Just the howl of an open circuit. *Dance* was starting to shake.

"I mean it. When you forged your First Tickets, anybody tell you what happens you Jump too deep in a gravity well?"

Silence.

"Want to find out?"

I cut the channel and hit the override. The good numbers slid right down the Jump-computer's throat. I counted six, then grabbed the angelstick.

The image in my screen slewed as one of the leggers whipped its tractors off us. *Dance* snapped the other one no problem and we made a slightly-less-than-textbook exit from Coldwater space, full throttles and god help anything in our way. We ripped a hole in the atmosphere big enough to drop a shaker into and by the time the stick dropped home we was twenty seconds past Transfer Point.

Safe. One more time.

But I had finally twigged to what that meant. The raid had gone real smooth, but smooth this time just meant double trouble next time, until you doubled out to where there wasn't no good numbers any more.

* * *

Now that it was mostly too late to change my mind I looked at the numbers I'd pulled out of Oob's "Too Secret To Look At" dumpfile. The navicomp would of given me names and addresses, but even without it I could see we was heading somewheres off the beaten track.

Toystore.

"I still do not precisely understand why we are going there, San'Cyr." Baijon looked pleased but not particularly disturbed by our recent almost conversion to nonfiction.

"Other than it's the only place in the Empire we won't get shopped and sold? It's that plan you said I had, bai."

"To go shopping?" He hadn't belted in to the worry seat. The straps and buckles clinked when he moved. "Our plan was to kill Archangel, was it not?"

"Oh, why the hell not?"

I got up and walked back out of the cockpit, jerking leads loose from the big bang I was wearing as I went.

Once the plan had been to get loose and go find Paladin, my one-time partner, Library, and all-around pain in the neck.

A little later, the plan had been to hide out while news of Mallorum Archangel's techleggery and High Book connections made him a non-player in the galactic game of ultimate power.

It didn't look like that was what you might call your viable option anymore. Not with what Archangel had from Library Archive. The only consolation was that Archangel didn't have any Old Fed Tech memories the way I did—but then, would he have noticed?

What Archangel did have was a wish-list for a Coalition without any hellflowers in it at all. More, he wanted what the hellflowers had: the Empire's largest cache of information on Old Federation Libraries or a reasonable facsimile.

I went back into the main cabin of *Ghost Dance*, where sophonts of distinction'd probably spent serious hours arguing over what to have for lunch. It didn't look quite so pristine mint as it had before Baijon and me'd took up light housekeeping here.

"Let me help you, San'Cyr." Baijon started pulling tape and grenades loose, turning me from a walking bomb back into a real live cyborg. This particular refinement'd been his idea. I'd just been planning on holding a gun to Oob's head.

Baijon didn't call me *"Kore"* anymore. It just meant "woman" in helltongue. I shouldn't miss it. Baijon was reinventing himself, taking out all the hellflower and leaving something that could deal with a *Malmakosim*.

Because Archangel was important enough for that.

Or because it was easier than dying nobly and with honor for a ideal that you'd already had proved to you didn't exist.

Baijon finished untaping me and then set to work sorting the grenades from the wrap in case we might want to blow up something later. I looked at my hand without the glove, but it hadn't grown any new fingers whiles I wasn't looking.

The trouble was, you couldn't just get up one day and decide that everything you ever knew was wrong. You could try, but it wouldn't work.

It hadn't worked for me.

"I be getting us something to eat, *ea*, che-bai? We got a long tik to where we going."

"They might simply blow us up when we reach this Toystore." Baijon, unimpressed.

"Gives us something to look forward to, ne?"

I'd always wanted to peel Baijon loose from his honor. From the first time I met him.

I'd changed my mind.

* * *

There was food for another five hundred hours in the galley. It was nice to know I had enough munchies to last out my life. I looked at all the baggies and boxes and tried to think what I was doing here.

Stinging Archangel. He'd bite. He'd let us get close to him. He wanted the Brightlaw Prototype, which might be anything from the ultimate holecard to a new way of making beer but what was in blissful theory a tame Library that'd do what it was told. Which might exist, and might not. And Archangel thought I had it. Or was it.

And I could be.

"You are not happy, San'Cyr." Baijon came in to the galley about the time I was thinking of rearranging the supplies by size and color. Anything to take my mind off my mind.

"You got any thought why I shouldn't be happy, Baijon? I got a thousand-year-old set of alien memories eating my mind, every *legitimate* and nightworlder in the Empire is after us, and for the icing on the brass cupcake Archangel's got the galaxy so spooked it's going to bolt into six kinds of war at once."

"But we won't have to worry about that, San'Cyr. We'll be dead." Baijon began rummaging about the shelves, looking for something to eat. "When will we reach Toystore and begin to kill Archangel?"

"You know, bai—I've never told you this—but being dead is not exactly my life's ambition, you know."

"Everyone dies." Baijon popped a meal-pak and began to eat it without waiting for it to heat. "That is why you are born."

"Real comforting."

"Is it more desirable to die *not* having slain Mallorum Archangel?"

No.

We couldn't stop the war. But we could lower the ante. Ice Archangel, and there wouldn't be any Old Fed weapons on the field.

"It is our holy purpose. It pays for all. It proves—" he stopped. "It proves we were right."

I didn't want to be right. I wanted to live.

But not as much as I wanted Mallorum Archangel dead.

"Terrific. We were right. They'll put that on our marker, bai: They're Dead All Right."

"And now you will tell me our plan."

Find out what Mallorum Archangel wanted. Get next to him with it and ice him—but for the really big payoff, stop the war he was winding up to rock and roll as well.

Nothing to it, once you knew how. Because reality ain't real anymore. It's what the computers and the data-web say it is. And what they got in them. Like Paladin. He was in there now, if I knew anything at all.

"It's a great plan. I been staying up nights over Archangel's wish-list. I figure, he wants a Library so much, bai, we buy and deliver him one."

Find Paladin and I controlled the nature of reality in the Phoenix Empire. He'd do me a favor or two.

He'd better.

16

Toys in the Attic

We made Transit to realspace in the geometric center of nowhere. There was a faint gray band of light off to starboard that was the main starmass of the galaxy, a few nearer dots for nearer systems or at least suns, but mainly nothing.

No relative motion. No depth perception. The black and white could of been painted on *Ghost Dance*'s canopy for all the sense of here and there it gave. And somewhere within a thousand cubic lights of stone cold empty was something relatively not all that bigger than my ship.

"It's . . . empty," Baijon said, which was no more inadequate than anybody else's comment on seeing the Big Dark up close and personal for the first time.

"You should see it standing on the hull in armor."

All communications frequencies was open and I had the sensor-sweeps out. So far, nothing. But Toystore was out here. Oob's numbers said so.

* * *

Toystore is a deep space station of no fixed address, which was one reason it could cost you so much to find out the current one. The other was that anything's for sale there—anything illegal under the Pax Imperador and too hot to factor through a Free Port.

What that leaves is very hot indeed.

The usual way you got to Toystore was knowing someone what knew someone until you got passed up the line far enough to spin serious credit to get a set of mystery coordinates loaded into your navicomp. Then you'd Jump with them, and you was home free if they liked you and dead if they didn't.

We hadn't done it that way, and Toystore probably knew it.

"Are you sure . . ." Baijon said.

"Sure that this was the coordinates behind the six sets of locks in Oob's dumpfile on the Coldwater dataweb? Je. Sure for anything else? Ne."

But Toystore brokers information. At the moment we represented quite a lot of potential factoids. I was hoping they'd be curious enough at least to let us in.

At worst, we could probably clear their space alive—assuming they ever bothered to do something as interactive as start shooting.

"Welcome to Toystore, Captain St. Cyr."

The voice came over my commo, but the picture didn't. That was courtesy of holo-tightbeam, just to let me know that they knew right where we was, thank you very much, and had tech and power to waste.

The tightbeam showed me a sleek young techie dressed like ready money and not a weapon in sight. He looked more than a little like a broker I knew hight Silver Dagger, and if he was half as dangerous I had new and additional troubles.

"If you would care to follow the tracer beam you will find an empty docking sleeve able to accommodate your ship. You may carry any form of personal armament you desire while visiting Toystore, but use of antisocial technology is strictly prohibited. Toystore reserves the right to place a lien on your property and transport if punitive fines in excess of your personal credit balance are levied, and accepts no responsibility for injuries or damage incurred by persons attempting to leave Toystore without a ship. Enjoy your stay."

Right on cue and don't think they hadn't planned it for effect, Toystore hit all of its self-lights and lit up like the Emperor's Birthday. My sensors binged and agreed with my eyes: all of a sudden Toystore was right there in front of us looking all floaty and pastel and beautiful.

So they *was* curious. Round one to us.

"More lies," said Baijon, unimpressed.

"He weren't lying, 'flower. He done told us we do anything they don't like, we get spaced without ship nor suit. Simple."

Baijon grinned. The idea appealed to him. Hellflowers do have a sense of humor. It just isn't what the rest of the galaxy thinks is particularly funny.

Ghost Dance slid right down Toystore's tracer beam and kissed the gunner's daughter. The flexible dock-socket slid closed around her and started hooking ship's systems up to the great outside before the goforths was cycled down. Toystore docking computer slid down the connects as soon as *Dance* was hooked up and piggy-backed a pseudomind on any sort of intelligence my resident computers might have. By the time we was absolutely at rest Toystore'd took control of all ship's systems right down to the air locks. They slid open and the cockpit hatch slid open and we was high wide and help-less until Toystore Main Memory returned control of our comps to us.

I might be able to purge them myself, but for damn sure any try at doing so would be construed as mopery with intent to gawk, and there was something here I wanted.

I wanted the Keys to Paradise.

* * *

The pseudomind interface gave *Dance* limited access to Toystore Main Memory. I read up on rules and regs and fees while Baijon made extensive inroads on some glitterborn's lost wardrobe.

Our resources consisted of a stolen Imperial Battle Yacht, a defrocked hellflower, and a body of knowledge that hadn't been current events for the last ten centuries. It might be enough to start a revolution.

Or stop one.

I figured we had credit enough to pay our freight about thirty hours worth. If we couldn't get the piece of techno-candy I wanted by then, we'd have to switch to Plan B.

It was real too bad there wasn't a Plan B. I wondered if the price Oob'd put on me was higher than the one the

Empire was offering, and if Paladin knew about either one. I also wondered if even Toystore had what I wanted, and if I could afford it if it did.

I wasn't even sure the Keys to Paradise existed.

You might guess, with the legal down on machines hellishly forged in the likeness of a living mind etcetera, that cybernetic tech was not exactly an open traded item, Brightlaw's Folly aside. But the Empire couldn't hold together without some of it. Paladin used to even think that the Imperial DataNet might someday grow up to be a Library if it got big enough, and there was a big shady area between tronics and numbercrunchers and things that might "think as well as a man but not *like* him."

One of the ways techies tried to get around the down the Tech Police have against building machines that think was by hanging cyber-bells and whistles on something already allowed to think on account of being born organic.

Mostly they didn't get away with it. But sometimes it took the Tech Police long enough to make up its mind that by the time they decided something belonged in Chapters 1-4 of the Revised Inappropriate Technology Act of the 975th Year of Imperial Grace (pat. pend.) it'd already been in use and production long enough that it left behind it a sizable bank of outlaw tech.

Like the Keys to Paradise.

* * *

"San'Cyr, why are we here?"

Baijon Stardust looked like one very rich mercenary. He was wearing a short cape, high boots, any number of fire-irons, a worried expression, and I had real doubts about the quiet good taste of *Ghost Dance*'s last tenant.

"Because I'm stupid." I was wearing something closer to quiet good taste that'd probably belonged to the last pilot. No blasters—you can wear but not shoot them on Toystore. A glove that made it look like my lost fingers was still there—not that it'd fool anybody much, with Toystore's scanners.

"If you were stupid, San'Cyr, we would both be dead,

I think. You said you wished to make Mallorum Arch-angel a . . . gift. And thus kill him. This I believe. But is the Empire truly so depraved as to offer such things openly?''

It took me a minute to figure out what he meant. I'd told him I was going to give Archangel a Library.

''Ne, che-bai, is only one Library I'd trust anywhere near Archangel, but I got to catch him first. To do that, I got to go to Paradise.''

Baijon frowned. ''This is not Paradise. You said this place was Toystore, a haunt or resort of the Empire's most vile and feckless technologists.''

''Is one way of putting it, as long as you don't let nobody hear you. Put another way, is the only place I can buy what I need to catch me a Library.''

''The Keys to Paradise?''

''Too reet, babby. Let's ankle.''

* * *

Baijon stuck closer'n my shadow; nothing in his as-sociation with me'd prepared him for this.

Nothing in *my* association with me'd prepared me for this.

The total citizen population of the Phoenix Empire is somewhere around ten thousand billion. If only one per-cent of them is bent (which is stone optimism), that's ten billion people. If only one percent of *them* is major play-ers, that's one hundred million. And if only one to the third power percent of the population of the Empire was up to things they shouldn't be at Toystore at any given nanosecond, that meant there was close to a million peo-ple here all looking for trouble.

* * *

The Graymarket is the entire central core of Toystore. It had a passing resemblance to any downport wonder-town: places to eat and places to deal, and places to get what you needed to deal.

It looked like Grand Central on the Emperor's Official

Birthday. Every method you might ever want to use to bend the Pax Imperador was being offered absolutely open by kiddies who looked like they'd never ducked a blaster-bolt in their lives. If I'd thought I'd been out of place on Mikasa and alMayne, I'd been local color compared to here.

There was holos two and three times life-size of people demonstrating illegal acts they would be happy to perform for a fee. There was offers of things for sale—half of them I didn't recognize, and the other half was nine kinds of forbidden. The level of pure unfamiliar information on offer was numbing.

But this was just the opening act, flashcandy for the rubes and hangers-on. Toystore's rep-making stock in trade wasn't this stuff. What Toystore dealt in was the hottest, most illegal kick of all.

Knowledge.

"San'Cyr, how do we find . . . what you are seeking . . . in all of this?" Baijon gestured at five tiers of wondershow.

"We don't. We hire a professional."

"But San'Cyr, you have told me we have 'barely enough credit to keep breathing if we don't jump salty.' "

"Said we hire a pro. Didn't say nothing about paying him."

* * *

The memorybroker's shop I wouldn't of recognized without the Intersign glyphs running parallel to the Imperial Standard Script. Baijon was the one what found which part of the wall was the door. If I was still in the business of being impressed by things I would of been impressed.

"Welcome to Toystore, Butterflies-are-free Peace Sincere. How may we help you?"

The sophont that oiled out to meet us was Core-worlds B-pop and spun Interphon straight from the Imperial Mint with an accent you could use to finance most of the con jobs in the Outfar.

"Perhaps a new life history? Some job skills? Your

credit is quite good . . . at the moment.'' He smiled in a way as said it was oke to be impressed with his superior way of weaseling info out of the Toystore Interstellar Bank.

I wasn't. On Toystore, everything's for sale.

"Not buying memory. Selling. Anybody wants to know why Tortuga Sector isn't answering the phone, they ask me.''

"Weapons systems failure,'' said the broker, unimpressed. Baijon looked indignant. I shrugged.

"Didn't ask for critical reviews, bai. I was there. I was on alMayne when it went up, too. And I was in the Roaq. That's my sale.''

Information. An eyewitness account, vetted, certified, and on cassette, of what I'd seen and what I'd thought about it. Inarguable. Anybody can say something's so. Thanks to the magic of modern technology now you can prove it, and hand somebody else the experience to boot.

"Well . . .'' The broker was playing coy, which is not a new experience in my life. "I suppose there might be some curiosity value in it. If you'll come this way we'll copy the memories, transcribe an abstract, and place them in our catalog. If someone is interested—''

"Wasn't born yesterday. You put what I said in your catalog. Somebody wants to deal, we deal then.''

"You're making things very difficult, Sincere. I don't know what you're used to on the Borders, but—''

"It's *Captain* St. Cyr, *chaudatu*-bai, and you're the first shop I came into, not the last. I come to sell. I told you what I'm selling and how. You know what you've heard about Royal and Washonnet and the Roaq. Now it's your turn, je?''

He didn't like it but I'd twigged him; he'd heard enough about current events to want to know more.

"Most of our clients, *Captain*, prefer to leave their information on consignment. Of course, we do, occasionally, make an outright purchase at a far lower scale of remuneration—''

I looked at Baijon.

"He means he wishes to cheat you now," Baijon translated helpfully.

The memorylegger turned enough colors to almost make me think he'd been insulted.

"I merely wished to point out that it is difficult to assign a monetary value to memories that one has not personally experienced. We would not be able to continue in business were we not known to be discreet and irreproachable; your information would lose no marketability or uniqueness by being left on deposit; in fact, frequently the resale value—"

"Not be living long enough to worry about that, bai, don't you worry your pretty head none. Come here to buy, got to sell to do it. Get what I want, I be gone, j'keyn?"

If there hadn't already been some trickle-out from the galactic garden spots I'd mentioned, I think Baijon and me'd of been tossed back out in the street for the Toystore version of the *legitimates* to find. But there had been, and I had the right words and enough of the music to make people sit up and whistle.

"Very well, Captain. And can we possibly assist you in making your purchase?" the memorylegger finally said through gritted phonemes.

"I swap all those memories I said—even—for one working set of the Keys to Paradise."

He didn't throw us out then, either.

*   *   *

They started out as a toy. Fake reality, like dreamtapes or memory-edit, except that with them you just get added or subtracted a rote thing and that's that. The Keys was *flexible;* you got the jinks sunk in your head and plugged in the game computer, you got a whole world to play with.

It needed a pretty big tronic brain to hold the game reality, and that was where the trouble started, because any comp that big is just naturally plugged into at least the planetary net, and if you could get to the planetary net you could get to something hooked into the Imperial dataweb.

But couldn't nobody get out of the programmed paradise, right? Nor know what to do if they did?

Wrong. The way I heard it, most people who turned the Keys just died, but at least one person went out where he shouldn't of been able to and came back too, and that was it for the Keys to Paradise.

I knew all about them because Paladin'd wanted me to have a set, which even if I'd been fool enough to want somebody to do that to my brain I didn't haul enough cubic to rate. But I knew about them—Pally'd been real good getting at stuff the Empire didn't want its average citizen to see.

And any technology that convenient, I was betting, wasn't lost.

* * *

"Now what do we do?" said Baijon on the way back to *Dance*.

"We wait."

* * *

We waited twenty hours. I wasn't really expecting a straight swap; what I was trolling for was a come-on from some techleggers who thought they knew what I wanted Keys for—because in addition to the bootleg technocandy we needed a cyberdoc to set the jinks and serious time on a DataNet terminal and somehow I didn't think Oob was going to let us come back and use his again.

But the offer didn't come. Soon we was going to be over the margin that'd let us take our ship with us when we left.

We could kyte before that. There was a Plan B after all, but it didn't have as much to recommend it as dumping Paladin into Grand Central Main Bank Memory and making him mind Archangel's manners. It was more like me walking up to Archangel and shooting him under excuse of being the Brightlaw Prototype he wanted.

I didn't think it'd work. But I was out of ideas that would.

We waited and watched hollycasts. I caught up on my talkingbook auditing—the adventures of Infinity Jilt, undercover girl space pirate for the Tech Police and her crew of hulking loyal wigglies.

This installment she had penetrated the secret starbase in the Black Nebula, where she found a tribe of outlaw techs selling Imperial know-how to the geat-kings of the Hamati Confederacy.

It struck me that my life was a little too much like the talkingbooks these days—only I didn't have Throne backing, I couldn't whistle up a crack squad of loyal and well-mannered Space Angels, and I didn't give a damn who sold what to the Hamati so long as I didn't have to do it.

Baijon audited real-world stuff—looking for news about Washonnet, of which there wasn't any. Half the time the 'casts made it sound like the hellflowers was having a love-feast, not a war.

The Roaq was still closed for renovations. A previously predicted and right-on-sked astrophysical disturbance had shut down Royal Directorate and the Chairman of the Charlock Corporation was petitioning Throne to keep it closed until a Board Meeting and elections could be held.

I just bet he was.

What good is knowing you can't trust anything you see and hear when you need it to navigate anyway? Knowing the Imperial news out of Washonnet and everywhere else was lies didn't tell me what was true. How was I or anybody supposed to think about anything, knowing everything I had available to think about was a lie?

Maybe nobody else knew. Maybe nobody else cared.

I don't know why I bother sometimes bringing peace and justice to the Empire at reasonable prices. What did I care who ran the dog-and-pony show? I didn't have any intrinsic objections to a change in Emperor. I wouldn't even mind an even-more-repressive galactic tyranny grinding Citizen Taxpayer under its brutal heel so long as it left the stars and planets in the usual places and didn't involve things like wiping out all organic life one more time.

It kept coming back to Archangel wasn't going to do that. Sure, we could probably claw our way up from the amoeba again, but doing stuff like that gets boring after a while.

Some of this I told Baijon. Some not. We didn't understand each other any better than Paladin nor me had, really.

On the twenty-first hour we spent waiting, the brokerage called and told me somebody wanted to buy.

* * *

"I do not trust him, San'Cyr. It is another trap."

"I ain't trusted nobody since I was fifteen, Baijon; you get used to it. But the 'legger wants his credit, and we got a radical rep, and sooner or later somebody's going to want to know how I pulled these coordinates off Oob's terminal in the first place. Then we cut a deal."

"Or they shoot us."

"Wondering which is what makes life such a designer thrill, bai."

* * *

There was one thing different from our last visit to the Graymarket, and she was standing outside the shop. She was even more out of place here than Baijon and me was, with a play-for-pay chassis and all mod. cons., wearing one piece of hold-me-tight superskin and a lot of paint, hanging roundaround outside the memorylegger's with the bright interested expression of a veteran tourist.

And that was real wrong. She wasn't a player, and she wasn't muscle, and ain't nothing else got any busines on Toystore.

Her face brightened right up when she saw us. Wrong number two.

"Oh, hello," she said brightly. "I'm sorry about the wait."

That's when I realized I knew her.

''We got trouble,'' I said to Baijon.

It was Berathia Notevan, the spy from alMayne.

* * *

I like being alive. It's been my hobby for whiles and in weak moments I hope to pursue it into old age.

It was why I stopped Baijon from going for his heat when he realized who she was. He ripped off a line of helltongue at her indicating that most of her parents had been assembled.

''What a wonderful coincidence that we happened to be here, too,'' she said brightly. ''Daddy always says I have a tendency to be overly optimistic, but once I heard that an Imperial Battle-Yacht had petitioned to dock here I just knew everything had turned out all right for you. It's too bad about Royal, though.''

''Ain't it just, your Gentle Docentship. And maybe I be wondering just how you come to be here when I left you on alMayne.'' I smoothed the glove on my left hand; a new nervous twitch that kept me from going for the blasters I wasn't wearing. Berathia laughed like I'd said something funny.

''Oh, you know how it is, work-work-work. Once the War College was bombed, I knew there really wasn't any reason for me to stay. And you'd already left, after all.''

''You was Kennor's holecard, right? The one supposed to do one thing or t'other when I showed up on alMayne, right?''

''Oh, there really isn't any point in dredging up ancient history now, is there, Captain St. Cyr? Besides, there's someone here wanting to see you—and you did come to Toystore to deal, didn't you?''

Sure. And did it with no options and no clout, other than being too valuable and entertaining to waste. We went through the front, into the back where the private rooms was.

''You don't need to worry about the fee—that's been paid,'' Berathia said, and opened the door.

Kennor Starbringer was waiting.

He was all alone and dressed pure hellflower, with the

Knife like Baijon didn't have no more strapped front and center.

"Well," said Berathia brightly, "now that we're all here . . ."

"Where is my son?" said Kennor, looking right at Baijon.

"But he's . . ." Berathia said, and stopped. Baijon twitched. I put a hand on his arm. Could of been feeling up the Hoplite armor for all the give there was.

"The *arthame*, what is the alMayne spirit-blade, is what Mallorum Archangel got rid of for him when we was on Royal, your Gentle Docentship."

Along with a planet, a moon, and a couple of space-stations.

I watched Kennor age half the rest of his allotted life-span in the next tik-anna-half. He sat down back behind the table again. He didn't look at Baijon.

"Did he . . . die with honor?" Kennor said to no one in particular.

"Honor died first," said Baijon sadly. "The woman the aunt of the Third Person of House Starborn—whom I will kill, father—"

"You are too late. Valijon—"

"He is *dead!*" Baijon wailed.

"My son." Kennor got up and rounded the table. He looked like he might put his arms around Baijon if Baijon was here. But Baijon wasn't. Kennor looked at me.

Keep him safe, Kennor'd said, and this was what I'd done instead.

"Why are you still alive?" Kennor said.

Baijon laughed, sounding crazy. "What news from Royal, Second of Starborn, and of the insurrectionists who were receiving Starborn weapons?"

Starborn weapons. Sure. I'd been right. And if I'd bothered to ask I bet Baijon would of told me. In order for hottoys to be transhipped from alMayne, someone on alMayne had to order them first. Someone with clout. Not a LessHouse like Meggie'd said. A GreatHouse.

Kennor Starbringer was backing the Brightlaw Rebellion. Not Amrath. Not the Coalition. *Kennor.*

"Royal is gone," Kennor said slowly.

"Lord Starbringer, there isn't much time. You *must* be seen to be aboard the *Lorelei Rake* when she passes the Washonnet checkpoint. *Alone,*" Berathia said.

"I have come for my son."

"He's dead," Baijon and me said, almost in chorus.

"And you killed him, Kennor-bai," I finished. "You started a war on alMayne. That's why you sent us there. All this farcing about ship and papers was just the excuse to get us to alMayne so Baijon could stand up and get flattened."

"I would have kept my word. There was a ship."

"And papers. Too bad we didn't know to ask for them when we beat your war off-planet by the skin of our never-you-mind. *Angelcity's* by way of being a old friend of mine, bai—and you set her up, too. But you got what you wanted. Baijon thought everybody'd rally round the boy who cried Library. You knew they wouldn't. And Archangel was waiting for all of us at our next stop."

There was a pause.

"And you have come to complain?" Kennor said.

"No," said Berathia. "She came for these."

She tossed a set of the Keys to Paradise on the table.

They was all in the original wrapping—the brainjinks, the scenario modules, all factory new.

"Illegal cybernetics. A neural interface. Wouldn't it be nice to know what somebody who came here in Prince Mallorum Archangel's own battle-yacht wanted with this?" Berathia added.

"Who are you really?" I asked Berathia the ratfink.

She smiled.

"An anthropologist. I told you that at Wailing, Captain St. Cyr."

And maybe it was even true, just like I was a legit small-freighter captain. But Berathia was a player, too.

"There are warrants out on the two of you from here to the Core. What possible use is a dreamworld?"

Kennor looked at his son and looked at me. I saw him figure it out.

Everything.

We'd told him about the Library in the Roaq, Baijon and me. Kennor'd had his basic Library-burning lessons

back at the War College just like every other hellflower.
I'd had an illegal transponder in my skull when he picked
me up and now I'd come here—from Royal—shopping for
something that could pour a human ego into the DataNet.
He knew I had a cybernetic arm and he knew how it could
be modified.

He *knew.*

He backed away from Baijon, slow. Baijon looked at his
face and backed away, too.

"And what do you do here?" Kennor said. It weren't
quite us he was asking. And something in the back of my
skull wanted to answer.

"Buying. Selling. Wondering how much honor goes for
in the galactic marketplace these days, Kennor-che-bai."

Once Kennor's kind and mine had been partners—

No. Not my kind.

But I wondered. If you'd been part of that much power,
was a thousand years time enough to cut the taste for it?

"What does your kind know of honor?" Kennor asked.
I made a fist, but the fake fingers wouldn't close.

"I know what you taught me, father," Baijon said.

"I taught *you* nothing."

Berathia started to look left out. Something flashed below my line of sight and I looked down. Kennor was holding a little silver hideout in his hand, own twin to the one
I'd killed Winterfire with.

So he was going to do it after all.

"Lord Starbringer!" Berathia sounded actually worried
for a change. "Toystore is *very* inflexible about its ag-
gression policies. If you shoot—"

"—I do as Archangel wishes. But no longer. Is the Prototype loaded?"

Berathia's mouth twitched. She was a pro, all right, and
Kennor was an amateur. He hadn't needed for to tell us
that.

"That wouldn't be the Brightlaw AI Prototype that
Archangel was looking for back at Royal, would it?" I
asked. "The one that was supposed to be on the same
ship as us? Just out of idle curiosity, Kennor-bai, what do
you think happened to Royal?"

He bared his teeth. "It became a symbol of unjust oppression."

I tried again. "What was Archangel trying to stop when he hellbombed it?"

"The Brightlaw Prototype," said Baijon. He looked from me to Kennor. He'd figured it all out. There was no illusions left.

The Brightlaw Prototype. A fake Library that did what it was told. Something so close to anathema that when the real thing came along Kennor Starbringer didn't blink twice. Because Brother Kennor'd been hip-deep in anathema for years.

"You set Baijon up to make alMayne do what you wanted. You set Royal up—you *knew* what Archangel would do there."

Kennor'd knew Archangel would bomb Royal. He'd made sure of it. Once Archangel saw Baijon and me with Meggie he wouldn't think three-times. Why shouldn't we be in Kennor's confidence—even if we wasn't? It was a perfect setup. We would of walked right down Archangel's throat with the Prototype or a convincing fake clutched in our little paddy paws.

"*Ten billion people, bai*—what you got that's worth that butcher's bill?"

"Peace," said Kennor Starbringer. "Does that amuse you, *Malmakosimra*? Peace at any price. For too long Archangel has held the Emperor a helpless prisoner and acted in his name. The *chaudatu* hand power into his blasphemous hands, thinking it is Throne that they serve and not the Destroyer, but at last he has overstepped himself."

If anybody but the hellflowers believed that Archangel and not the Brightlaw Rebellion had fragged Royal.

"Now his allies will turn on him. Once more alMayne will lead the Coalition—and the Coalition will lead the Directorates."

Right into trouble. I've always said hellflowers was crazy. Kennor Starbringer was so far round the twist he couldn't see the bend in the road—or maybe that was hellflower logic in the service of greater galactic realpolitix.

"The Azarine Coalition will free the Emperor and restore power to him—to a certain degree. The Coalition will dictate terms to the Emperor—and alMayne will lead the Coalition. Your days are numbered, and those of your tainted kindred. Once the Gentle People have taken their rightful place as guardians of all life even the *possibility* of your kind will end.''

Paladin had a word for it, like he did for everything else. Theocracy. Rule by revealed truth. And it'd make Archangel's version of everybody's future look like a garden spot.

''You can't do this,'' I said, and it sounded stupid even to me.

''It is not right,'' Baijon added. Nice of him.

''What does your kind know of right?'' snarled Kennor. ''Is it right that Archangel should enforce a tyranny the like of which the Empire has never seen, destroying the Gentle People and setting the *Malmakos* to rule men? Would he forbear to do so should we ask him—in honor—to refrain? He has no honor. And honor cannot therefore oppose him. I had to find another way.''

''But we are not meant to rule,'' said Baijon, miserable.

''You say that now, knowing what you know? We are humanity's masters. The race needs a master—for its safety, if nothing else. The Empire cannot support a war. I will not risk one. Archangel's plan depends on subtlety— it is worth the destruction of Royal to unmask his ambition. Now there will be peace.''

Logical. As logical, true-tell, as a genocidal Library Archive I knew a little too well. Had the Libraries thought that, oncet? Was that how the war had started?

I didn't get time to worry about it. Just then lights and gravity flickered, a blip that set me back down on my feet a little too hard.

''You'd better go, Lord Starbringer,'' Berathia said. ''You know what the bargain was. I don't think you'll want to be here when they arrive.''

Kennor looked at us. ''Tell your master, when you see him next—''

''Came to Toystore looking for to ice Archangel, bai,'' I said.

''You can tell him so when you see him,'' Berathia said. She turned to me and smiled. ''Surely you don't think

Throne doesn't know about this place, Captain St. Cyr? Why do you think you were kept waiting around so long? Toystore has vigorish to pay, too—to the Empire. They're handing you over to Archangel the moment he gets here.''

Kennor was up and moving. He looked at Baijon, deciding whether to shoot.

"Al-ea-alarthme, chaudatu," Baijon said to his father, teeth bared. Kennor brushed past him and didn't look back.

The downside under my feet shook, and Berathia's I-know-what's-going-on-and-you-don't expression damped a couple of amps.

"That's what they think," I said to Berathia. Toystore was neutral, Toystore was safe. Everybody in the night-world said so. That's the last time I believe anybody's publicity.

But coming here'd got me what I needed.

I dived for the Keys Berathia'd tossed to the table and dumped them down my shirt.

"C'mon, babby!" I said to Baijon. "We gone!"

"No, wait!" said Berathia.

"You got a better way out, right?" I said. "How many times you think we going to fall for that?" She took a good look and didn't stand between us and the door.

The Graymarket was empty when Baijon and me went through. All the screens was showing warning countdowns, but I didn't need that to tell me Toystore was probably in more trouble than it wanted. They'd called in Archangel. And even if it was to sell me out so they could keep their Most Favored Techlegger status, they wasn't going to find it that easy to kick Archangel out of bed again.

They thought they was justified. Just like Kennor, when he set up one planet for war and another for death. It's all how you look at it, I guess.

Does the end justify the means? Archangel backed Charlock to get Throne. So Kennor backed Brightlaw to get Archangel. And now that Archangel and the hellflowers was done with it, wasn't nothing left in Tortuga worth having for neither Damaris nor her uncle.

We came to the end of the tier and there was some

Toystore *legitimates*. They was standing on their rep, expecting us to go with them quiet. Maybe thinking we didn't know we'd been sold out.

This time when I pushed for it in my mind it was there—the thing that let me see around corners and twenty minutes into the future. I saw Baijon bringing up his heat and didn't bother wishing for mine because hellflower logic had got him the same answer a Library gave me.

Archangel wanted us alive at any cost.

I couldn't of pulled the trigger on them. That was part of what I'd lost. But Baijon could. He dropped two and that got me armament so I gave him a lightshow backdrop and then we bulled through what was left of them and away. Now all their cybertech was tracking our hottoys, but that was a joke. Toystore wouldn't detonate them. Archangel wanted us alive.

* * *

We beat it back to *Dance* in the curious absence of any opposition or even audience whatever. Berathia's theory that Archangel was coming to collect me was high on my list of reasons why, but it wasn't the only contender.

Toystore offered a lot in the way of privacy, but not in the docking area. *Ghost Dance* was right there where we'd left her, wide-open to anyone as cared to drop by and guarded only by Toystore's good intentions.

But her neighbors wasn't. When we'd left here about a hour back, I could see six ships from where I stood. No more.

Where were they? And if gone, why?

"An excellent place for a trap," Baijon said crossly, looking at our open hatch.

"Je. And if they don't want to get permanent with us, bai, there's lots of temporary measures." In spite of which, we still had to get inboard.

"I will go first, San'Cyr." Baijon pulled his blaster and slid along the wall to where *Dance's* nose poked out. He was in before I could come up with a reasoned argument about him not going.

What was left for Baijon Starbringer? Father, lover, home, and honor. Gone.

Did the means justify the end?

Silence and the sound of someone running our way. One person, and I bet I knew who.

"It is clear, San'Cyr," Baijon announced just as a body caught up with the sound effects.

"You idiots!" Berathia said. "You can't leave in that thing—they won't let you!"

Lights and power went off-on again, which was another good reason to get out of here.

"Watch us."

Berathia followed me into *Dance*'s cockpit, talking the whole way.

"Look, I admit I wasn't completely honest with you back on alMayne but that's my *job*—I'll tell you what I was tasked for now—"

"Ancient history, 'Thia." I vaulted into the mercy seat and started peeling back my sleeve. "Baijon-bai, I pop these locks you can start getting us out of here, je?"

"*Ea,* San C'yr." Baijon put himself into the worry seat and started strapping in.

"Listen to me: *you can't get out of Toystore this way.*" Both of us ignored her.

I asked Toystore for it nice one-time whiles I ripped off my glove and shook the jacks loose out of my arm. They laughed in my ears but by then I was plugged in.

/*This is of-*Dance./

/*This is not of-*Dance./

I swept all of Toystore's reasons to be cheerful out of my Best Girl's brain. It was so easy I couldn't think why it'd ever been hard. Baijon was watching me, waiting for the office. He followed right on my tail, buttoning us up and pulling goforths on line, just like I'd taught him. For one weird instant it was *me* he was playing, not the ship, and then I was out and Berathia was staring at me.

"Thing is, jillybai, you start farcing with Old Fed Tech something's almost bound to happen."

We pushed off from Toystore with pressors only; getting even the sublight power up would take longer than I wanted to sit. The docking cradle socket ripped loose as we pushed free. Bits of it went drifting in all directions and nearspace sensors started accumulating memory.

But it was already too late. Berathia yelped and then said something naughty as promised grief to someone.

The view from *Dance*'s cockpit came clear.

We'd disengaged from Toystore right into a host of shakers and friends. Archangel'd brought the wife and kids to pay his little call.

* * *

I wished I could stay and watch—a full battle array was something I'd never thought to see even oncet. Two of the shakers from Royal was there and their support ships around them, in a mathematically compelling pattern of density and flux. An infinite killer. The wings of night.

I twisted *Dance*'s tail and Toystore slid away. We was in the middle of the hostile technology now and running for the edge. Lights flashed on the control panel: our flight recorder and ID beacon was being tapped and telling Fleet its version of the truth.

If Archangel could pull something like this together— and use it—things was falling apart faster than anyone— me, Kennor, Paladin—had thought.

But the array didn't have a Library and it didn't have the Brightlaw AI. Communication between ships was strictly speed-of-light, and wasn't nobody in this host going to do anything without Archangel's especial say-so.

No one fired.

Not at us. Not yet.

They had another target.

Toystore began to glow. They was fighting back and heavy with it, but slow as a jagranatha and lots more fragile. Toystore went invisible behind flaring shields as the big boys stood back and hammered on it.

"Fools only deal with Archangel," Baijon said. He sounded satisfied but not happy. "Now they bear witness to the truth beyond shadow."

"He can't be doing this," Berathia said, sounding

scared for the first time since I'd known her. "The Empire *needs* Toystore."

But Archangel didn't. Brother Archangel'd raised the stakes. In his brave new world was room for only one techlegger.

Later I could play back my gun-cameras and see when Toystore blew. Fleet didn't get it all its own way; I saw the pattern of disorder swirling out of whatever Toystore dumped on them—a pseudomind to crottle their warcomps, maybe. But then Toystore went to heat-light-and-energy, and Archangel's starfleet reconfigured to start picking off anyone who'd managed to get free.

Just like Royal.

A singleship wing closed up around *Dance*. Now we got down to cases. They'd be out to cripple us. We had to be ready to kill.

I tried to be. I wanted to be. If anything called for it, this did.

Kennor'd set up Royal. He'd planned it.

I had to maneuver the ship to aim. I needed a gunner.

Kennor'd planned Royal to make Archangel show himself high wide and public. To trigger the High Book investigation that would bring Archangel down.

Baijon pulled the weapons console over. His practical knowledge came out of the talkingbooks, but the controls was simple.

Kennor'd paid out ten billion people he didn't own to get Archangel. He'd spent his own and only son. But the Empire held billions more. Prey for Archangel.

Saved by Kennor. If his plan worked.

The singleships made their first attack run. The schematic of *Dance* unreeled in my head: nose cannon, tail guns, midships catapult. I twisted her tail and *Dance* sang for me.

I spun her into position and called the shots for my gunner and every volley missed.

"Let me!" said Berathia. She got up out of her seat and tripped, disoriented by the lightshow beyond the canopy.

"No!" shouted Baijon.

We was pulling more interest from Fleet now. Energylances crossed right in front of my Best Girl's nose. I slewed her offsides, joycing up the hit. Baijon fired. He got it right this time.

An acceptable trade. Royal in exchange for all the rest. Kennor's bargain.

The singleships made a second attack run. Two of their pilots took the Long Orbit. I didn't need to call shots this time. Each time *Dance* hit her marks Baijon fired just like he could read my mind. A hole was opening up in front of us now: office to kyte if I could get Jump-numbers into the comp.

I'd seen Royal. Kennor'd seen a whole future full of Royals once Archangel got rock-rolling. Desperate? Yes. He'd done what he did because he was desperate.

Justified?

"Ready-ready-we-ready!" My left hand was tapping numbers into the touchpad and all I knew about them was that they was somewheres safe—according to Archive.

Safe for Archive Library a thousand years ago might be safe for us now.

The end justified the means.

Did it?

Didn't it?

"Get us out of here!" wailed Berathia. The world beyond our ports was gone in a halation of unfriendly energy as one of the big rigs targeted us. More to come and we couldn't survive many.

I sent numbers to memory and redlined the goforths. Baijon gave me the office and I pulled the angelstick for the drop. *Ghost Dance* was everywhere at once and then gone.

Justified.

* * * * *

Valijon's Diary:

Does the end justify the means?

Once I had a father, immaculate in honor, whose sole desire was that the Gentle People should be again what they once were, for our souls' health. It is fitting irony that

as my father once reached for the purity of our Imperial
past, I have reached farther, into a past remembered only
in nightmare.

Long ago, before the Empire, the Gentle People all were
kings and princes and ruled everywhere—so we are told
as children.

It is but a tale we are told. The truth is far uglier. In that
long-ago time we did rule . . . as pawns of the Machine.

We are told—in the way that Loremasters speak to
shaulla—that because of what we were and did in the days
of the Old Federation the war came, and so never again
must we seek such power lest it lead us to compromise
with the Machine.

Truth and tale share one shadow. Kennor Starbringer
mocks those who have forgotten the Machine—he curses
its name while calling up its pale descendant to serve him
as we once served its ancestor. Kennor Starbringer, too,
has forgotten truth.

The end does not justify the means. The end is the sum
of the means, as the road traveled determines the desti-
nation.

I was born into a world with only one enemy. But I have
grown, and see beyond the walls of my birth, and see that
enemies are many, but their goal is all one.

In the end, the Gentle People whom I must disown are
right in one thing: truth is the compass of one's own hand.
The Machine is not the ultimate abomination, but its cause:
the loss of humanity. And it is not the only cause.

And now I know that the time is long past to speak of
roads and choices, ghosts and history.

Now I must reach out and seize my truth.

DAW

Epic Tales of Other Worlds

ELUKI BES SHAHAR

☐ **HELLFLOWER** (UE2475—$3.99)
Butterfly St. Cyr had a well-deserved reputation as an honest and dependable smuggler. But when she and her partner, a highly illegal artificial intelligence, rescued Tiggy, the son and heir to one of the most powerful of the hellflower mercenary leaders, it looked like they'd finally taken more than they could handle. For his father's enemies had sworn to see that Tiggy and Butterfly never reached his home alive. . . .

DORIS EGAN

☐ **THE GATE OF IVORY** (UE2328—$3.95)
Cut off from her companions and her ship, attacked and robbed, anthropology student Theodora of Pyrene finds what began as a pleasure trip becoming a terrifying odyssey on the planet Ivory, where magic works. For all her studies and training are useless, and she is forced to turn to fortune-telling to survive. To her amazement, she discovers that she is actually gifted with magical skill—a skill, however, that will plunge her into deadly peril.

JOHN STEAKLEY

☐ **ARMOR** (UE2368—$5.50)
Impervious body armor had been devised for the commando forces who were to be dropped onto the poisonous surface of A-9, the home world of mankind's most implacable enemy. But what of the man inside the armor? This tale of cosmic combat will stand against the best of Gordon Dickson or Poul Anderson.

Buy them at your local bookstore or use this convenient coupon for ordering.

PENGUIN USA   P.O. Box 999, Bergenfield, New Jersey 07621

Please send me the DAW BOOKS I have checked above, for which I am enclosing $_____ (please add $2.00 per order to cover postage and handling. Send check or money order (no cash or C.O.D.'s) or charge by Mastercard or Visa (with a $15.00 minimum. Prices and numbers are subject to change without notice.

Card #_____ Exp. Date _____

Signature_____

Name_____

Address_____

City _____ State _____ Zip _____

For faster service when ordering by credit card call **1-800-253-6476**
Please allow a minimum of 4 to 6 weeks for delivery.

DAW

Charles Ingrid

☐ **RADIUS OF DOUBT** (UE2491—$4.99)

THE MARKED MAN SERIES

In a devastated America, can the Lord Protector of a mutating human race find a way to preserve the future of the species?

☐ **THE MARKED MAN** (UE2396—$3.95)

☐ **THE LAST RECALL** (UE2460—$3.95)

THE SAND WARS

☐ **SOLAR KILL: Book 1** (UE2391—$3.95)
He was the last Dominion Knight and he would challenge a star empire to gain his revenge!

☐ **LASERTOWN BLUES: Book 2** (UE2393—$3.95)
He'd won a place in the Emperor's Guard but could he hunt down the traitor who'd betrayed his Knights to an alien foe?

☐ **CELESTIAL HIT LIST: Book 3** (UE2394—$3.95)
Death stalked the Dominion Knight from the Emperor's Palace to a world on the brink of its prophesied age of destruction. . . .

☐ **ALIEN SALUTE: Book 4** (UE2329—$3.95)
As the Dominion and the Thrakian empires mobilize for all-out war, can Jack Storm find the means to defeat the ancient enemies of man?

☐ **RETURN FIRE: Book 5** (UE2363—$3.95)
Was someone again betraying the human worlds to the enemy—and would Jack Storm become pawn or player in these games of death?

☐ **CHALLENGE MET: Book 6** (UE2436—$3.95)
In this concluding volume, Jack Storm embarks on a dangerous mission which will lead to a final confrontation with the Ash-farel.

Buy them at your local bookstore or use this convenient coupon for ordering.

PENGUIN USA P.O. Box 999, Bergenfield, New Jersey 07621

Please send me the DAW BOOKS I have checked above, for which I am enclosing
$_____ (please add $2.00 per order to cover postage and handling. Send check or money order (no cash or C.O.D.'s) or charge by Mastercard or Visa (with a $15.00 minimum. Prices and numbers are subject to change without notice.

Card #_____ Exp. Date _____
Signature_____
Name_____
Address_____
City _____ State _____ Zip _____
For faster service when ordering by credit card call **1-800-253-6476**
Please allow a minimum of 4 to 6 weeks for delivery.